MACHINE
CITY

OTHER TITLES BY SCOTT J. HOLLIDAY

Detective Barnes Series

Punishment

MACHINE CITY

SCOTT J. HOLLIDAY

THOMAS & MERCER

This is a work of fiction. Names, characters, organizations, places, events, and incidents are either products of the author's imagination or are used fictitiously. Any resemblance to actual persons, living or dead, or actual events is purely coincidental.

Text copyright © 2018 by Scott J. Holliday
All rights reserved.

No part of this book may be reproduced, or stored in a retrieval system, or transmitted in any form or by any means, electronic, mechanical, photocopying, recording, or otherwise, without express written permission of the publisher.

Published by Thomas & Mercer, Seattle

www.apub.com

Amazon, the Amazon logo, and Thomas & Mercer are trademarks of Amazon.com, Inc., or its affiliates.

ISBN-13: 9781503903401
ISBN-10: 1503903400

Cover design by Michael Heath | Shannon Associates

Printed in the United States of America

*This book is dedicated to my sister, Heather.
I never met her, as she was born before me and died
from an undetected brain tumor at three months old.
I know she lives on in my mother's heart, but I like to
think that mentioning her name and telling her story
gives her back a little of the life she never had.*

The moment we want to believe something, we suddenly see all the arguments for it, and become blind to the arguments against it.

—*George Bernard Shaw*

PROLOGUE

DETROIT, MI—Officials issued an AMBER Alert Monday as the Detroit Police continue the search for 10-year-old former *Starmonizers* contestant Cherry "Little Cher" Daniels, who disappeared from her Corktown home Tuesday night.

Cherry's mother, Hannah, pleaded for her daughter to be returned to safety.

"We'll do anything, just bring her home safely," Daniels said, staring into a WXON news camera at the scene outside of her home. "She's a good kid. She gets good grades. She's nice to people. You all know her."

Little Cher captivated audiences during the nationally televised children's singing competition show, eventually taking fourth place due to her soulful renditions of Motown classics such as "What's Going On," "Papa Was a Rollin' Stone," and "Superstition."

Hannah Daniels stated she came home from work on Tuesday evening to find that her daughter, a latchkey kid and a walker from the nearby elementary school, was missing. The last time Hannah could recall seeing her daughter was the same morning when she sent Cherry off to fifth grade at Cross Elementary.

Police have reported there was no sign of forced entry in the home.

The Wayne County Sheriff's Office has stated that crews spent all day searching the city for the girl. A spokesperson for the Detroit Police,

Lieutenant Detective William Franklin, told WXON, "It's all hands on deck for Little Cher. We're doing everything we can."

Cherry's mother describes the girl—who is 4′ 6″ tall, weighs about 90 lbs., and has blonde hair and brown eyes—as "full of laughter" and "everyone's best friend."

Little Cher has so far been unable to turn her competition success into fame outside of Detroit but has performed at local events, including last season's Governor's Ball for charity and the national anthem at the Lions Monday night game this past season. She is currently scheduled to perform at Cobo Hall on the final day of the upcoming Auto Show.

1

Former Detroit homicide detective John Barnes sat on the wooden steps that led up to his porch, his leather tool belt unbuckled and set at his side. There was a framing hammer in the steel loop, 16d sinker nails in the main pouch, a twenty-five-foot measuring tape buttoned in its place. He sat with his forearms on his knees and a beer held loosely in his right hand, dangling in the space between his legs. It was Friday afternoon, and the foreman had let the crew off early. Barnes had come home to an empty house, pulled the beer from the fridge, and headed out to the porch, letting the cheap screen door bang and rattle as it closed behind him.

He took a swig, set the bottle down, and examined his hands. They were calloused and muscular now, lightly coated with drywall dust and blue snap-line chalk. His silver wedding ring was battered and beautiful. He clapped his hands and rubbed them together, sending dust into the air. He then ran his fingers through a full head of hair. His surgically repaired shoulder ached. There was titanium in there now, beneath the scars. Same with his knee. They both gave him trouble at times.

Barnes placed a hand on the scar above his heart. He pressed down on it like a button. It tickled and stung. He waited for the victims in his head to comment, but they were quiet now. Had been for some time. He smiled and leaned back against the stairs, placing his elbows on the step above and behind him. He kicked out his legs and crossed them at the ankles.

A school bus appeared at the end of his road. The air brakes sounded off as the bus came to a stop at the corner. Jessica was waiting there alongside two other mothers. It was a warm autumn day but growing crisp as evening approached. Jessica wore a sweater and a long skirt.

Richard J. Barnes hopped off the bus with both feet and landed like a paratrooper, Batman backpack firmly attached. He ran a few circles around his mother before taking her hand. They spoke with each other as they headed down the sidewalk toward home.

The boy's face lit up when he saw his dad.

Richie ran out in front of his mother and down the sidewalk toward home, arms pumping at his sides. His hair flew back and his backpack shifted across his shoulders. Never had the boy looked so much like his namesake—Barnes's kid brother, Ricky, dead and gone now for more than twenty-five years.

"You're home!" Richie said. He clambered up the steps and hopped into his father's arms.

Barnes caught Richie with a huff and a laugh. He stood and hugged his son to his chest, the boy's feet dangling at his father's thighs. Richie smelled of scratch-and-sniff strawberry and pencil shavings, paste and construction paper.

Barnes looked up to find Jessica walking up the sidewalk toward the porch. Her hands were clutched together at her waist. She wore the strained smile of a worried mother, a concerned wife. "Everything okay?" she asked.

"My day ended early," Barnes said. He rolled his eyes toward the developing storm clouds overhead.

Jessica stopped walking, looked stunned.

"Don't worry," he said. "I've still got a job. It's only—" A lightning bolt flashed across the sky. The thunderclap followed quickly, rattling the home's front windows and the porch's wooden slats. Richie squeezed

4

Barnes tighter, buried his face into his father's neck. Barnes smirked at Jessica. "The weather." He set Richie down on his feet.

The sky darkened and the storm clouds swelled as Jessica stepped onto the porch and stood with Barnes beneath the awning.

"Want to see what I made at school?" Richie said. He started peeling off his backpack.

"I sure do."

"Not right now," Jessica said, placing a hand on the boy's shoulder. "After dinner."

Richie's delighted face went hangdog. The wind picked up and tossed his hair. *Too long for a boy*, Barnes thought. *It should be cut*. He lifted his son's chin with two fingers. "After dinner. Okay, Dynamite?"

Richie smiled. "Okay, Hurricane."

Barnes held out his hand in monkey bite formation—index and middle finger opened like scissors, the fingers curled in toward his palm. Richie responded with his own monkey bite formation, which they connected and clamped together for their secret handshake.

Jessica held the screen door open. Richie sped past her into the house, sending her skirt swirling around her legs. She eased the door closed and stayed on the porch. "It's Dynamite and Hurricane now?"

The professional wrestling characters from young Johnny and Ricky's favorite arcade game, *Mania Challenge*, were technically Dynamite Tommy and Hurricane Joe, but to the boys they were Dynamite Ricky and Hurricane John.

Come get some, Hurricane.

You're dead meat, Dynamite.

Barnes offered a wry smile.

"You sure everything's okay?" Jessica said.

"Of course. What is it?"

Jessica tilted her head and put a hand on his cheek. She regarded him for a moment, examining his face. A lock of her hair fell across her eyes. She pulled it back behind her ear. "It's nothing."

"It doesn't feel like nothing," Barnes said.

She leaned in and kissed his lips. Her touch was light and soft, tentative as a bird. A shy girl snatching a kiss from an aloof boy. She pulled back and regarded him again, eyes searching.

"What's going on?" he said.

"Just come inside, okay?"

Barnes bent down to pick up his tool belt, but the sound of an approaching vehicle interrupted him. As the rain began to fall, an unmarked sedan pulled up to the curb with Lieutenant Detective Franklin in the driver's seat, plus a man Barnes didn't recognize in the passenger side. Probably Franklin's new partner. Raindrops bubbled on the sedan's windshield. They *ticky-tacked* the aluminum awning over Barnes's head.

"I'll leave you three alone," Jessica said, raising her voice above the increasing downpour. Barnes turned, but the screen was already closing behind her. The door banged shut. She walked down the hall, a fuzzy vision through the mesh.

The sedan's suspension squawked as Franklin emerged from the driver's side. His big head appeared above the car's roof, which was growing slick and shiny from the rain. Franklin appeared to have aged two decades in the six years since the two had worked together. The black in his hair was hanging on, but it was mostly streaked with gray. His dark skin was ashy at the edges. He still wore the finest suits, though some of them—this one included—were in their golden years.

The other man stayed in the car. He stared out through the windshield with his head tilted back in a cocky sort of way. New cops were like that. Made of steel until the city heat softened them. Barnes had been new once, too. He recalled walking a beat in uniform, arresting dopers and domestic abusers, chasing runners and subduing fighters. Afternoons kicking in door after crack-house door, hauling in the same perp a dozen times. Small-time criminals were processed through the system quicker than crap through a goose. You brought them in at night and then passed them by on the sidewalk the next morning.

"Morning, Sam."

"Morning, Ralph."

Then came the rookie hazing after he made detective. Salt poured in his coffee while the old guard stared on, waiting to bust their guts while he cringed from the taste. A bubble-wrapped desk. His car filled with shaving cream. They'd started out calling him Slick, but the nickname never stuck. The Calavera case had changed all that. So much time on the machine. The voices, the physical abuse, the murders he relived, over and over. Hard to call him Slick when his face eerily resembled the skeletal mask of the man he chased. Hard to bust his balls when his body was broken and his mind was filled with voices.

The serial killer's deeds had been Barnes's personal trials of Job, and that was just the time he spent on the machine. Getting shot three times in real life didn't help. He'd nearly bled to death in Whitehall Forest, his back against the door of that old boxcar to trap Calavera inside.

Franklin strolled through the falling rain toward the porch, stepping on the wet spots collecting on the pale concrete. His shoulders were no longer wider than his waist, but they were still impressive. His arms and hands were like heavy plate weights stacking up to connect with his powerful frame. The wooden porch steps creaked as he came up.

"Beer?" Barnes said.

"No thanks. Here on official business."

"Is that right?"

"How are you feeling?" Franklin said.

"I feel like I'm wondering what *official business* means."

Franklin opened his jacket and reached inside. He slid out a white envelope, the back side facing out. "I got a letter here . . ." He put on a pair of reading glasses and looked at the front of the envelope. "It's addressed to Detective John Barnes of Homicide, care of Detroit Police, First Precinct."

"And?"

"What do you say to that?"

Barnes looked puzzled. "I say let me read it."

"It's not addressed to you."

"How's that?"

"You still a detective?"

"No," Barnes said, "but it's got my name on it, right?"

Franklin handed Barnes the letter. "Don't open it yet. That's not why I'm here."

Barnes glanced at the envelope. The return address was DILLMAN & ASSOCIATES ESTATE LAW, NEW ORLEANS, LA. He folded the letter in half and slid it into his pocket, crossing his arms over his chest. "Shoot."

"We need you."

"We?"

"The police."

"No thanks," Barnes said.

"A favor, then," Franklin said. "For me."

"That's dirty."

Franklin raised an eyebrow.

"What could the Detroit police need so badly that you'd call in a favor on me?"

"We need someone on the machine."

Barnes blinked. He stepped backward. Coldness emerged in his needle-scarred elbow pits. Numbness raced up toward his head, turned toward his internal organs. His scalp tingled. He ran his fingers through his hair. "You're kidding, right?"

"I'm not."

"Fuck you for even asking, *partner*," Barnes said. "You know what that thing did to me."

"A man's life is at stake."

Barnes balled his hands into fists. "You're damn right there is. Mine!"

"Flaherty."

"Who?"

"Detective Adrian Flaherty," Franklin said. "Remember him?"

"What's he got to do with me?"

"He's gone missing."

"So find him. You're a detective."

"You know the machine is outlawed now."

"And?"

"Thought you might still have contacts."

"You can have them."

Franklin sighed.

"Oh, I see," Barnes said. His chest began to heave. "Everyone saw how the machine fucked up Barnesy, so now no one wants to take the ride. Outlawed for investigative and recreational use, servers retired, machines dismantled, but Barnes still knows of a few, eh? He's got contacts, maybe even a med card. Hell, he's probably still a munky. How am I doing so far?"

"Spot-on."

"Well then, here's the news of the day, *partner*. I don't have a med card, and I haven't been on that thing in years. In case you hadn't noticed, I've got a life that I'd rather not have destroyed, so to hell with your favor."

Rain had filled the gutters, clogged with leaves and beginning to overflow. Water peeled down in sheets from the awning, framing falling leaves like they were suspended in glass. Franklin looked out over the street. "Sorry I asked."

Barnes took a beat. He calmed his breathing, unclenched his fists. He snatched up his beer, took a slug, and then followed Franklin's sight line. The big man was looking between the houses across the street. There was a coyote there. Skinny. Starving. The neighborhood seemed overrun with them lately. More and more wild animals were circling back into suburban neighborhoods as the spread of humanity kicked them out of their forest homes. The two men watched the coyote sniff around between the houses, look up suddenly at a passing car, and then return to sniffing. Barnes moved his eyes back to Franklin's sedan and found the man in the passenger seat, now a blur of cop-shaped color behind the fogged-up glass.

"That your new partner?" Barnes said.

Franklin pursed his lips. "You could say that."

"What happened to him?"

"Who?" Franklin said.

"Flaherty."

"Abducted, we think."

The coyote slunk in behind one of the houses. Through the drumming rain came the faint rattling of a chain-link fence. The thing must have been struggling to crawl beneath it, losing back fur along the way.

"This has something to do with that girl," Barnes said. "Cherry Daniels, right?"

Franklin nodded. "Little Cher."

"Let's see if I can add two and two," Barnes said. "Cherry Daniels goes on AMBER Alert, Flaherty tracks her down, gets close, and ends up missing, too?"

"You're in the ballpark."

"Got any leads?"

"A few," Franklin said. "But hey, I gotta run, okay?" He offered his palm.

Barnes shook his former partner's hand. "Sorry I can't help."

"I shouldn't have asked," Franklin said. "Take good care of that family you've got." He stepped into the rain and headed down the sidewalk but stopped halfway to his car. He turned back. "Hey, remember that time we sat on the precinct roof taking potshots at the old Denbo water tower?"

Barnes smirked. He nodded.

"What was it you said?"

"I bet Jimmy Hoffa's in there."

Franklin smiled. "That's right."

"Just a theory."

Franklin continued to his car and pulled open the driver's-side door.

"Wait," Barnes said, catching his old partner before he ducked into the vehicle. "Two questions."

Franklin set his forearms on the car's wet roof. Raindrops collected in his hair and dripped onto his shoulders. The low dinging of the vehicle's door-ajar indicator sounded off repeatedly. He said, "Shoot."

"Who would I have been?"

"On the machine?"

Barnes nodded.

"Flaherty, himself. I know you never liked the guy—hell, not many of us did—but he was a thorough detective, and damn good with that machine. Instead of taking notes"—Franklin tapped his temple—"he recorded his memories. Felt it was the more reliable method." Franklin shook his head. "Pretty much everything was locked down when the police servers were archived, but I know he stashed some of the stuff he was working on"—he swirled a finger in the air—"out there on the web. What's the second question?"

"Who would have the stones to abduct a police detective?"

Franklin began ducking into the vehicle. "That's what we're trying to find out."

Barnes watched Franklin drive down to the next block and turn. His taillights flickered as he rolled the stop sign. Once the sedan was out of sight, Barnes pulled the folded envelope from his pocket. He read the return address again—DILLMAN & ASSOCIATES ESTATE LAW, NEW ORLEANS, LA. He tore the seal apart, retrieved the letter, and read it:

Barnes,

Find me on the machine. It's about Ricky.

Freddie Cohen

2

Freddie Cohen, middle school bully to Barnes's younger brother. Barnes hadn't thought of him in years. As he understood it, Cohen came into some money, bought up a chain of Piggly Wiggly grocery stores in the suburbs of New Orleans, and moved down there to operate them. Word had it he'd become a big shot in the Big Easy, a string puller with the local crime syndicates and the government. The letter was from an estate lawyer, though. Maybe someone opted to pull old Freddie's string instead?

A memory bloomed in Barnes's mind. Elementary school. Seventh grade. The kickball diamond. Ricky had come home late for taco dinner the evening before, walked out of Whitehall Forest with a knot above his left eye. He'd convinced Mom and Dad that he'd fallen out of the boys' tree fort and bumped his head, but big brother knew better. That night, in the dark stillness of the bedroom they shared, Johnny piqued his ears to the sounds of Ricky's muffled crying.

"You didn't fall out of the fort," Barnes said.

Ricky didn't respond, just sniffled.

"Freddie hit you."

A silent moment, and then Ricky said, "Don't hurt him, Johnny."

"Why not?"

"He's not like other people."

"What's that supposed to mean?"

"It's just . . . it's okay, ya know? I'm not mad at him."

"I am."

The next day Johnny Barnes found Freddie Cohen on the diamond. The kid was holding the kickball hostage and yelling at the younger boys the way a bully does—the way an insecure, overweight kid with an advantage does. He was red-faced and terrifying, so long as you were too small to consider retaliating.

Johnny wasn't too small.

"Hey," he said, stalking toward Freddie. The minced gravel crunched underfoot like the teeth Johnny planned to knock out, the bones he planned to break. The scents of dirt and sweat invaded his nose. His hands shook with adrenaline, his heart raced, his eyes felt like they were bulging. The sixth-graders quickly formed a loose circle around the expected seventh-grade combatants. "You hurt Ricky."

"So?" Freddie said.

Johnny feinted forward. Freddie stepped back. He dropped the kickball to bring up his fists. The ball bounced and rolled away.

"Just being fat don't make you tough," Johnny said.

The other children snickered.

Freddie's hands fell. His wet lips quivered. He stood there with his arms at his sides and his head low. Barnes took two steps and shoved him. The bully fell and *whumped* the ground. He flailed like a turtle on its back.

The circle of snickers rose into laughter.

Johnny knelt beside Cohen and moved his face within inches of the bully's own. He smelled like Jolly Ranchers. Johnny gripped the kid's chin with one hand, squishing his cheeks and pushing out his lips. Cohen stopped squirming. His nostrils flared, his brow was wet. His frightened eyes were sunken deep and peering out from puffy slits.

"Touch him again," Barnes said, "and I'll *really* hurt you."

Cohen stared up at him, his buried eyes pleading.

"Got it?"

Freddie nodded.

Now sheltered from the rain beneath his front porch awning, and with Freddie Cohen's simple letter in his hand, Barnes found he felt sorry for the overweight kid. He recalled their ten-year high school reunion when Freddie played big shot throughout the evening, buying everyone drinks and practically gorilla-slapping his chest as he brayed about his successes. Barnes had slipped out the back door, convincing himself he was sparing Freddie another altercation, but the truth was that he'd felt sorry for him then, too. He'd relived that so-called fight many times throughout his school days and in the years afterward, never able to admit he felt guilty over it. In the presence of others he'd reveled in the fact that he was able to drop that witty comment at just the right time, not twenty minutes later. He'd reveled in taking the bully down a peg and standing up for his kid brother. The story was told in the school hallways, at recess, at lunchtime. There were always high fives to be slapped, shoulders to be punched, and more laughter at Freddie Cohen's expense.

But there were no high fives from Ricky, no shoulder punches, no laughter. He'd heard word of his big brother's deed, and his only response had been, "Thanks for not hurting him."

The brothers were in the woods beyond their trailer park home when Ricky spoke those words. It was the following afternoon, the same Saturday when Ricky died. They were walking along the banks of the Rouge River, heading out toward their tree fort with an eight-foot two-by-four between them, the board snagged from that construction site on Middlebelt where all the new condos were going up. The plan had been to cut it into sections and make steps to replace the rope that took them up to their fort.

They stopped when they came across a coin purse lying on top of the leaves. It was a black rubber thing with a Batman logo on the outside, the kind of purse you squeezed and the mouth gasped open.

The boys exchanged a glance and dropped the two-by-four, their saw, their hammer and nails. Johnny picked up the purse and squeezed it open. Six quarters inside. That worked out to three games of *Mania Challenge*—mano a mano, Dynamite Ricky versus Hurricane John—on the cabinet at the gas station just the other side of the tracks at Calvary Junction.

"I've seen that before," Ricky said. "I think it's—"

"Who cares?" Johnny said. "Finders keepers, right?"

Ricky shrugged, palms up.

The boys sprinted out of the woods. They came to the back patio breathing hard. John snatched up his BMX, but Ricky hesitated. His bike chain was badly rusted. Dad had bought them new chains earlier that week and John had already switched his out, but Ricky hadn't.

"Come on, Johnny," Ricky said. He gestured toward his orange-and-brown chain. The thing looked as brittle as candy. "Help me."

Barnes mentally slammed a door on the memory of his brother's death. He'd made peace with it long ago and refused to let the seed regrow. Still, the damn thing tried to sprout its way around his mental barrier. The memory was like living vines slithering beneath a door and over the threshold, fingering through the cracks, pushing through the keyhole. In his mind Barnes shouldered the door to keep it closed. He stomped the vines on the floor, punched at those probing their way through the cracks and holes.

The sound of shattering glass grabbed Barnes's attention. He looked through the screen door to see Jessica in the kitchen, her hands over her mouth, the broken remains of a glass bowl at her feet. Barnes went into the house.

"You okay?" he said.

She pulled her hands away from her face. Her cheeks were wet with tears. She showed him defensive palms. "I'm fine."

"Let me help you," Barnes said. He bent down to pick up some shards. The mess was complete with steaming spaghetti noodles and marinara sauce.

"Don't," she said. "Just go upstairs and clean up. I'll make something else."

"We'll order a pizza," Barnes said.

Richie's voice came from upstairs. "Yeah! Pizza!"

Barnes smiled.

Jessica said, "Just go."

"Hey now," Barnes said. He reached out to her, but she drew back.

"Just. Go."

"Okay."

Barnes started up the steps to the sound of pattering feet above—Richie making a break for his bedroom. By the time Barnes reached the top step, the only sound was Jessica's sobbing between clinks of glass dropping into the trash.

Richie's door was open a crack. Barnes lightly rapped on it, opened it. "What's up, Dynamite?"

The boy was lying prone on his bed, face smashed into the pillow he'd scrunched up beneath his chest. The room was neater than young Johnny and Ricky had ever kept theirs. Everything was in its place and situated just so. Barnes resisted the urge to knock a few dolls off a shelf and say, "Live a little, kid." One doll in particular stood out, the iconic Eddie Able figure Barnes had bought the boy for his birthday last month. Eddie was a freckle-faced, towheaded cherub dressed in whatever career he was *able* to do. Your choice—a policeman, doctor, carpenter, whatever. Pull his string and he spoke, his mouth moved, his head turned, his eyes blinked. *I'm Eddie, and I'm able! I love you!* Barnes had chosen a fireman's getup for Eddie, including the red hat and suspenders, yellow jacket, and yellow boots. It was precisely the same version Ricky had gotten when he'd turned five some thirty years ago.

But Barnes's son had frowned when he unwrapped the gift. He'd looked at it, confused. It was the same with the Batman backpack he'd opened only moments before.

Jessica gave Barnes a sidelong glance.

"What?"

"Thank your father for the gift," Jessica told Richie.

"Thanks, Dad."

Eddie Able was quickly supplanted by the refurbished iPad mini she'd gotten the boy, and the doll was left to collect dust on a shelf above the toys Richie actually played with. Based on the less-than-enthusiastic response, Barnes canceled the surprise visit from a real live Eddie Able for Richie's party that weekend, some guy in a fiberglass head and clown-size shoes. Barnes kissed off his $200 deposit.

At least the kid used the backpack.

"What's wrong with Mom?" Richie said, his voice muffled by the pillow.

"She's okay," Barnes said. He came over and sat at the foot of the bed. "Just having a tough time, I guess."

"Why?"

Barnes sighed. He thought for a moment, then said, "Remember last month, when we lost Goldie?" There were two remaining goldfish in a tank downstairs. There had been three—Goldie, Whitey, and Bugs. Goldie went belly-up in July. The resulting backyard burial was fit for an Egyptian king. "Remember how sad we all felt?"

The boy nodded.

"Mom feels like that right now, I think."

Richie turned to Barnes, his eyes wide. "Did Whitey die?"

"No."

"Bugs?"

"No," Barnes said. He smirked and tousled the kid's long hair. "Nobody died. It's just . . . sometimes mommies and daddies can feel sad, even if no one died, ya know?"

Richie smashed his face back into the pillow. "No."

Amen to that. Jessica's sudden turn in personality was as perplexing to Barnes as it was to Richie. The other morning she had awakened him by sliding over to his side of the bed wearing only a smile. Things got underway nicely, but she seemed to lose steam and after a few minutes gave up and slunk off into the shower. That afternoon he found her out in the backyard, down on her knees in the grass with her hands over her face. When he approached her to ask what was wrong, she jumped up in a rage, shoving him backward and slapping him all over. He tripped and fell over a plastic water table. She stood above him with dirty knees, fists clenched.

"What the hell?" he'd said.

She just turned and went back into the house with no explanation.

What could he tell Richie?

A strange, breathless voice emerged in Barnes's mind. *"Ask him. If he. Wants to play."*

Barnes went rigid with fear. Blood drained from his face. He'd beaten the voices, hadn't he? He hadn't heard one in . . . Jesus, who knew how long? Yet here was this voice from within. And worse yet, he didn't recognize it.

"Shhh," Barnes thought. It was the same way he'd quieted the voices in the past. He closed his eyes and fought off a shiver.

"Dad, are you okay?" Richie said.

"Yeah," Barnes said. "I'm okay." He took a beat and then opened his eyes. "Did you wash your hands for dinner?"

"Are we getting pizza?"

"Go wash up."

Barnes went downstairs to find that Jessica had cleaned up the kitchen, but she wasn't there. He discovered her on the living room sofa. The lights were off. She was sitting in the dark, staring at the blank television.

"I'll order a pizza," he said.

"Use that voice speaker thing," Jessica said. Only her lips had moved. Her eyes remained fixed on the dead screen.

Barnes turned his eyes to the small black tower on the kitchen counter. Barnes got gooseflesh just looking at the speaker, never mind having a conversation with it—the robotic female voice was nearly the same as the one from the machine.

"No thanks," he said. He held up his smartphone. "I'll go old school." He called Ziti's, placed an order for pickup, and disconnected the call. He slid his phone back into his pocket. Freddie Cohen's envelope was in there. He pulled out the letter and read it once more.

It's about Ricky.

Again, Barnes's elbow pits went cold, his scalp tingled. He rubbed a hand through his hair.

The machine. Just the thought of the device was anathema to Barnes. He recalled the prick of the needle entering his skin, the tubes and suction cups, the sterile feeling of the serum moving through his veins and entering his brain. The machine was invented to aid detectives in homicide investigations, to let them investigate the victim's death firsthand. Sure. And Coca-Cola was invented to cure morphine addiction.

Machine usage had spread like proverbial wildfire. First came recreation, then came punishment, then came baby in the mind-fuck carriage. Machine junkies—munkies—walked the streets like crackheads on the hunt for a rock roast. They weren't themselves anymore but innocent people victimized by a virtual reality machine that, by the preexisting definition of the word, wasn't technically virtual. It sure as hell wasn't television. Nor was it a mask you put on so you could ride a computer-generated roller coaster or be tricked into thinking you're bungee jumping. The sound wasn't in stereo, the vision wasn't HD. The fear you felt was real, the pain you absorbed was real, the death you experienced.

The ax.

The lingering push and pull had been the most difficult part of riding the machine. The aftereffect of other people's memories fighting for time in Barnes's mind. Ignoring them was akin to trying not to think about a purple dinosaur.

And there it was.

But he'd done it once before. He'd beaten the voices and regained himself. He could do it again.

Couldn't he?

He said, "Be right back," and snatched up his jacket and keys as he headed for the door.

3

Barnes pulled into the alley behind Ziti's Sub and Grub in Corktown. He killed the engine and rubbed his hands over his face. His heart beat to match the tempo of rain pounding the windshield. It was dusk now. A streetlamp at the corner zapped into life. Its hue made diamonds of the raindrops on the glass. Barnes pulled the keys out of the ignition. His hands shook so badly the keys jingled on the way to his pocket. He hopped out of the pickup truck and closed the door behind him.

The rain's humidity gave weight to the grease-trap stench of the alley. A nearby dumpster was a rusted skeleton of its former glory, the dual lids long since missing. Black and white garbage bags peeked out from the shadowy depths, sleek with rain, bloated and overrun with rat-size holes. The cinder-block wall along the back of the alley separated the restaurant from a field of weeds as thick as saplings, the field in which Andrew Kemp's body had been found. The teenager who, through the latter's use of the machine, took over Antonio Reyes's mind and turned him into the infamous Detroit serial killer, Calavera. Reyes, or Kemp, whichever you preferred, was currently at the Bracken Psychiatric Institute for the Criminally Insane. Last Barnes knew, Calavera was reliving each of his victim's deaths weekly on the machine. Reliving Barnes's near-death, too. They'd recorded the three days leading up to Calavera's capture at that boxcar in Whitehall Forest, recorded every moment of Barnes's physical pain and mental misery, including the bullets blasting holes in his body, so the pain could be transferred back to the man who originally doled it out.

Barnes touched the scar above his heart, felt the tickle and sting. Same with his right shoulder and left knee. The scars metaphysically burned, seeming to recall the salt Barnes had poured into them while they were still open wounds. He grinned to imagine the agony Calavera had endured on the machine. It might be outlawed for use outside of prison walls and psych wards—save for the ill who qualified for med cards—but on the inside the machine still doled out plenty of punishment. Not just physical pain, and not just torture, but as Barnes knew all too well—the voices. Even his own voice would be in Calavera's mind, tormenting the killer from within.

The thought brought a chill.

Barnes stepped through the rain to the back door at Ziti's, his old machine haunt. There was a time when outlawed machines could be found in secret joints like this all over Detroit, but since the crackdown it was nearly impossible to find an unlawful place to hook in. The machine's trajectory was like that of marijuana. At first everyone knew someone who used, and probably knew someone who dealt, but then the government got involved, started handing out medical cards to those they determined were in need. Now a med card could get you into any memory shop in the country, but merchants who played it straight had bullshit memories to sell. Running a memory shop was like running a movie theater that only showed G-rated films. Candy-coated recollections from kids at theme parks, crunchy people on nature walks, hour-long hugs, workplace affirmations, missionary sex. People with med cards wanted escape from the horror of their real lives, the physical destruction of their bodies, or the slipping gears in their minds, and the only legal place to go was inside a kid on a Tilt-A-Whirl? What a scam.

To get the hard stuff you had to go underground. At Ziti's, that meant literally.

Barnes rapped his knuckles on the gray steel door. There was a flash of shadow through the peephole, and then a voice from behind the door. "Fuck off."

Barnes took a beat and knocked again.

The voice came again. "The two words were *fuck* and *off*. When you put them together, you get *fuck off*."

"Come on, man," Barnes said. "I know Raphael."

"Who?"

"Look, I don't know his real name, but he keeps two katana blades tucked into his pants, so he's like Raphael with his sais, you know? The Ninja Turtle?"

Locks clicked and clacked. The door swung open, releasing the scent of french fries and pizza from within. The man standing there was dressed in a stained apron and a T-shirt ringed in sweat. His face was scruffy. He held a bread knife in one hand, a sub bun in the other. "You know Danny?"

"I mean, yeah, from back when I used to come by here more often."

"Have you seen him?"

"Not since, I don't know . . . it's been a while."

The man cocked his head, knitted his brow. "You ain't seen him?"

"Is he missing?"

"Motherfucker ran off with Brenda and a week's take. I find him"— he brandished the bread knife—"he's fuckin' dead."

"Duly noted," Barnes said.

"What do you want?"

"I ordered a large double pepperoni to go," Barnes said, and then he showed the man a fifty-dollar bill. "But first I'd like a ride."

The man's expression changed. "A ride on what?"

"You know what I mean."

The man leaned out into the alley and looked both ways. "That your truck?"

Barnes looked back at his old pickup. The wheel wells were rusted out, the windshield was cracked, and the paint job was a study in nicks and scratches, but the engine kept purring. Tucked against the cab was a secure toolbox, the only thing less than fifteen years old. "Yep."

The man nodded at the fifty. "Double that."

"Really?"

"You got a med card?"

"Think I'd be here if I did?"

The man pursed his lips. "Maybe."

"No," Barnes said. "I wouldn't."

The man nodded. "Still, though, the price doubles."

Barnes produced another fifty.

The man snatched the money and stepped back to let Barnes inside. To Barnes's immediate left was the familiar dank stairwell that led to the machine room beneath Ziti's. He stood at the top of the steps with his heartbeat building to a frenetic pace, his elbow pits tingling, his throat suddenly dry.

"Go on, then," the man said, clapping Barnes's back. "Munky see, munky do."

Barnes stepped down into the darkness.

The cellar contained boxes of onions, stacked cans of tomato sauce, and a chest freezer poorly lit by a dusty overhead bulb on a wire. Barnes maneuvered through the maze of boxes and pallets until he came to the back wall. He slid sideways behind an industrial-size refrigerator and made his way along until he found the familiar hidden door. He knocked. A head-level mail slot slid open, revealing a woman's eyes.

"Do I know you?" the woman said.

"Don't think so," Barnes said.

"You paid Harrison?"

"The guy upstairs?"

"You tell me," she said.

"Gimme a break," Barnes said. "I just parted with a yard to some dude pining about a girl named Brenda running off with—"

The man from upstairs called down the steps. "Dawn! Let him in! Use Danny's med card!"

The slot closed and the door opened.

Barnes stepped inside the machine room. The last time he'd been in the space there'd been three hospital beds inside, three machines. They were down to one machine now and an old, padded leather table. A bald-headed man in a button-down shirt and tie sat on the lone table with his head hung low, hands at his sides, palms to the padding. His sleeves were rolled up and a cotton ball was taped to his right elbow pit, old needle tracks around it.

"Shhh."

Barnes looked at the woman who'd let him in. Dawn. She held a finger to her bright red lips, shushing him. He noticed a spiderweb tattoo on her knuckle. Her wrist was inked as well. Chickadees on branches. The art traveled down her arm and up into her sleeve. She was tall and physically fit with black hair cut into a Mohawk, black pants, and black boots. An imposing presence in the small room. Sticking out from the waist of her jeans was the yellow butt of a Taser.

"He's just coming out," Dawn said. She gestured to a chair along the near wall. "Have a seat."

"I'm fine standing," Barnes said.

The man sitting on the table looked up at them without lifting his head, only his eyes. They were bloodshot and mostly hidden by his brow. His facial skin was slack, his lips wet.

"You all right, Jack?" Dawn said.

"You know," Jack said, his speech slow, "a long time ago being crazy used to mean something. Nowadays, everybody's crazy."

Barnes turned to Dawn. "Manson?"

She nodded. "Ol' Jack used to come in here for Tom Brady and Mike Tyson."

The man stared at the side of her face as she spoke to Barnes.

"Predictably, he graduated on to Peter North," Dawn said. "At some point all of you men do. That lasted a few weeks, and then one day he asked if I had Dennis Rader."

"The BTK Killer," Barnes said.

"That's the guy. So I go, 'No, Rader hasn't sold his memories yet . . . but I got Manson.' He sold his stuff a couple weeks before he kicked off, you know? Anyway, you should have seen this guy's face light up." She turned to the man. "Ain't that right, Jacky boy?"

"Everyone's got something to blame," Jack said, his eyes shifting between Dawn and Barnes, "because no one wants to look inside themselves."

"Hey," Dawn said, "snap out of it." She snapped her fingers in front of his face. He blinked and recoiled. The skin on his face began to tighten, his hanging jaw slowly closed. He dropped his forehead into a hand and squeezed his temples.

"Give him a second," she said. "He was on a binge. They tend to hold on a bit longer."

"A binge?"

"You never tried one?"

Barnes shook his head.

"I guess some hacker figured out a way to stitch snippets from a bunch of memories together in one file, like cut and paste, you know? Saves you from going under a bunch of different times for the different memories you want. Jacky here binged on a series of Manson snippets in one go. It's like mixing a whole bar-night's worth of shots into one big glass." She gestured throwing back a glass and then rolled her eyes. "Intense."

Barnes turned his eyes to Jack, whose body was beginning to shiver. He'd seen the transformation before, felt it before, more times than he cared to recall. He scratched at his scalp. "You sure he's all right?"

"He's fine," Dawn said.

From behind his hand, Jack said, "Believe me, if I started murdering people there'd be none of you left, because . . ."

"Because what?" Dawn said, leaning into the man's face and smiling. Her teeth were dazzling white. "Because your children are coming, Charlie?"

Jack pulled his hand away and gazed at her with eyes that were somehow both fierce and dispassionate. You could imagine him playing curiously in a brutalized victim's blood, steam still rising from the gore. Barnes instinctively reached into his armpit where a .45-caliber Glock used to hang. Nothing there now.

Still shivering, Jack blinked and his eyes changed, his demeanor shifted. To Dawn he said, "What did you say?"

She patted his knee. "Just wanted to know how you feel."

Jack smiled. "I feel great." He turned to Barnes. "Hi there."

Barnes nodded back.

Jack hopped down from the table. He rolled down his sleeves, plucked a suit jacket from a nearby hook, and put it on. "See ya tomorrow."

Dawn held the door open for him. "See ya."

She closed the door behind him, locked it, and turned to Barnes. "You want Manson, too?"

"You can't let him out of here like that," Barnes said.

"Why not?" Dawn said. "He's in the Sect. He'll be fine."

"The Sect?"

"The Sect of Shifting Sands," Dawn said. "Duh."

Barnes raised his eyebrows.

"Gabriel Messina? The Shivering Man?"

Barnes shook his head.

"Let's put it this way," Dawn said. "If you're in the Sect of Shifting Sands, you can handle a little Charlie Manson."

"What are they, a bunch of machine nuts?"

"Forget I mentioned it. Who are you looking for?"

"Freddie Cohen."

"Never heard of him."

"Figured that."

"Personal?"

Barnes nodded.

"Man," Dawn said, "I haven't served a personal in months." She went to the machine and pulled out the keyboard tray beneath the bulk of the apparatus.

Barnes looked closely at the machine. First time he'd seen one in a while. Basically it was a black box, almost like a desktop computer, but with a few tubes here and there, a bottle of serum, suction cups, and the needle. An artificial heart pumped somewhere inside, sending serum through the body into the brain. The machine may have seemed like an ordinary device, but the goddamn thing had presence. Above its power switch was a red LED light that blinked slowly, as if monitoring a dying pulse.

"No med card, eh?" Dawn said.

Barnes turned up his palms.

"We've been using the shit out of Danny's card," Dawn said, "not that he doesn't deserve it. Dumbass ran off so fast he forgot it. Anyway, if it comes back canceled you may be out of luck. What'd you say the name was, again?"

"Cohen," Barnes said. "Freddie. Maybe Frederick."

"Should I even bother searching CogNet?"

CogNet. Short for Recognizant Network. It was where all legal memories were stored, accessible to anyone who had a med card and bought from a licensed memory merchant. A great place to hook in if you wanted to experience life inside a Stepford Wife. You could spend an hour high-fiving teammates as Tom Brady or painting happy little trees from within Bob Ross. If you wanted to get really crazy, you could be J. K. Rowling reading a book. Not writing one, though. Those memories weren't for sale.

"Doubt it," Barnes said.

"Okay," Dawn said, "then it's straight to the Echo Ring."

The Echo Ring was the illegal side of memory sharing. Peer-to-peer, like Napster in the beginning. Licensed machines could be jailbroken to tap into either CogNet, the Echo Ring, or both, but there was risk.

Tapping the Echo Ring using a med card was akin, penalty-wise, to a misdemeanor, while tapping without a card was more like a felony. Prison time instead of a fine. A cuff around the wrist instead of a slap.

Dawn flipped a handmade switch on the machine, turning the connection over from CogNet to the Echo Ring. She typed on the keys for a moment. "Got a few Frederick Cohens in here. You know his date of birth?"

"No," Barnes said.

"Know his middle name? Maybe his location?"

"You can find him by location?"

A smile built slowly on Dawn's face. "You sure you've done this before?"

Barnes deadpanned.

"I can find him by location three different ways," she said. "One, by his address. If he was willing to give it, which I doubt. Two, by the location where he hooked in. Or three, the location of his memories."

"What do you mean, location of his memories?"

"It's a recent upgrade," Dawn said. "If there are any visual or audible clues in a memory the machine can pick them up and try to determine the location. Like, say someone remembered walking past a street sign or eating at a particular restaurant"—she patted the machine—"this baby can likely figure out where they were in the world."

"Can you search by Louisiana for hook-in location, Detroit for the memory?"

Dawn tapped some keys and pressed "Enter."

"One hit," she said, "no pun intended. The file's called Ricky."

"That's the one," Barnes said. He took a beat and then asked, "Is it a binge?"

"No way to tell."

"Let's have it."

Dawn picked up a green-and-white med card from atop the machine. It depicted Danny's familiar face in black and gray, plus a series of numbers. She slid the card through a reader on the machine and theatrically tapped the "Enter" key.

"How did Danny get one of those cards?" Barnes said. "Last I knew, he was healthy."

"He got cancer," Dawn said. "Didn't you know?"

Barnes shook his head.

"Actually, maybe it was Alzheimer's," she said, smirking. "Or was it dementia? Oh, I remember now, it was kidney failure."

The machine made a positive noise, like collecting coins in a video game, and a bar across the top of the machine's small screen went green. "Looks like we're good to go." She picked up something from the machine's table, turned, and smiled mischievously at Barnes, the item hidden behind her back.

"What?"

She showed him a set of battery-operated clippers and popped her eyebrows. "Mr. T or Breakdown Britney?"

"Shit," Barnes said. He'd forgotten about the suction cups to the temples, the inescapable evidence of a munky's machine use. He rubbed his hands through his hair and scratched his head. "Screw it. Take it all down."

Dawn was as quick as an army recruiter with her clippers, all the while whistling an ancient pop song Barnes vaguely recognized, something to do with feeling like tonight will be a good night. In minutes he was as bald as a PFC, rubbing a hand over the bristle on his scalp.

"Lose that jacket and hop on up," Dawn said, slapping the black bonded leather of the padded table.

Barnes peeled off his jacket and hung it on a hook. He reached to roll up his shirtsleeve before recalling he was only in a T-shirt, so no need. He sat down on the table, swung his legs up, and lay back. Dawn held out a short dowel rod for him to take. The thing was riddled with enough bite marks to rival a third-grader's pencil. Barnes gripped it in his fist while Dawn snapped on black surgical gloves and brought the needle toward his elbow pit.

"I guess you *do* know the drill," Dawn said, noting Barnes's needle tracks. But she stopped short of piercing his skin. She cupped a hand on his arm. Her touch was warm, despite the latex. "You need to relax. You're shaking all over."

"Sorry," Barnes said. His mind was suddenly overrun with incoherent whispers, like a tangle of snakes, hissing and sinking their fangs into his brain matter.

Voices.

Some words could be heard in the din.

"*Why?*"

"*Please.*"

Barnes felt sick to hear them again. He considered hopping up from the table and running off, but . . .

. . . *It's about Ricky.*

He squeezed the dowel hard enough to whiten his knuckles. He locked eyes with Dawn. "Been a while."

"Take a deep breath," she said.

Barnes closed his eyes and tried to still his mad heart, to quiet the voices. He breathed deeply and slowly until he felt the needle sting his skin. Then he held his breath until Dawn said, "All set."

He exhaled shakily as the cold serum mingled with the blood in his arm. The whispers faded.

She applied the machine's suction cups to his temples. "You ready?"

Eyes still closed, Barnes nodded.

"Better put in that bit."

Barnes brought the dowel rod to his mouth but stopped short of biting it. He opened his eyes and said, "Can you sing?"

"Excuse me?"

"Can you sing?"

Dawn pinched her face. "I ain't exactly Little Cher, God help the poor girl, but I can hold a note or two. Why?"

"Raphael used to sing."

"Danny, you mean?"

"Yeah."

"What'd he sing?"

"Anything," Barnes said. "Whatever came to mind, I guess. Not Britney Spears."

Dawn smirked and nodded. "Fair enough." She put her hand on the machine, ready to turn the dial and connect Barnes with whatever Freddie Cohen had in store.

"Put in that bit," Dawn said, "and close your eyes."

Barnes bit down on the rod. He closed his eyes.

Dawn turned the dial. The machine clicked and hissed. The serum moved through his veins. She began singing, softly and slowly, "There is a house in New Orleans, they call the Rising Sun. And it's been the ruin of many a poor boy . . ."

Through his bit Barnes sang, "And God, I know I'm—"

The machine's surge arched Barnes's body, heels to head, like he was being electrocuted. A Vitruvian Man test pattern appeared before his closed eyes, overlaid with the words *Please Stand By*. A female voice from within his mind said, "*Prepare for transmission.*"

4

The scent of pine, the sound of droning insects and labored breathing. His own. Barnes's lungs burned. He found himself walking through a forest in the late afternoon, struggling over fallen logs and up and down little hills covered with crispy leaves and waving ferns. The inside of his mouth was coated with saliva and the remnants of a Slo Poke caramel sucker, or maybe a Tootsie Roll. He was tired and hot and sweating. The straps of his backpack cut into his shoulders. The weight and bulk of Freddie Cohen's body was disorienting. Barnes felt as if he were walking underwater.

"Come on, Freddie!"

Cohen looked up to find the source of the voice. Ricky. He was standing on a ridge thirty yards ahead, sporting jeans and a white T-shirt, holding a shoebox against his hip. He smiled widely, showing front teeth that seemed too big for his mouth. Barnes felt the sensation of Freddie's unfocused gaze. Time seemed to slow, and there was a flutter in his belly to see Ricky, alive and happy, still running through the woods, still on an adventure.

The nostalgia soon turned over to nausea. Tears pressed at Barnes's eyes as he thought, *I'm so sorry, kid.*

At the sight of Barnes's kid brother, Cohen's pounding heart seemed to spread inside his chest, sending a tingling sensation to the extremities. It felt good to be the reason for Ricky's smile. He quickened his pace up the ridge, smashing through the undergrowth, taking scratches and scrapes along the way.

When Barnes looked up again, Ricky was gone.

Freddie redoubled his effort to finally make the top of the ridge. He stooped over, hands on his knees, and sucked big breaths. Drops of sweat tickled his brow.

"Put your hands on your head."

Freddie looked down the back side of the ridge to find Ricky with his fingers laced together on top of his head, mimicking breathing heavily. Barnes followed Ricky's advice, lacing his fingers over Freddie's greasy hair. Sure enough, the big kid's hot lungs opened up and let in more air.

Ricky stood next to a weeping willow near the riverbank. Barnes recognized the tree; it was the only willow for a half mile in any direction in Whitehall Forest. He and Ricky would know—they had walked, ran, or stomped through every bit of these woods. Mom used to tell her grass-stained, mud-coated sons, standing happily at the trailer's back door after boomeranging home, "You two have covered every foot and furlong of that jungle, and I'll be damned if you don't bring it all home with you." The boys would snap off the willow's flexible branches and whip the shit out of each other, running in circles, screaming and laughing, until one of them caught a face shot and claimed temporary blindness. Barnes felt the memento burn on his cheek, recalled sneering at Ricky with one eye closed, his brother pulling an *oh-my-God-I'm-sorry* face with clenched teeth.

Freddie started down the ridge toward Ricky's position, stepping carefully over loose rocks and moss-covered waterlogs that crumbled underfoot. Once he reached the bottom, Freddie playfully slapped the younger boy's shoulder with the back of his hand. "You're so fast."

"Let's do this," Ricky said. He produced a gardening trowel from his back pocket and showed it to Freddie.

Barnes recognized Mom's trowel. It had a worn wooden handle with *CB* etched into the end—Cassie Barnes. She tended her patio pots with the tool along with the patch garden she had planted in their scant yard. She also used the trowel's back as a paddle. Just seeing it made Barnes's butt sting.

Ricky dropped to his knees and started digging at an open spot between the willow's thick roots. To Freddie, he said, "What'd you bring?"

Freddie came down to Ricky's height one knee at a time. He slid the backpack off his shoulders, reached inside, and pulled out a folded edition of that morning's *Detroit Free Press*. "First thing is today's paper. It proves the date."

"That's real smart, Freddie," Ricky said. Their eyes met for a moment. Freddie Cohen felt dizzy about it.

"What else?" Ricky said.

"*Giant-Size Fantastic Four*, number four," Freddie said, displaying the comic book wrapped in cellophane. "Don't worry. I have another one at home. Let's see, I've got this week's *TV Guide*, Destro, a menu from Mancino's, a picture of Rufus, and some duct tape."

Ricky laughed. "You brought a picture of your dog?"

Barnes felt Freddie's cheeks burn.

"Hey, man," Ricky said, chuckling, "it's all right. I'm just crackin'."

Freddie shrugged.

"So crazy that you brought that menu," Ricky said.

"Well, what'd you bring?" Freddie said.

Ricky opened the shoebox. "I've got Zandar to go with your Destro, a Twinkie, plus a couple of my dad's smokes, but those aren't for the time capsule." He plucked the two Merit Ultra Lights out of the shoebox and put one behind each ear. He then pulled out a manila envelope looped closed with red string. "The rest is stuff for my brother."

"What kind of stuff?" Freddie said.

"Aw, he's real good at thinking things out, ya know? I figure if he finds this time capsule, I'll give him some clues to follow."

"Follow for what?"

Ricky winked and smiled. "That's for me to know . . ."

Freddie rolled his eyes. ". . . and for me to suck an egg about."

Ricky handed Freddie the shoebox. "Get it all in there and seal it up." He went back to digging between the roots.

Freddie padded the bottom of the shoebox with the newspaper. He delicately placed the comic book on top of the paper, curling it up against the side walls. He picked up Ricky's manila envelope and sniffed it. Barnes found the scent of his family's trailer, plus the smell of Magic Marker from where Ricky had written "Johnny" on one side. Freddie placed the envelope over the comic book, added the *TV Guide* and the menu, and then piled on the G.I. Joe action figures, the Twinkie, and finally the picture of Rufus, his Maltese. In the picture, the dog was sitting on the couch in the Cohen family living room, its jaw lowered onto its paws.

Freddie closed the shoebox top. He picked up the duct tape roll and sniffed at the edge, found that pleasant little glue scent. He carefully sealed the shoebox edges. He then wrapped the tape all around the box, turning it into an impenetrable gray fortress.

"Ready?" Ricky said. He'd dug the hole a couple of feet deep, having chopped through a wrist-size root with his trowel.

"Won't the roots grow through the box?" Freddie said.

"Not this close to the tree," Ricky said. He looked up. "Look at the canopy. It goes all the way out." He pointed to the edge where the great willow's branches ended, but Freddie never turned his head. He studied the movements of Ricky's arm and his shoulder, the pulsing veins near his neck. "Any new roots will grow out there."

The boys buried the time capsule and tamped the dirt flat above the hole. Afterward, Ricky picked up the duct tape and turned his back on Freddie. He pulled a Magic Marker from his back pocket.

"What's up?" Freddie said.

"Hold on a sec," Ricky said. He peeled off a long strip of tape and began wrapping it around something small that Barnes couldn't see. He stopped for a moment, wrote something on the inside of the tape, and put the marker back in his pocket before he kept wrapping. Once he was done he threw the tape roll into the open zipper of Freddie's backpack and began climbing the willow.

"Be careful," Freddie said. He stepped beneath the tree and looked up as Ricky climbed. Ricky was quick from branch to branch, holding whatever he'd wound in tape between his teeth. He got so high up that Freddie lost him in the mix of branches.

For several minutes Freddie was alone, the time capsule beneath his feet and only the sound of the rushing water to keep him company. He felt sweaty. He wondered if Ricky might be up for taking a dip to cool off but pushed the thought away when he imagined that Ricky would bust his balls if he kept his shirt on. He recalled his family trip to Virginia Beach earlier that summer. He'd kept his shirt on while wading in the ocean because Dad said he had bitch tits. "Take your shirt off, Freddie. No one cares about your bitch tits."

"Leave him alone, Don!"

Ricky came down the tree. The duct-taped item was gone. They went down to the riverbank and sat on two boulders, shoes dangling perilously close to the water. Ricky popped the cigarettes into his mouth and produced a mini Bic lighter. He lit both and then handed one to Freddie.

Freddie puffed without inhaling. He tasted the acrid smoke, felt the heat of the orange-hot cherry. Barnes's throat burned. Freddie blew out, casual as can be.

"You never smoked before, eh?" Ricky said.

"Of course I have," Freddie said. He took another short puff and blew it out.

Ricky nodded. His cigarette was lipped, eyes squinting like an old pro. He took a drag, scissored the cigarette between two fingers to pull it from his mouth, and drew his knees up to his chest. "This is the spot me and my brother come to sometimes," he said. "Used to catch fish around here. Brook trout and little chubs, ya know?"

Yeah, Barnes thought. They used to cook those brookies on sticks, skin on, over a little campfire and eat them like corncobs. Just a little salt and pepper was all they needed. The packets stolen from Mancino's earlier that morning.

Freddie nodded.

"Last summer one of those chubs swallowed a hook and we couldn't get it out. The fish died, and now Johnny doesn't want to fish anymore. He's sensitive, I guess."

Barnes harrumphed. The little liar. It was Ricky who'd cried over that dead chub. They'd tried like hell to pull out the hook as the damn fish gasped and twitched, but its guts just came out with the hook, turning it inside out.

Freddie said, "It's okay to be sensitive, ain't it?"

Ricky offered no reply.

Silence wedged its way between them like an uninvited guest. The two boys smoked and stared until Ricky took a final drag from his cigarette and flicked it into the water. It sizzled at the surface, bobbed under, came back up, and was carried downstream. He stood and dusted himself off. "Let's go."

"Wait," Freddie said. He threw his cigarette into the water and struggled up from his boulder to a standing position.

"What's up?" Ricky said.

"I just . . . I just want to stay a little longer, if that's okay?"

"It's Thursday, man," Ricky said. "Mom's making tacos."

"Just a little longer," Freddie said. "Come on over here." He took Ricky by the hand. Barnes noted how cold his brother's hand felt. All the time, no matter what, Ricky's hands were cold. Mom used to tell him, "Cold hands, warm heart."

Ricky yanked his hand from Freddie's grip but followed the older boy back to the willow.

"I want you to stand with your back against the tree, okay?"

"Why?" Ricky said.

39

"It's a game," Freddie said. "Just trust me."

Ricky rolled his eyes. He went to the tree and stood with his back against the trunk. He spread his arms and raised his eyebrows. "Now what?"

Barnes's palms were suddenly clammy. Freddie rubbed them against the front of his shorts, felt the lump of the coin purse he carried in his front pocket. "Close your eyes, okay?"

Ricky's hands fell back to his sides. His eyebrows knitted. "No way, dude. You're gonna sock me."

"I swear to God I won't."

"Gimme the duct tape."

"What?"

"Gimme that duct tape so I know you won't tape me to the tree."

Freddie rummaged through his backpack, found the tape, and handed it over.

Ricky held the roll with two hands in front of his waist. He closed his eyes. "Okay, so what's this game?"

Freddie Cohen moved close to Ricky. He stood for a moment, just watching the younger boy's face, watching him swallow, watching his eyes move beneath the lids. He smelled of cheap fabric softener, something like grapefruit. Waves of fear pulsated through Barnes's body. Freddie's hands shook, his knees trembled. Barnes's mouth still tasted of smoke.

Freddie leaned in and kissed Ricky's lips.

When it was done, the older boy stepped back.

With his eyes still closed Ricky said, "You shouldn't have done that, Freddie."

"I'm sorry," Freddie said.

Ricky opened his eyes. "You should have asked me."

"You would have said no."

"You're right. I would have said no. And you wouldn't have had to trick me to find out I'm not gay."

"Don't tell anyone, okay?"

"I'm mad at you."

Freddie produced the coin purse from his pocket. It was a black plastic purse with a Batman logo on the outside. "Here," Freddie said, "take it. It's all I've got."

"I don't want your money."

"Then what do you want? You can't tell anyone."

"I won't tell anyone."

"Promise me," Freddie said.

"No."

Ricky pushed off from the tree and started to walk away, but Freddie grabbed his arm and stopped him.

"Promise me!"

"Promise not to tell anyone you're a fag? Is that what you want?"

Freddie threw Ricky back against the tree. "I'm not a fag!" His heart pounded crazily inside Barnes's chest.

"Then what am I *not* supposed to tell anyone?" Ricky said. He offered that half-cocked know-it-all smile Barnes knew all too well. That smile that made you love him and want to smack him at the same time. Freddie felt that pang of love, that desire to smack. "You're going to tell, I know it."

Ricky stared off.

"Please, don't."

Ricky pursed his lips.

Freddie punched him.

Ricky's head slammed back against the tree. His body slumped and then toppled forward, face-flat in the leaves.

"Oh no," Freddie said. "Oh God." He turned Ricky over, found he was breathing, saw the mouse forming above the younger boy's eye. He lightly slapped Ricky's cheek. "Ricky. Come on. Wake up."

Ricky stirred but didn't open his eyes.

Freddie stood up and backed away. He collected his things and stuffed them into his backpack. He threw it over his shoulders and began to walk off. He turned back for a final glance and saw his Batman coin purse on the ground near Ricky. He ran back, picked it up, and started back toward the ridge.

Barnes's breathing was strained when Freddie reached the top. He headed back the way he came. It was dusk now, and the woods looked different. A red hue on everything. Crickets chirred. Freddie made his way down the ridge and stuck close to the river as he had on the way in, still clutching the coin purse. The breeze picked up, carrying a scent that seemed out of place. Something plastic-y, like the Bondo auto body repair kit Dad used on that old Camaro he was always working on. There was a coppery, oily scent, too.

A cracking branch stopped Freddie cold. The crickets went silent. Leaves rustled as something moved through the trees. The sound had come from across the river.

Barnes looked over to find a six-foot Eddie Able standing at the riverbank.

Freddie blinked. His jaw fell open. He dropped his coin purse.

Eddie Able was dressed as a plumber, but he was a monster, Freddie knew. Not the kind of monster with fangs and claws and scaly skin. Not the kind that might howl or scream bloody murder in the night. No. This was a thinking monster, one smart enough to disguise the horror that it really was, clever enough to wrap itself in a vision that appealed to the innocence of its prey. Its blond hair was shellacked on top of a big fiberglass head. Its pupils were black mesh designed to be seen through from inside out. The evening sun caught a glint of the human eyes set deep within. A little red patch above the breast read EDDIE in stitched white. It wore big brown work boots the size of clown shoes. A brass zipper trailed down the front of the monster's outfit, and its gloves were those puffy, four-fingered deals cartoon characters wore. Only these gloves weren't white, but red.

But then again, no. The gloves weren't technically red. They were white gloves that'd been splattered red.

And they were dripping.

The Eddie thing raised one of his splotchy red gloves to its fiberglass mouth, extended a thick finger, and mimicked *Shhh*. When it pulled the finger away it left behind a sticky red line from its button nose to its dimpled chin.

Freddie ran.

Darkness and silence.

"End of transmission."

The Vitruvian Man test pattern.

Please Stand By.

5

Barnes lay on the table beneath Ziti's, eyes still closed. His body was overwhelmed with fright. He felt reduced to a child, felt the urge to run and hide, to find a blanket and crawl under it. He recalled the only other time he'd been frightened by Eddie Able. The doll had recently been introduced to the public, and with so much sales success there was an afternoon TV show quickly slapped together. To add to the excitement, it was announced that the show would be taped at WXON studios in Detroit, where Eddie Able's regional sales had gone off the charts.

After weeks of waiting for the premiere, Johnny and Ricky sat through the first episode on the edges of their seats, eyes riveted to the seventeen-inch screen in their trailer living room. The show's format was similar to that of *Bozo the Clown* or *Howdy Doody*. A life-size Eddie played games and interacted with an audience of children as well as his campy counterparts. When the show was nearly over and it was time to sign off, Eddie turned to the camera and the stage lights dimmed, leaving him alone in the spotlight. The camera panned closer and closer while he spoke. "So long, kids," Eddie said. "See you next time." He waggled a finger as his head began to take up the entire screen. "Don't grow up too fast, and hey, come to think of it"—he tapped his lips to mimic thinking, tilted his head, and then looked directly into the camera with those blacked-out eyes—"wouldn't it be *bliss* if you never got old, like me?"

The stage went dark.

Several days had passed before young Johnny was willing to pull the string on Ricky's Eddie Able doll again. He was certain it wasn't geared to say the words that the real live Eddie had signed off with, but he wasn't taking any chances.

That first episode was the only time that sign-off was used. In the second episode, and thereafter, Eddie ended with a simpler, "Hey, kids, don't grow up too fast!"

"You all right?"

It was Dawn. Her voice cut through Barnes's fog to draw him out of his reverie. He blinked his eyes and sat up, spat the bit into his hand.

"Ended kinda rough there," Dawn said. "All that time you were happy, and then whammo, you were screaming."

"I was?"

"You know what?" Dawn said. "I think I do know you. You're a cop, right?"

"Used to be," Barnes said.

"I remember your face," she said. "You were with the boys that busted that crack house on Fenkell. I was just a girl then, but it really helped clean up the street. My parents talked about it for months."

Barnes nodded. He didn't recall that particular case, but crack-house busts were as common as morning coffee to Detroit cops before the machine changed the drug world landscape. One day they were kicking in the doors on baseheads with glass pipes, the next they were arresting anyone with a set of clippers and a strong internet connection.

"Wouldn't have pegged you for a munky," Dawn said.

Barnes reached up to pull the suction cups from his temples but stopped short. "Do me a favor. Check to see if there's anything from an Adrian Flaherty in there."

"You got the money?"

Barnes handed her a fifty. "Will this cover it?"

"Sure," Dawn said, "but keep your pants on. I gotta run this card again." She slid the card through the reader and pressed "Enter." They waited in silence for a moment, and then the machine made a negative noise, the death of a video game sprite.

"Shit," Dawn said. "Danny's luck just ran out."

Barnes looked at the machine's screen to see that the green bar across the top had gone red. "What's that mean?"

"That means our only option is to go bare balls in the Echo Ring," Dawn said, "and I won't be doing that for fifty bucks. Harrison will kill me."

"You've done it before," Barnes said. "Else you wouldn't be hiding this machine down here in the basement. You'd be running this operation like a real memory shop."

"You know so much, huh?"

"What don't I know?"

"Remember that show *To Catch a Predator*?"

"They entrapped pedophiles by posing as kids in chat rooms, right?"

"Right. Well, they're doing the same on the Echo Ring now. Used to be it was just harmless sharing, everything was underground and no one cared, but once the crackdown got serious, the FBI started setting traps. Try tapping into a juicy memory, you could be inviting the feds right to your door."

"How could they find you?"

Dawn winked. "Big Brother is always watching."

"Well," Barnes said, "you willing to take a chance?"

Dawn held out an open palm.

He sighed. "I've got twenty more, but my kid is waiting on a double pepperoni from upstairs."

Dawn shoved the keyboard back in. "Business is business."

"Even for the guy who helped clean up your street?"

She stared down at the machine for a moment, drumming her fingers on the plastic. Without looking up, she said, "My parents had already decided to move, you know? They couldn't afford much, but they were going to find a way to get us off that street. They had their eyes on some shack in mid-Michigan, nothing around but trees and campfire rings. I didn't want to leave my friends behind and sure as hell didn't want to start a new life in some backwards hick town who'd view me in a black shirt as satanic panic, end up like the West Memphis Three." She looked at Barnes. "You boys saved my ass."

"Glad to be of service," Barnes said.

"What was that name again?"

"Flaherty." The breathless voice, speaking from within.

"Shhh."

"Adrian Flaherty," Barnes said to Dawn.

Dawn pulled out the machine's keyboard, started typing. "F-L-A-H-E-R-T-Y?"

"Yep."

"Locations?"

"Probably Detroit and Detroit."

"Let's see," Dawn said. "I've got a Homicide Detective Flaherty in here with three files. That your guy?"

Barnes nodded.

"You gotta be kidding me," Dawn said. "You want me to go Echo Ring on a *cop's* files?"

"There's no way they'd be dumb enough to entrap you with a cop's files, right?"

Dawn stared at him.

"I'm trying to save that cop's life," Barnes said.

"Sure you are."

"Cherry Daniels," Barnes said.

"Oh, come on," Dawn said. "Don't sell me that shit."

"This cop, Flaherty," Barnes said. "He was on Cherry's case. Suddenly he disappeared. If I can find him, I can find her."

"You said you weren't a cop anymore."

"I'm not. I . . . It's complicated, all right, but I *am* trying to save him. And her."

Dawn sighed. She looked at the screen. "I've got ColdCase, all one word, plus Franklin, and FiveLives, also one word."

"Franklin? That's my old partner."

"That's what it says."

"Gimme Franklin," Barnes said. He chomped his bit and lay back.

"Want me to sing again?"

Barnes shook his head.

"Okay then," Dawn said. "We'll do it my way." She tapped "Enter" and turned the dial. A click and a hiss. She leaned in close to Barnes's face. "Good night, sweet prince."

Barnes's body arched. The Vitruvian Man returned to his closed eyes.

The scent of disinfectant. Stainless steel doors. Muzak. Barnes felt butterflies in his guts, like when Mom used to take the backcountry roads and speed over the intersection hills. The elevator doors opened to reveal a hospital hallway. Adrian Flaherty stepped out and showed his badge to a nurse at the reception desk. She nodded. He turned the corner and kept walking.

The hospital hallway felt familiar to Barnes.

Flaherty was at Sinai Grace.

He took a left into Franklin's single-bed room. Barnes's former partner was sitting up in bed, watching the overhead television. There were circles shaved into his temples and a plastic mug with a bendy straw on the table by his bedside along with a half-eaten meat loaf and some dire mashed potatoes on a plastic plate. To one side sat a dormant squeeze box that had once done Franklin's breathing for him; to the other side was a computer monitoring his vitals and feeding an oxygen tube to his nose.

"Aw, hell," Franklin said. He picked up the remote and turned the TV off. "What happened?"

"Calavera," Flaherty said. "Barnes got him."

"You're shittin' me."

Flaherty shook his head.

"But they sent you?"

"Barnes took three rounds, point blank. Ambulance took him to Providence."

"He gonna make it?"

You're damn right I am.

Flaherty shrugged.

"So what's this, then?" Franklin said.

"Follow-up." Flaherty produced a notepad and pen. "We need to start building our case. We got a three-day memory pull off Barnes, but we'll need more to convict Calavera. Whatever you've got on him, whatever you guys discovered."

"Bullshit," Franklin said. "There's plenty of time for that after I'm out of this bed. And you won't need Barnes's pull. He's gonna live."

Flaherty pulled up a chair, sat next to the bed. "Okay then, maybe I'm here for something else."

"Shoot."

"I've been on the machine."

"So?"

"As you."

Franklin's face darkened. "And?"

Flaherty held Franklin's gaze, said nothing.

"Tyrell Diggs, right?" Franklin finally said.

Flaherty nodded.

"You gonna arrest me for shooting a crack dealer a hundred years ago?"

"No," Flaherty said. "As far as I'm concerned, you did the world a favor that day, never mind the statute of limitations. I want to know what else you knew about him."

"Diggs?"

Flaherty nodded.

"Just a boogeyman who lived on my block. Sold crack to good people. Cost them their lives, like scumbags do."

"Anything other than crack?"

"I don't know what went on in that house besides drugs, man. It ain't like I hung out there."

"But you were there."

"One time," Franklin said.

"I know. I saw what you saw."

"Then what's this about?"

"Think back, Billy," Flaherty said.

"You think back, you know so much."

"You know more than I do," Flaherty said.

"What do you want me to tell you?"

"Think back."

"No. First tell me what this is about."

"Just help me," Flaherty said. "Do me a favor."

Franklin harrumphed. He shook his head, rolled his eyes, and then closed them. "I tell you one thing, that place smelled like piss."

"And the floorboards creaked," Flaherty said.

"Where there were any. It was a total shithole."

"Was there anyone else in the house when you shot Tyrell?"

Franklin ruminated for a moment and then shook his head. "None that I saw, but it was a crack house. Could've been baseheads upstairs, downstairs, wherever."

"Tell me about the walls."

"They were just walls, man. I mean, the wallpaper was for shit, and there were holes punched out here and there, but basically they were just walls."

"No art?"

"Shee-it," Franklin said, smiling, eyes still closed. "You ever taken down a crack house, Flaherty?"

"What about posters?"

Franklin rubbed his chin. "Wait. Yeah, there were a few posters. *Scarface*, *The Godfather*, gangster paraphernalia. Every crack house in the world."

"Eddie Able?"

Franklin opened his eyes. "Eddie Able?"

"You know, that doll for boys? Came out around that time, maybe a couple years before. It was a big hit. Mothers fought over them at the toy stores. Still does pretty well today, from what I understand."

"So?"

"There was an Eddie Able poster on the wall in Diggs's crack house. You saw it. I saw it through you."

"Okay," Franklin said, "now that you mention it, sure. Blond hair, dressed like a policeman or something."

"In that poster, yeah, but not all of them dressed like that."

"How's that?"

"Eddie isn't just a doll," Flaherty said, "but a concept. The character was successful enough that they rented out life-size versions for kids' parties and such. Some guy inside the suit."

"Like Mickey Mouse?"

"Yeah, sure."

"So, what?" Franklin said. "One of these dressed-up Eddies do something?"

"Question is, why would a crack dealer like Tyrell Diggs have an Eddie Able poster on his wall, stashed in there with all his gangster shit?"

"It was a crack house, dude. They probably thought it was funny."

"No," Flaherty said, "think back. That poster wasn't stuck up with thumbtacks like the others. It was framed in glass. Professionally done."

Franklin sighed. "My partner's been shot, I got one tube in my nose and one in my dick, and you're coming at me with this doll crap. What's up?"

"You were already gone when they took Diggs's crack house down," Flaherty said. "Back to college, I assume. I was in middle school. But just this morning, out of curiosity, I pulled the file. Found out Diggs was involved in something other than drugs. Something our guys never released to the public. I'm not even sure what to call it. The basement of that house was set up like a dreamland for children—puzzles, toys, doll-houses, arcade games, pinball machines, you name it. The door at the bottom of the steps was dead-bolted like a prison, and there was a photo album containing pictures of neighborhood kids reported missing."

"Kiddie porn?"

"Not that we know of, but our boys obviously liked Diggs for the missing kids. Only they couldn't pin it on him."

"That's why they didn't release the case facts?"

"Right. They were looking for Diggs's silent partner. Never sniffed him out, but a couple of the kids in those pictures are all grown up now—those that survived, anyway—and they're coming out of the woodwork to talk about what happened."

"And they ain't talking about Diggs?"

"They're talking about Eddie Able."

"What else did they say?"

"Haven't gotten that far yet."

"I don't get it," Franklin said. "These guys abducted kids so they could . . . what? Play dress-up with them? Show them their cool toys?"

"That's the part that doesn't click. That's why we need to look harder. Discover the motivation, create the profile, and track this silent partner down."

Franklin looked off in thought. "Who owned the house?"

"Diggs. Thought maybe he got it for a song when the real estate market tanked, but no. He paid fifty thousand, cash."

"No way," Franklin said. "That kind of money? Someone fronted him."

Flaherty nodded.

"And we never got this other guy?"

"Case went cold, but it's still open. Guy's probably still active, all these years. Could be linked to dozens of missing children's cases."

"What're you gonna do?"

"I'm gonna start digging."

Darkness and silence.

"End of transmission."

The Vitruvian Man test pattern.

Please Stand By.

6

Barnes sat on the edge of the padded table, his feet dangling above the concrete floor of the basement at Ziti's. The noise in his head was too loud. Impossible to think. The needle had been removed from his arm, a cotton ball and a Band-Aid put in its place. The suction cups had been taken from his temples. His muscles were sore, his eyes burned.

"—pperoni home to your kid."

Barnes turned toward the sound. A woman standing there. Pretty. Tattooed. Mohawk. Sunrise or something. "What'd you say?"

"I said, you better get that double pepperoni home to your kid. Before it gets cold, you know?"

Barnes nodded slowly. The movement was exhausting.

"Come on," the woman said. "Here we go." She helped him off the edge of the bed to his feet.

"Thanks," Barnes said. He felt wobbly. He tried to recall her name. "Um . . ."

"Dawn," the woman said.

"Right." He stabilized himself against the table.

"Here's your jacket," Dawn said. She held it out to him.

Barnes didn't take it. He closed his eyes and gripped his forehead with one hand. His body trembled. Cohen. Ricky. Franklin. Tyrell Diggs. Flaherty. Eddie Able. Voices whispering from within. The science was understood now, the danger of the machine had been determined, the reason it was outlawed. Neurons were forming in Barnes's brain, connecting to their new host and growing. Not just other people's memories, as Barnes well knew, but their personalities. Over time he could hold them back and with disuse they would eventually fade, but as of now he was a reformed munky fresh on relapse.

As the junkies of old might say, *What a rush.*

He held still and fought not to shiver. The noise in his mind began to fade. The fog cleared away. He released his head and looked at Dawn.

She smiled and showed those brilliant whites. "Back with us?"

"I think so," Barnes said.

"At least you weren't screaming this time."

He took his jacket from her and put it on.

She opened the door and let him out. "You seem like a decent guy. Maybe don't come back for a while, huh?"

Barnes nodded.

Dawn nodded with him. "Maybe not at all."

Barnes started out the door but then stopped. He turned back to Dawn. "This Echo Ring," he said. "It's definitely peer-to-peer?"

"Yep."

"So those memory files are on someone's home computer?"

"Most likely."

"Can you get the IP address?"

Dawn went back to the machine. She pulled out a notepad and wrote down the IP from the peer computer that contained Flaherty's stashed files. She came back and handed him the note.

64.199.1.7

"Thanks," Barnes said. He pocketed the note, left the room, and slid along the wall behind the refrigerator. He made his way through the dimly lit basement and back up the stairs. His pizza was waiting on a ledge near the back door. He fished in his pocket for his wallet while looking into the kitchen to find Harrison. The man was tossing dough into the air, spinning it out. Their eyes met. Harrison nodded at the pizza box. "On the house."

Barnes picked up the box and backed out the door.

Outside was dark. The rain had stopped. Barnes set the pizza on the passenger seat and climbed inside the truck. He dropped his head to the steering wheel and closed his eyes. His body ached. Adrenaline rolled like napalm. He was sweating, but cold. He couldn't release the vision of Ricky standing happily on that ridge in the woods, couldn't release the joy he felt followed by the pain, the guilt. He was Ricky's monster, Ricky's Lenny Small, the thing that loved him to death.

He picked up his cell phone and dialed Franklin, waited through the rings until he got to voice mail: *"You've reached Lieutenant Detective Franklin, Detroit Homicide. If this is an emergency, please dial 911. Otherwise, you know the routine."*

After the tone, Barnes said, "You've got some explaining to do. Call me back."

Barnes dropped the phone onto the pizza box and started the truck. When the headlights popped on they revealed a Melodian standing next to the dumpster. He was soaking wet from the recent rain, staring at the back door to Ziti's.

Melodians were members of Melody Sharpe's angel squad. They were easy to spot because they all wore reverse Mohawks to indicate their non-use of the machine. Initially it just looked like male-pattern baldness (though the look was strange on her female followers), but after some time the hair on their temples grew long and they ended up with the same style as men of the Hasidim. Many wore hats while at their jobs or running errands.

Melody Sharpe was an inmate psychologist who ran an independent study of the machine's effects on the criminals who were forced to use it. She was the first to suggest it wasn't only memories that lingered in the brains of machine users but that personalities were beginning to form. Melody's findings were initially dismissed, but then one of her most ardent opponents, a California senator named Randall Shakely, became less and less vocal in defiance of her results. Turned out he'd been spending time on the machine as a teenage girl in rural Arkansas, and Melody scared her.

The girl's name was Brittany Tuck. Her memories were a collection of her sitting around painting her toenails while listening to electronica, playing video games, and occasionally prancing around in front of her bedroom mirror wearing nothing more than a set of butterfly wings, but she figured they may be worth a couple of bucks, so into the Echo Ring they went.

Randall Shakely, having essentially become Brittany Tuck through his use of the machine, stopped showing up at Congress and his own office, and one day he didn't come home for Prince Spaghetti night. His wife reported him missing. The police picked him up at a high school sweet-talking some of the boys on the football team. He inadvertently became the poster boy—poster girl, as it were—for Melody Sharpe's antimachine stance, and a new faction of the Sharpe angel squad was born: the Brittanians. Men and women dressed as teenage girls, sporting high socks, skirts, and high-schooler backpacks. Melodians and Brittanians often banded together to protest at memory shops or known underground machine locations. Mostly they were harmless picketers, but this guy? He was at a crossroads.

Barnes pulled forward. The Melodian either had to move or get run down. The man stepped to the side but held out his hand, indicating Barnes should stop. He did. The man gestured for Barnes to roll down the window. Barnes obliged.

"There's a machine in there," the man said. His jaw shook as he spoke. Raindrops glistened on his bald head and dripped from his chin. "Right?"

"Yeah."

"What's it like?"

"It's not worth it," Barnes said.

"Who were you?"

Barnes sighed. "Does it matter?"

The man took a beat and then quickly uttered, "I don't like my life."

As Barnes rolled up the window, he said, "Join the Brittanians." He pulled out of the alley and turned toward home. His cell phone rang as he accelerated down the street. He snatched it up and answered. "You bastard."

"Is that. Any way to talk. To a friend?"

It wasn't Franklin. Barnes pulled the phone away from his head and checked the caller ID. UNKNOWN. He put the phone back to his ear. "Who is this?"

"Oh, John," the caller said. "My feelings. Are hurt."

"Gee, I'm sorry. Now who the fuck is this?"

"I know. What you must. Think." The voice was weak and whispery. The caller struggled to speak. He took sharp intakes of breath between his stunted phrases. "You think Franklin. Is toying with you. You think he wrote. The letter from Cohen."

"Say what?"

"You think he's. Trying to pull you. Into an. Investigation. Using Ricky as bait."

"Look, jerk-off," Barnes said. "I don't know who you—"

"Using the fact. That you failed. Your kid brother."

Barnes went silent. His mind raced as he tried to place a face with the voice.

"And then," the voice said. "There's that. Terrifying. Eddie Able. In Cohen's. Twenty-five-year-old. Memories. Plus the poster in. Diggs's crack house. No way it's. Coincidence."

Barnes took his foot off the gas pedal. "Who are you? How could you know these things?"

"I've been them, too," the caller said. "Cohen. Flaherty. Franklin. I've even. Been you. Detective."

"That means you're police."

"Perhaps. I'm just a concerned. Citizen."

"Last chance, pal," Barnes said. He stepped on the accelerator again. "Your name or I'm gone."

"Find the shoebox. John."

Barnes slammed the brakes. The truck screeched to a halt. "What?"

No reply.

Barnes took the phone away from his ear and stared at it. The call had been disconnected. The LED screen was blank. Barnes sat in silence but for the running engine and the keys swinging in the ignition. The black screen seemed to grow bigger, the world around it went out of focus. A high-pitched sound from far away. The screen grew wider, deeper. A hole.

A car horn honked as the driver pulled around Barnes's truck. "Get off the road, asshole!"

Barnes set the phone down on the passenger seat. The pizza box was on the floor. He pulled a U-turn and headed north toward Whitehall Forest.

The overgrown two-track came to a dead end in the woods west of Featherton Road. The pickup truck's headlights blasted through the white birch and pine trunks, exposing zigzag branches like gnarled fingers. Barnes killed the engine and the lights went out. He got out of the cab, reached behind his seat to find a Maglite and a spare claw hammer. He closed the door and checked that the flashlight worked. He turned off the light and went to the front of the truck where he stood in silence, allowing his eyes to adapt to the darkness.

A breeze hushed through the trees and whistled in the undergrowth. The river rushed in the distance. The truck's engine ticked as it cooled. The purple ghosts on Barnes's eyes began to fade. More and more of the forest could be seen—the tree trunks, the branches, the lilting ferns. His body became taut, as though the cool earth beneath his feet was filling him up like a balloon, testing the strength of his skin. Stand still long enough and he might burst.

Barnes clicked on the flashlight and began moving through the trees toward the sound of the river. When he arrived at the bank, he followed it west until he neared a clearing. The markings were familiar here, even in the dark. The trees, the rocks, the boulders. He would soon step into the clearing where Calavera had lived in his boxcar, where Barnes had apprehended him.

His scars burned. Memories of the killer's deeds emerged, the brutalized victims once thriving inside Barnes's head. He no longer heard their voices, or so he had thought, but their presence was always felt. His spine went numb where he'd psychosomatically taken the pickax. His ribs throbbed. His head ached. Flashes of the weapon swinging toward him, his eyes closing, his head banking to the side, their screams like distant calls. He'd been suicidal that day. Willing to die at the hands of a serial killer so long as he made his collar. It was only luck that'd kept him alive, maybe divine intervention. The brush with death had changed him, made him cherish the life he'd so foolishly pushed across the table, all in on a bad hand. He'd fought like a dog to recover, to win himself back, to outlast the voices and the pain, hadn't he? Memories of his time in the hospital were spotty at best. Just flash details—an IV bag touched by the sun, faces looking down at him, the distant blip of a machine, a bendy straw in a plastic cup, meat loaf and mashed potatoes. They said recovering munkies experienced lost time during the days and weeks—even months and years—they'd walked around as someone else. How much time had he lost? More flash details had eventually emerged. Jessica in her wedding dress. *I do*. A tear on her cheek, trailing down toward her smile. The scent of pink paint as it was rolled onto a kid's bedroom walls. Takeout Chinese on an overturned cardboard box. The house empty but theirs now, the mortgage said so. Richie, just a baby, crying in the middle of the night. The sting of a milk bottle tested against a forearm.

How much time had he really recovered? However much it was, he'd be damned if he'd let it fall away again.

"Then why are you here?" A voice from within.

Barnes stopped at the edge of the clearing. He vaguely recognized the voice. Someone he thought he'd edged out. Apparently someone growing in strength from his time on the machine.

"Shhh."

He waited for the voice to reply, but it didn't.

Barnes stepped into the clearing to find the boxcar was still there, rusty red in the darkness and now coated in graffiti. Barnes stood still, unable to proceed. He thought the boxcar would have been lifted away by a police chopper years ago. The circular beam of his flashlight only lit parts of the structure at a time. The elaborate and colorful graffiti, jumbled, crazy, mostly illegible. But there were instances of gang signs, at least one skull and crossbones, and an Adidas logo. Someone had painted a series of cartoon faces going from calm to angry to insane. Someone else had painted *Fuck the Police!* in white letters. His flashlight revealed that the door was closed and locked. The torn remains of blaze-orange crime scene tape stuck across the opening. He supposed the land and car might be caught in a probate dispute involving Calavera's remaining family, most, if not all, of whom would be living across the border in Mexico. To them the relatively low value of a dented and rusty boxcar on a half acre of useless land might seem like an estate. Could take a decade or more to sort it out.

He turned his flashlight away from the car and pointed the beam into the woods beyond. The trees crowded the river at the far edge of the clearing. One step at a time he trudged forward, gaining back the strength being near the boxcar had robbed from him. He snapped and cracked through the branches that closed off the clearing to the banks of the river. Nocturnal creatures cleared a path, some dashing away with a startling sound, others simply stepping aside and curiously watching him go, their eyes aglow with his artificial light.

The willow was on the opposite side of the water. Barnes flashed the trunk and then slowly moved his light up into the canopy. The tree was dying. It tilted out over the water more than it ever had before. Falling over glacially. One day it would just topple.

There were no logs or stones to help him across without having to step into the flow. He'd have to get wet, like it or lump it.

His shoes were soaked through and his pants were wet to the thighs when he reached the other side. He'd come an inch away from freezing his nuts. He squelched around to the far side of the willow and located the two roots between which Ricky had buried the time capsule. He dropped to his knees and set down the flashlight, pulled out the hammer and turned it around so the claws faced forward. He hacked at the ground. Once the soil was soft enough he began digging at it with his hands, scooping away muddy black earth between his legs like a dog.

His fingertips scraped something solid. He picked up his flashlight and pointed the beam into the hole to find a line of gray duct tape. He dug around until he found the edges of the box. He outlined it, pried it loose, and placed it on the ground next to the hole. The tape had held up well over the years. Barnes brushed off the mud, and the shoebox looked nearly as new as the day it had been buried. He produced a jack-knife and sliced away the tape that held the top in place. He removed the lid and pointed his flashlight inside the box.

Staring up at him was a little Maltese dog on a couch, its eyes as black as piss holes in snow. The Polaroid picture was on top of a Twinkie. The shape of the treat was intact, but when Barnes picked it up it felt as light and brittle as Styrofoam. The snack had a green-gray hue now.

Destro and Zandar were in fine shape. The two Cobra-affiliated action figures were ready to battle G.I. Joe and his American Heroes. Barnes set them aside with the Twinkie and Rufus.

The prices on the Mancino's menu made Barnes shake his head. Was there really a time when you could buy a cheeseburger for sixty-nine cents? He supposed you could find one that cheap today, but it wouldn't be a Mancino's burger.

A quick flip through the *TV Guide* brought a rush of memories Barnes hadn't expected, not the least of which was the ceremony associated with the small magazine showing up in the mail each week. To retrieve the guide Dad would stand in his socks and reach out the front door to the mailbox attached to their trailer. He'd then open a little leather booklet cover, pull out the old guide, toss it into the trash, and slide the new one in. The contents of that old guide were dead and gone. Never had information been rendered so useless. And the new guide, well, it held the future. At least for a week.

Beneath the *TV Guide* was Ricky's manila envelope—"Johnny" written in Magic Marker in Ricky's handwriting. Barnes set it aside, choosing to examine what remained in the box first. Freddie Cohen's comic book was down there. Giant-Size Fantastic Four, number four. Mint condition. The cover depicted the members of the Fantastic Four battling Madrox, the Multiple Menace. He flipped through the pages and read a couple of speech bubbles—*Who are you? What do you want from me? I don't care if you're the tooth fairy, meatball!*—but nothing seemed to take hold. He set the comic book down.

The headline on the newspaper's front page was benign, something to do with foreign automakers kicking Detroit's ass. Same headline could be printed today. He flipped through the sections—Sports, Metro, Lifestyle—unable to connect with what he saw.

His mind was on that manila envelope.

He packed all the contents back into the time capsule and crossed back through the river, making his way east along the riverbank on wet feet, willfully ignoring the clearing and the boxcar where he'd taken down Calavera.

He came to his truck, got inside, and turned on the overhead light. He pulled out the envelope and unwrapped the red string that held the seal. There was a sheet of ruled notebook paper inside, the scent of which took Barnes back to doodling on the edges of his assignments while his teachers sounded like they were straight out of Charlie Brown. At the bottom of the envelope was a metal ring and what looked like a wristwatch. He tipped the envelope sideways. The ring and watch fell into his hand. The watch was a cheap army-style thing Ricky used to wear on occasion. The ring was a brass decoder Ricky had ordered from the back of a wrestling magazine. He'd saved up enough in loose change and battered one-dollar bills to get Mom to write a check and send it off to God knows where, delivery in four to six weeks.

Ricky went nuts when he got the ring, leaving numbered messages all over the house. Trouble was, it was his ring, so initially he was the only one with the means to decode his messages. Mom had threatened to take the ring away after she found the code 6-1-18-20 on notes all over the house. Using the decoder ring while Ricky was at school, and discovering its simple cryptography, she deciphered F-A-R-T, *F* being the sixth letter of the alphabet, *A* being the first, and so on.

After a scolding Ricky got to keep his ring, but any more FART or BALLS codes around the house would result in permanent ring disposal. This threat had been driven home by the nunchaku (or numbchucks to any preteen Detroiter who'd stayed up past midnight for *Martial Arts Theatre* with Charlie Lum), Water Weenies, and plastic handcuffs from Gibraltar Trade Center that'd mysteriously gone missing over the years.

Barnes slid the brass decoder ring over his left pinkie finger. It barely fit, but he found he could slide the alpha ring to reveal an individual number in the digit slot. He set the ring to A-1.

The watch wasn't much of a sentimental piece. Ricky had won it from Eric Shield, who dared him to play ding-dong-ditch-it at the Masterson trailer. The boys stole a bottle of root beer schnapps and spent all night sipping courage to hype themselves up for the event, which had become a rite of passage for kids from the park. You couldn't call yourself a man from Flamingo Farms if you didn't have the sand to ring the Masterson doorbell and run like hell while Earl Masterson or one of his brood screamed obscenities and shook a fist on the porch.

Johnny recalled when he himself had rung the bell and run only the summer before. At the end of his run he felt like a king, despite having puked up his share of apple pucker behind Gary Baldwin's inflatable pool.

But this time it was Ricky's turn. Johnny and Eric watched as he silently approached the Masterson front door, which was wooden with a diamond-shaped window, and as he stepped onto the porch Eric shined his dad's deer-spotting flashlight on the door to reveal a terrifying face peering out at them through the diamond window. Ricky screamed and all three of them ran. The next day Ricky and Johnny came back to see that the Mastersons, having endured too many ding-dong-ditch-its, had taped a record sleeve of Ted Nugent's *Cat Scratch Fever* inside the window. Uncle Ted's crazy face was what had scared them so badly.

Though Ricky never technically rang the bell, Eric Shield still gave him the watch. (He felt bad, having known about Nugent's face in advance.) There was nothing special about the watch other than it kept time on a twenty-four-hour clock instead of just twelve. The battery was long since dead. Barnes put the watch in his jacket pocket and pulled the ruled paper from the envelope. A note. Ricky's handwriting.

Johnny,

If you're reading this, you're either a bastard or I'm dead.

Don't double your trouble. Go balls out. Solve the riddle or suck an egg:

I am not in closed drawers,

But I do cut a shine.

I am yours,

But you are not mine.

Ricky

Barnes thought on the riddle for a moment, but he came up empty. He smirked. Ricky, the clever little punk. He slid the note back into the envelope and put it back in the shoebox. He set the shoebox on the passenger seat and retrieved his cell phone to find a voice mail from Franklin.

"Meet me at Roosevelt's."

7

Roosevelt's Bar was situated a little too close to Keisel Street for it ever to be a hip spot. To make matters worse, an E. coli breakout in a tub of coleslaw had nearly shut the place down several years back. After that most people stayed away, save for the munkies and crack zombies with enough leg power to propel themselves over from Machine City.

Barnes pulled into the parking lot, got out, and went into the bar.

Franklin was sitting at a booth against the back wall of the joint, a half-empty draft beer in front of him. His new partner was with him. The guy's leg was propped awkwardly beneath the table, a horsehead cane leaning against the booth at his side. Franklin signaled with three fingers to the bartender as Barnes weaved through the mix of empty two-tops and four-tops.

Barnes sighed and rubbed two hands over his bristly scalp as he plopped down into the booth across from Franklin and his partner. There was a news anchor on the television overhead, next to him the familiar video clip of Little Cher at her audition for *Starmonizers*. The girl was cute with pigtails tied up with red ribbons, but her voice out-sized her tiny frame. The set was muted, but the closed-captioning was on. At the bottom of the screen the words passed by . . . POLICE ARE BAFFLED BY THE DISAPPEARANCE OF "LITTLE CHER" CHERRY DANIELS, WHO IS STILL ON AMBER ALERT. SHE WAS LAST SEEN WALKING DOWN THE SIDEWALK BETWEEN A NEIGHBOR'S HOME AND HER OWN . . .

"You stroll in here soaked to the crotch and sporting a shaved head," Franklin said, "and *I've* got some explaining to do?"

The bartender appeared, set down three shots, and left. Bourbon. Barnes threw back a shot and then slapped Freddie Cohen's letter down on the table. "This is bullshit."

Franklin said nothing. He downed his shot.

"You wrote it," Barnes said.

"I didn't."

"We were partners," Barnes said. He leaned in toward Franklin with a quick glance toward the new guy. "We were friends."

"We're still friends," Franklin said.

"Why are you doing this?"

"Who were you on the machine?"

"Like you don't know."

Franklin waited. Above his head the news story switched over to the interview with Hannah Daniels, Little Cher's mother, from the night of the abduction. Barnes hadn't noticed before, or maybe he attributed it to her state of mind at the time of the interview, but the woman looked drunk. To Franklin he said, "Freddie Cohen."

"Is that name supposed to mean something to—"

"You know it does," Barnes said, pounding a fist on the tabletop and causing the shot glasses to dance. The full glass in front of the new guy nearly spilled out, but he caught it before it tipped. Barnes flicked the letter across the table. "Read the letter you wrote."

Franklin slid on his reading glasses. He opened the letter, lifted it to the light, and read it. Afterward, he looked up at Barnes, his eyes just above the paper. "Was it?"

"Was it what?"

"About Ricky?"

"You couldn't. Save him." The breathless voice. *"You failed him."*

"Shhh."

Barnes held Franklin's gaze for a moment and then looked away. "Yeah."

"I'm sorry," Franklin said. "If I had known"—he indicated the letter—"I wouldn't have delivered this."

"Why not?"

Franklin set down the letter and removed his glasses. "A few hours ago you were a happy father and husband with a head full of hair. Now—"

"Now I'm a munky." He gestured toward Franklin's partner. "Who the fuck is this guy?"

"Meet Dr. Hill," Franklin said.

Dr. Hill offered his hand to shake.

Barnes left the doctor hanging, kept his eyes on Franklin. "Doctor?"

Franklin nodded.

"What's this about?"

"You need help, John," Franklin said. "I dragged you into this because I thought Flaherty might have left a few clues as to who wanted him out of the picture, which could lead us to Little Cher. But you were right, I never should have asked. Let me help you now." He indicated Dr. Hill. "Let *us* help you. Dr. Hill is a psychiatrist, he works exclusively with—"

"Eddie Able," Barnes said, cutting Franklin off.

"Come again?"

"That's who I saw when I was Cohen. Eddie Able."

Franklin cocked his head and blinked. "The toy?"

"Not the toy," Barnes said. "The life-size version. Some maniac in a suit, his hands covered in blood."

Franklin exchanged a glance with Dr. Hill.

"And then again when I was Flaherty," Barnes said.

"Hold on," Franklin said. "You were Flaherty, too?"

"He had files stashed away, just like you said, on the Echo Ring. One with your name on it."

Franklin rubbed his hands down his face. "Aw, shit."

Barnes smirked. "Starting to come together now, isn't it?"

"Look," Franklin said, "I don't know what you saw in this Freddie Cohen's memories, okay? But this Eddie Able thing, you need to stay away from it. It's a cold case that Flaherty reopened, and it's nothing to do with you."

"You're saying the cold case has nothing to do with Cherry Daniels?"

"I'm saying you need to focus on what matters."

"So it's just pure coincidence," Barnes said, "that you show up at my door with a letter from Freddie Cohen's estate, asking me to go back on the machine, where I find a blood-soaked psychopath dressed up as Eddie Able, and in the next breath you're asking me to go be Flaherty on the same goddamn machine, where I find he was also working a cold case involving a guy who dressed up for little kids' birthday parties as Eddie fucking Able?"

Franklin put both his hands up, palms out.

Barnes addressed Dr. Hill. "You're a shrink, huh?"

"I can help you sort things out," Dr. Hill said.

"Ignore him." The breathless voice.

"Shhh."

"We need to marginalize the other voices you carry," Dr. Hill said, "giving you a bigger slice of the pie. It makes you stronger, mentally. Once your slice is big enough, you can kick the others out."

"I don't get it," Barnes said to Franklin. "You wanted me on the machine to help you find out what happened to Flaherty, to help you find Cherry Daniels. Now you bring along a psychiatrist? For what?"

"Look," Franklin said, "I would have introduced you earlier had you agreed to get on the machine when I asked. Dr. Hill was set to monitor you while you were under and after you came out, make sure you're doing okay mentally and that we don't put you under too much pressure."

"But I refused."

"The Barnes I knew," Franklin said, "the *detective* I knew, risked everything for a collar. Like a dog with a bone, only your bone was the machine. I wouldn't have asked in the first place, I wouldn't have set all this up, except for something Flaherty said before things went to shit."

Barnes waited.

"He said, 'Barnes will know how to find me.'"

"What? When did he say that?"

Franklin's face went grim. "A month ago."

"And when did he go missing?"

"His wife reported it last night."

"You said he was abducted."

"Car never left the driveway, credit card hasn't been used, no girlfriend on the side, as far as we know. Fits the bill that someone snatched him up."

"Let me get this straight," Barnes said. "A month ago this guy *predicts* he'll go missing and lets you know I'll be able to help you find him?"

"I thought he was just acting crazy," Franklin said. "Tired or something. Too many cases. Too many unsolved."

"Last night he finally goes missing," Barnes said, "just as he said he would, and you came to *me*?"

"He was close on this Daniels thing," Franklin said. "Maybe this guy saw Flaherty coming. Maybe Flaherty knew more than what's in his reports."

"The girl's been gone two days," Barnes said. "How does that jibe with his prediction from a month ago?"

"There's more," Franklin said. "The stuff in his reports. It all points to a bigger picture."

"What stuff in his reports?"

"A bunch of notes about cold cases," Franklin said. "Mostly this Eddie Able thing. He's had a hard-on for that case going on five or six years. Links every missing kid to it, every runaway, every homicide. Plus . . ." He shook his head.

"Plus what?"

"Madrox," Dr. Hill said.

"Madrox?"

"Just that single word," Franklin said, "written in Magic Marker on a few of his more recent cases, including Cherry Daniels."

"What's it mean?"

Franklin shrugged.

Dr. Hill looked away.

"All right, then," Barnes said. "Maybe you can tell me about the Sect of Shifting Sands?"

Both Dr. Hill and Franklin eyed him cautiously.

"Ooh, now that got your attention. Who's the Shivering Man?"

"Don't go there," Franklin said. "The Sect is just a bunch of machine fanatics."

"A cult," Dr. Hill said.

"They're led by Gabriel Messina," Franklin said. "Some call him the Shivering Man because he's got dozens of personalities inside him and he's constantly changing."

"Shifting sands," Barnes said.

"Yeah," Dr. Hill said.

"Messina's got a powerful mind," Franklin said. "He's able to draw up any one of his personalities at any time. He's a godlike figure to Sect members. Got maybe a hundred followers."

"The Melodians and Brittanians hate him," Dr. Hill said.

"How come I never heard of this guy?" Barnes said.

"He's underground," Franklin said. "Keeps a low profile these days, like one of those mountain gurus. People come to him for wisdom and help. Always comes at a price, though."

"Used to be he'd show up with his people at memory shop protests," Dr. Hill said, "to beat back the Melodians and Brittanians, but he's more like David Koresh now. Jim Jones."

"I'll be sure to skip the Kool-Aid," Barnes said. He picked up the third shot of bourbon and downed it, clacked the glass down on the table. "Maybe Flaherty was right."

"How's that?" Franklin said.

"If what you're saying is true," Barnes said, "that Flaherty predicted he'd go missing, he must have known something, right? And if he was as thorough as you say, he would have recorded the memory. So, maybe I know how to find him after all."

"This was never meant to be a rogue operation," Franklin said. "You were supposed to be professionally monitored. Supervised."

Barnes turned to Dr. Hill. "He left two other files. Did you know that? One of them was called ColdCase."

"Don't," Franklin said.

Barnes collected the Cohen letter and stuffed it into his pocket as he stood up to leave. He smiled. "Why not? I already shaved my head."

8

Barnes walked across the parking lot toward his truck. A voice from behind called out, "Wait up!" He stopped and turned to see Dr. Hill hobbling toward him on his cane.

"No," Barnes said. He started again toward his truck, zigzagging between the parked cars. He arrived at the driver's-side door and got in. He put in the key and was about to turn it when a knocking came to the passenger-side window. Dr. Hill. He made the old-school rotating hand movement for rolling down a window.

Barnes used the electric button to roll the window down. The truck was old but not *that* old.

"We need to talk," Dr. Hill said.

"No, we don't."

"We do," Dr. Hill said. "You don't understand what's happening to you."

"And you do?"

"I've been there, okay? I've traveled down that road."

"So have I," Barnes said, "and I beat the voices. I'm me again."

"Says the guy with the shaved head."

Barnes turned the key and started the engine. He shifted into reverse and looked over in time to see that Dr. Hill had reached into the vehicle and popped the passenger door open. He was in and sitting down before Barnes could pull away.

"Look," Dr. Hill said, "I know you don't like the idea of talking to me about this stuff, but it could help."

"How?"

Dr. Hill reset himself in his seat, seeming to want to find a comfortable way to situate his bum leg. Once he stopped moving, he said, "I used to get these shivers, you know? That's how I knew when I was losing control of my mind and letting someone else run the show for a while. I'd get this cold feeling inside, and my whole body would shake. You ever get that?"

Barnes fought back the very feeling Dr. Hill described, the coldness, the shiver. He stomped hard on the sensation. "I've got control."

Dr. Hill looked him up and down and said, "Why do you think they outlawed the machine?"

Barnes sniffed. His hand was still on the gearshift, the truck still in reverse. "It fucked people up, just like any drug, even the legal ones. Alcohol fucks people up every day, save for those who can handle it."

"In the simplest sense, you're right; the machine fucks people up. But the problem is bigger than that."

"I'm sure you're going to expand," Barnes said. He shifted back into park, took his foot off the brake. The truck settled.

"Remember the Knowledge Reform?"

"Rings a bell," Barnes said, though it didn't.

"It started out by asking the question, what if every person was highly educated? What if every kid *really* had a chance, not some bullshit token bone, not affirmative action, but a real chance from the beginning? The government decided to give it a shot. The reform went into action, and all sorts of pathways were made so that any person from any socioeconomic background was given an opportunity to get a degree and make something of themselves."

"Sounds like a good plan," Barnes said, still struggling to recall the program. He'd lost time as a munky, sure, but enough to be completely unaware of national education reform?

"Sure it does, and if you opposed it you were labeled an elitist asshole who just wants the world's riches for himself."

"Your point?"

"My point is that the world needs janitors. Not everyone should be educated, not everyone should be wealthy. Not everyone should live the high life, else there'll be no high life left to live. If everyone's a CEO, who will pick up the garbage or clean the toilets?"

"I don't know, man. Robots?"

Dr. Hill smirked. "Maybe someday."

"So what, then, the reform didn't work?"

"It was canceled during the recent change up top. Democrats enacted it, Republicans killed it."

"Sounds about right. But how does the analogy relate to the machine?"

"We all want a better reality. We all want to live the kind of life we've been conditioned to believe we should live. That's why things like the Knowledge Reform were enacted in the first place. Unfortunately, most of us just get a raw deal, and that's all there is to it. It can't be helped."

"Jesus," Barnes said. "I thought shrinks were supposed to help people feel better about themselves."

"When the machine came around," Dr. Hill continued, "it was sold as a device to aid in homicide investigations, then evolved to punish criminals and otherwise just show people a good time. Harmless fun, right? Virtual reality."

"And if you opposed it?"

"You were a Neanderthal who opposed progress. But what happens when half the world can suddenly be whatever they want to be? What happens when, compared to a ride on the machine, reality is nothing more than a slog through a monotonous life? People stopped dreaming. People stopped striving."

"People stopped cleaning the toilets," Barnes said.

"People stopped choosing reality."

Barnes looked at Dr. Hill. "You one of those people?"

"For a time, yes. I *chased the man*, as they say, the Vitruvian Man. The thing is, the machine isn't like recreational drugs. When you get high from heroin or crack, or even something as innocent as weed, you're still you; you're just excused from yourself for the moment, so to speak. You might see illusions or have strange thoughts, but it's just a phase, and everyone around you can see it. They know you're struggling, and they pay you little mind when you're high or drunk or spacing out. But what happens when, say, a trusted government official is asked to make decisions on behalf of a city, a state, or even this entire country, only the man really making the decisions is the porn star he rode the night before?"

Barnes chuffed. He shook his head.

"How many of us are really happy?" Dr. Hill said. "How many of us spend our days wishing for something more? So many want just a little of what the other guy has, and with the machine they can have it. Trouble is, they don't always come back. Mothers and fathers go missing. They just walk away. Kids are left orphaned. Teachers stop showing up for school, and the next day they're found in a crack house down the street, or maybe in another state, wondering why people can't seem to get their name right."

"I'm Justin Timberlake, goddammit!" Barnes crowed. "Why do you keep calling me Earl?"

"Exactly."

"So, who were you?" Barnes said. "Who was your big fix?"

"Does it matter?"

"Well, maybe you're not Dr. Hill, eh? Maybe you're Gene Simmons."

Dr. Hill produced a card from within his jacket pocket. He handed it to Barnes. It was a Machine Anonymous business card. He was a sponsor. "This is who I am."

Barnes tapped the edge of the card against his knuckles. He gestured toward the bar. "What's he got on Cherry Daniels?"

"Franklin?"

77

"Yeah."

"We're tracking down a potential witness, someone saying they saw a suspicious car on the street near Cherry's house, but so far that's it."

"Is Flaherty really involved in this?"

"Absolutely. We need to find him."

Barnes nodded.

"I met a kid one time," Dr. Hill said. "High school kid. Captain of the football team, good grades and all that, world in his hands. Thing was, he loved Soundgarden. I guess his old man was a big fan. One night, the kid gets a chance to ride Chris Cornell, you know?"

"And he eventually killed himself, right?"

"Just a couple weeks later," Dr. Hill said. He looked Barnes in the eyes. "Question is, what was the crime? Homicide or suicide?"

"Meaning, did Chris Cornell kill that kid, or did Chris Cornell just kill himself again?"

Dr. Hill looked out the window. "Or did that kid, when he chose to get on the machine and resurrect the man from a digital grave, kill Chris Cornell?"

Barnes shrugged, shook his head.

"What did Freddie Cohen want you to know?" Dr. Hill asked.

"That he was sorry for hurting my brother."

"Do you believe him?"

Barnes looked off through the windshield. "He loved Ricky, too."

9

The house was nearly dark. Faint light poured from the kitchen windows. Barnes took the pizza box off the passenger-side floor and got out of the truck. The street was quiet, save for the buzzing of the sodium-arc streetlights. The porch steps creaked beneath his feet. The screen door yawned on its hinges as he pulled it open. Once inside, he eased the door closed behind him, applying low pressure until the bolt clicked home.

Jessica was alone in the kitchen. The light came from the hanging lamp above the table where she was sitting. The scene resembled an interrogation room. A cup of Red Rose tea sat in front her, the bag on a spoon next to the cup. No steam rose from the liquid. Her elbows were propped on the Formica. Her eyes were red from crying. She went rigid when she looked at him, no doubt from the sight of his bald head. New tears formed and fell.

Barnes set down the pizza box and flipped it open. The pie inside looked like a domestic violence incident. He closed the lid and sat down across from her. Her tea smelled like vodka.

"Why are you doing this?" Jessica said.

Barnes hung his head. He thought back to when he and Jessica had first met. She was a teacher then. He was hot on the Calavera case and she had been so understanding. But the killer had entered her home, riding Barnes's coattails through the door. He'd bound her hands and feet, tortured her, painted her face like a death bride. Only a last-ditch act of mercy had saved her life. How had she managed to forgive him, much less stick by his side, marry him, and give birth to their son? He had flash memories of arguments, of the front door slamming behind him as *he* left, in front of him as *she* left. Could be any married couple in the world, right? Memories of reuniting, apologies, makeup sex. The scent of bacon at breakfast, smiles and laughter over eggs and coffee. She'd stayed at her mother's, admitted they'd spent the night bashing him. Him rushing out the door in response to a call from dispatch, her waving in the doorway, pregnant in a hoodie and sweatpants.

"It's who I am," Barnes said, looking up at Jessica.

"A munky? That's who you are?"

"A detective. A man is lost. A little girl has been kidnapped."

Jessica placed her hand on top of his. At first her touch felt light and loving, but she wrapped her fingers around his palm and squeezed hard. A sharp pain shot up Barnes's forearm.

"I won't let you destroy this family."

"I would never do that."

"You're already doing it."

Barnes opened his mouth to reply but found no words.

"I need you to leave," Jessica said.

"I'm sorry," Barnes said, "I—"

"No!" Jessica said, squeezing his hand harder than he imagined she could. The pain made him grit his teeth. "No explanations. No lies. Just leave. Now."

Barnes stood up. His chair fell back and clacked the floor.

Jessica didn't release his hand. She glared up at him, her lips curled in rage. "Leave!"

Barnes tried to step away, but her grip was terrible. Their hands shook wildly with her ferocity. "Let go," he said.

"Leave!" Jessica said.

Barnes closed one eye to the pain. "How can I leave if you won't let go?"

She pulled him down, closer to her face. Her nostrils flared before she spoke. "Please leave . . ."

"Let. Go."

She let go.

Barnes backed out of the kitchen and turned into the hallway, shaking the pain out of his hand. He went up the stairs to the master bedroom, rummaged through the closet, and found his old service pistol on a high shelf, a .45-caliber Glock inside its shoulder holster. The gun's chamber was empty. He popped the magazine and found it full. He ratcheted a round into the chamber and holstered the gun. He slid into the holster and put his jacket back on. His badge hung from a hook. He reached for it but then stopped. He left it where it was.

He turned to leave the bedroom to find Richie standing in the doorway. He was in his pajamas, rubbing his right eye.

"So sweet." The breathless voice.

"Shhh."

"What's up, sleepyhead?" Barnes said.

"What happened to your hair?"

Barnes went to Richie and squatted down to the boy's height. He leaned the crown of his head toward him. "Want to feel?"

Richie rubbed his hand over the bristle of Barnes's head. "Cool."

Barnes joined Richie in rubbing the bristle.

"I thought we were getting pizza?" Richie said.

Barnes looked up. "I'm sorry, bud. I got distracted." He absently spun the decoder ring on his pinkie finger.

"What's that?" Richie asked.

Barnes showed the ring to the boy.

"Neat," Richie said. He reached out to touch it.

"I got this ring from my brother," Barnes said. "Your uncle."

Richie stopped short. "My uncle?"

"Aw. Let him. Play with it." The breathless voice.

Richie screwed up his face. "What?"

81

It took a moment for Barnes to realize the voice's words had come out of his mouth. His core went cold. He closed his eyes and fought not to shiver in front of the boy.

"Are you okay?" Richie said.

"No." The breathless voice.

"Shhh." Barnes fought the shiver until he won, until the presence of the voice's owner was pushed back into the corner of his mind. He smiled at his son. "You do have an uncle."

"No I don't."

"Trust me, kid. You do."

"You never talked about him before."

"It was too hard, I guess."

"Why? Is he dead?"

Barnes nodded. "A long time ago."

"How did he give you the ring then?"

"When we were boys," Barnes said, "your uncle always used to send me on scavenger hunts. I guess maybe he knew I liked to find things, you know? He'd have me out in the woods or at some supermarket looking for clues. It got to the point where I didn't even know he'd set up some mystery for me until I was halfway through it. He'd come up with these intricate riddles to solve."

"That's why you became a detective."

"Right." Barnes smirked and chucked Richie's chin. "Maybe you'll be a detective yourself."

"What's *intricate* mean?"

Barnes smiled. "Hard."

"He sounds like fun," Richie said.

"He was a good kid. You remind me of him."

"I wish I could've met him," Richie said.

"Me, too." Barnes tousled the boy's hair. "Now off to bed, huh?"

Richie bolted down the hallway toward his room.

Barnes went downstairs. He glanced into the kitchen to find Jessica still there, her head on her forearms, which were crossed on the table.

"Leave her be." The familiar voice.

He headed for the front door and reached for the knob. A noise stopped him. He looked back over his shoulder and up the steps. Richie was there, clutching the balusters like the bars of a jail cell. He formed a monkey bite and held it out. Barnes formed one in response. They silently performed their secret handshake across the empty space.

The night air was muggy from the recent rain. Barnes rolled the windows down on his truck. His cell rang as he backed out of the driveway. He checked the caller ID—UNKNOWN—and answered. "What?"

"You found. The shoebox. Yes?" It was the same caller as before, that same breathless voice as the one speaking from within his mind.

"Fuck you," Barnes said. He disconnected the call and threw the phone down. He pulled up the street and turned onto the main road.

The cell rang again.

Barnes picked the phone up, connected the call, and put it to his ear.

"What was. In there?" the caller said.

Barnes still couldn't place a face or a name with the voice.

"Silent treatment. Eh, detective?"

"You tell *me* what was in there," Barnes said. "You've been Cohen. You must know."

"Couple of. G.I. Joe. Villains. A comic book. A picture. Of a fat. Kid's dog. Yes?"

Barnes said nothing.

"I don't care. About the box. Detective. What was in the. Envelope?"

"Why should I tell you?"

"Because I can. Help you."

"You don't know me. I'm not even sure you're . . ." Barnes pinched the bridge of his nose.

"*Shhh.*"

"I see," the caller said. "You think I'm. A voice inside. Your head. Don't you, John? One you. Weren't able to. Fully suppress?"

Barnes didn't reply.

"You think. If you look at your. Cell phone screen. Right now. You'll find it blank. Because this call. Is in your mind. Well, go ahead. And look. I'll wait."

Barnes took the phone away from his ear and stared at the screen. He faintly heard the caller whistling the theme song to *Jeopardy*. The line was connected. He watched the call timer go up by one second, then two, then three. He put the phone back to his ear.

"Still there. John?"

"It doesn't mean anything."

"If you. Say so."

"How can you help me?" Barnes said.

"Tell me. What was in the. Envelope."

"It has nothing to do with the case," Barnes said. "Nothing to do with finding Flaherty or Cherry Daniels."

"Are you. Certain?"

"How could it?"

"That may be. Revealed. In due time."

"*Listen to him.*" The familiar voice. "*Solve the riddle.*"

"*Shhh.*"

"No," Barnes said as he pulled into a convenience store lot and parked. "First I need to know who you are. What's your stake in this?"

"Just a concerned. Citizen. No more."

"That's not enough," Barnes said. He disconnected the call and put the phone down. He sat gazing through the windshield at the convenience store, the overhead fluorescent lights, the clerk in a red vest slumped on the counter, bored. Aisles of chips and candy bars, magazines, beef jerky.

Bourbon behind the register.

Barnes left his phone in the truck and went into the store. He came back with a pint in a brown bag. He unscrewed the cap and sniffed at the bottle's contents, eyes closed. His mouth watered. His blood flow seemed to slow, his heartbeat dialing down a notch. He tilted the bottle back and filled his mouth with the whiskey. He swished it, savored it, and swallowed the burn.

Barnes capped his bourbon and picked up the phone. Ten missed calls from UNKNOWN while he was in the store. The phone rang again. He connected the call and brought it to his ear.

"Maybe I'm. The guy," the caller said. "Who's got Flaherty. Chained up. In his basement. Maybe if. You don't play nice. I'll stick a butcher. Knife. In his guts. And yank it up. To his neck."

"Maybe you already did that," Barnes said. "Maybe you've already killed both Flaherty and Cherry Daniels, and now you want me, too."

"Forget Little Cher. She's dead and. You know it. Flaherty will be, too. What was in. The envelope?"

It's all in my head, what difference does it make?

Well, hearing voices is one thing, but talking with them? Exchanging ideas?

They'll lock you up.

"Detective," the caller said.

What if he's real?

"The envelope."

What if he can help?

"Please tell me."

"A letter from my kid brother," Barnes said. "Plus a decoder ring and a cheap watch."

"What did the. Letter say?"

"There was a riddle."

85

"What was it?"

"I am not in closed drawers," Barnes said, "but I do cut a shine. I am yours, but you are not mine."

"Hmm. Tough one."

"Ricky was a smart kid."

"What's not in. A closed drawer?"

"Easy," Barnes said. "Light."

"That sounds right," the caller said. "Okay then. How about. But I do. Cut a shine?"

"Something my mom used to say. Whenever Ricky and I would be acting out, making fools of ourselves, she'd say we were 'cutting a shine.'"

"Your mother. Was she. A good woman?"

"Yes."

"And your father. A good man?"

"A better man than you."

"Most are. I think," the caller said. "The second. Line of your riddle. Is literal. The relationship. Between light and dark. For one to exist. The other is required. What literally. Cuts a shine?"

"Don't know," Barnes said.

"What about. I am yours. But you are. Not mine?"

"What can you own that can't own you?"

"Lots of things," the caller said.

"Relate it to light and dark," Barnes said.

"The sun? The moon?"

"Can't own those."

"But they. Shine on us. They give us light."

"Sure," Barnes said, "but . . . wait. I've got it. It's not light and dark, but light and *shadow*. If light cannot be in a closed drawer, neither can shadow. And what cuts a shine but a shadow?"

"Careful now," the caller said. "You're close. To it."

"You already knew, you bastard?"

"Tsk, tsk," the caller said. "Vulgar language. Will not help. I am merely. Telling you what. You already. Know. The answer you. Have given me."

"Shadow."

"Yes," the caller said. "A man has. A shadow. But the shadow. Doesn't have him."

"Jesus," Barnes said, "that's right."

Silence on the line.

"Hello?"

More silence. Barnes took the phone away from his ear to find the call had been disconnected. He dialed Franklin.

"I guess you don't care if I sleep, eh?" Franklin said when he picked up.

Barnes checked the clock on the dashboard: 2:04 a.m. "Sorry. Look, I need you to set up a trace on whoever calls my cell phone."

"Say what?"

"I've been getting phone calls from a guy who claims he might have Flaherty locked up in his basement. No number coming through on caller ID, though, just UNKNOWN."

"Hold on," Franklin said. "You got a call from our guy?"

"At first I thought maybe it was . . ."

"It was what?"

"A voice. In your. Head." The breathless voice.

"Shhh."

"Nothing. Next time he calls we need him tracked."

"Did he mention Cherry Daniels?"

"He didn't deny it when I brought her up. He said he wanted to help me. I asked who he was, and he said maybe he was the guy holding Flaherty. He threatened to gut him if I didn't let him help me. Claims he's been on the machine as Freddie Cohen, Flaherty, and me, even you."

"Then he's police."

"That's what I thought. We need to track him."

"A guy like this, he's calling you from a burner. Plus he won't be at the same location each time."

"It's worth a shot."

Franklin motorboated his lips. "Yeah. All right. I'll run your call records and we'll start tracking you."

"Good."

"Where you at?" Franklin said.

"What do you mean?"

"I hear traffic. Did she boot you?"

Barnes rolled up the windows. "We'll get it figured out."

"I'm sorry, buddy," Franklin said. "I never meant—"

"We're good," Barnes said. He disconnected the call and pulled out of the parking lot.

10

Shadow.

Barnes lifted his hand and examined the decoder ring on his pinkie finger. He was sitting on the edge of a bed in a room at a rundown motel called The Fleabag. How kitsch. He set down the nearly empty pint and dialed in the letters of SHADOW to find a number combination—19-8-1-4-15-23.

1981 could represent a year. Combine it with 4 and 15 for April 15, 1981? He pulled the newspaper from the shoebox. The print year wasn't 1981, the month wasn't April, and the date wasn't the fifteenth. He set the newspaper aside and checked the back of the Rufus picture. Nothing written there. He picked up the comic book. The edition was printed in 1975. *Giant-Size Fantastic Four*, number four, featuring Madrox, the Multiple Menace. On the cover, the Fantastic Four were being attacked from all sides by what looked like an army of men, but really it was just one character, Madrox, who could split into multiple versions of himself.

"Run with this." The familiar voice.

Barnes locked his jaw and gripped his temples. The idea of following the commands of a voice inside his mind was . . . well, crazy. Such a notion fought against the work he'd put in to defeat the voices in the first place. He thought, *"No."*

"Please."

"Shhh."

He set down the comic book and picked up the Mancino's menu. He flipped through the pages. Nothing caught his eye. He examined the front, taking in a photo of the restaurant owners standing in the dining room, waving. Joe and Martha Briggs. Dad said they'd bought the restaurant from the original owner before it went under and that they'd restored the place to its former glory. Dad had loved that diner. He'd dragged Johnny and Ricky there for breakfast every chance he got. "Belly up, boys," he would say as they took their usual stools at the counter, Ricky on Dad's left side, Johnny to his right. Dad always ordered a Beast omelet with extra-crispy hash browns. Ricky got french toast. The countertop was decorated with license plates from every state in the union, thermoformed under a layer of clear resin.

So crazy that you brought that menu.

Barnes picked up Ricky's letter and read it again—the note, the riddle, his signature.

Don't double your trouble.

It didn't feel like something Ricky would say. Had to be a clue of some kind, but . . . Barnes felt exhausted. His brain, scrambled eggs. He lay back on the bed, forearm on his forehead, and cleared his mind of mystery, of the past. He thought of home, their little house in the suburbs, the bang and rattle of that cheap screen door, Richie scratching through homework at the kitchen table. And Jessica, so grim, so stoic these days. Something had changed in her. The girl he met was adventurous and full of light, full of laughter. Her smile used to exorcise his pain. How long had it been since he'd seen that smile? He couldn't calculate it. He'd heard of postpartum depression, but how long could that last? Richie was five, for God's sake. Not so long ago the house had been wide open, the windows and doors allowing sunlight in, allowing a breeze to move through air filled with classic rock—AC/DC and the Allman Brothers, Van Halen, Styx. "Renegade" would get Richie on his feet every time, bouncing around the living room with burgeoning dance moves, his parents clapping and laughing around him. Barnes found the tune in his mind, found the chorus, and hummed it to himself. He pictured Richie giggling and spinning, trailing that long hair his mother refused to cut . . .

Barnes awoke to an argument outside his motel room window.

"You'll do exactly what I tell you, bitch." A male voice.

"Stop. You're hurting me." A female voice.

Barnes stood. His head swam from the bourbon, his mouth felt coated with fiberglass. He checked his armpit for the .45, found it. The alarm clock read 4:13 a.m.

"Bitch, you don't even know pain," the male voice said. "Now get the fuck back in there before I introduce you."

Barnes sensed action beyond the drapes, silhouetted movement revealed by the streetlights.

"No! Fuck you, Daryl."

The sound of a slap moved Barnes to his feet. He went to the door and slowly turned the handle. The bolt released and he eased the door open a crack. There was a munky-hook prostitute facing away from him, leaning against a concrete-and-pebble stone planter-cum-ashtray, her right hand on her right cheek. Her back was heaving with sobs, and Barnes could see her ribs through her tight-fitting top. She wore steep heels and a miniskirt that failed to cover the bruises on her thighs. The sides of her head were shaven, her remaining hair styled over to one side like punk rock angst. Men and women like her riddled the postmachine landscape. People with experiences for sale. Undoubtedly she'd filled up a machine with live sexual encounters, and if she were able to net a john he'd ride the machine for his money while she watched TV and smoked a cigarette. The pitch was that your ride would be *realer than real*. Why have sex with her using your dumpy body, you oaf? Why nail her when she's having an off night? Be handsome when you do her. Catch her on that one night she's willing to go over the line. Make her cum harder than she ever will again.

Realer than real.

Yeah, and flash-frozen is fresher than fresh.

Barnes turned his head to find the pimp that'd slapped the woman, but he seemed to have fled.

"Now that you and pain have made acquaintances," the pimp's voice said, "you'll get the fuck back in this room."

Barnes looked around, confused. The pimp seemed right on top of him, but the man was nowhere to be found. Barnes pulled his gun and opened the door a bit more, stuck his head out.

"I'm not going back with you, Daryl," the prostitute said.

Barnes looked in the direction she was facing, but there was no one beyond her. She was talking to . . .

. . . shit, she was talking to herself.

The girl straightened up from the planter, still facing away from Barnes. She steeled up her spine and threw back her shoulders. "I'm *never* going back with you, bastard."

Barnes holstered his gun and waited, watched from behind as she transformed from the prostitute back into the pimp. Her stance became shifty, swaying, like a boxer beginning to warm up. She gestured with her hands when she spoke in a deep tone. "Watch your tongue, bitch. I'll cut it out, make room for more money."

She transformed again, goose pimples in a wave over her skin as she became herself. Spine of steel, shoulders cocked. She reached into her little purse and pulled out a tiny nickel-plated pistol . . . but again she shifted, gun paused above the unzipped hole of her purse. "Bitch," she said, "you must be trippin', pulling that little thing on me."

"Enough," Barnes said.

The hooker released the gun. It fell back into her purse. She dropped her head into her hands, and her body began to tremble. Her bangles and necklaces rattled.

Barnes waited.

When the trembling was over, she turned to him and smiled, wiping tears off her cheeks. She had trace raccoon eyes from a recently broken nose, a week to ten days ago. "Hey, baby. Wanna party?"

"Where is he?" Barnes said.

"It's just me and you here, sweetie," she said, stepping toward him. She reached out a hand toward his chest, placed her palm flat against him. "Just me and you."

Barnes looked down at her hand. Her touch was delicate and warm. A primal sensation moved through him, caused him to close his eyes and breathe in. She smelled faintly of perfume, maybe hair spray, cigarette smoke. The hooker's caress turned into a knot on his chest, a fist closing and twisting Barnes's shirt. He opened his eyes to a white-knuckled grip.

"You messing with my bottom bitch?" The pimp's voice.

Barnes wristlocked her—strong enough to immobilize, light enough so she wouldn't scream—and removed her hand from his shirt.

"You like it rough, huh?" she said, back to being the hooker, smiling through a mess of makeup and tear tracks.

"Which room?" Barnes said.

"114."

"What will I find in there?"

She smirked and winked, dragged her available hand in a seductive pattern from her chest down her belly. "A little slice of heaven."

Barnes made the wristlock hurt.

The girl yelped and cringed.

Barnes walked her into his room, opened the nightstand drawer, and pulled out the Gideon Bible. With one hand he splayed it open. "The gun," he said, gesturing with the Bible. "Slowly."

She produced the gun from her purse and dropped it between the pages.

Barnes clamped the gun with the book, set it down on the nightstand. "What's your name?"

"Terri."

"All right, Terri. Let's move." He guided her by the wrist two doors down to Room 114. He released her. "Open it."

Terri fished in her purse and came out with the motel room key. Barnes stood behind her, his head swimming with alcohol, pain behind his eyes. There was a smell that'd gotten stronger as they neared the room. Something rotten and familiar.

Death.

Terri opened the door and the scent wafted out. Decaying blood and feces. She walked into the room, seemingly unaffected by the stench. She dropped her purse on the rickety table near the door and clicked on a lamp to illuminate the scene. Something that probably resembled Daryl was laid out spread-eagle on the far bed, his body going green and gray, melting into the mattress. Must have been there for a week or so, now. Probably about as long as Terri's black eye. Undoubtedly there'd be a bullet hole in his chest or head, but Barnes refrained from investigating. Just like Barnes's room, there was a bathroom in the back, a metal rack for hanging towels and clothing, the closed-loop hangers permanently attached, and an old glass-tube television on a stand along the far wall and across from the beds.

Terri sat down in a cheap chair next to the table. She slid a Virginia Slims from a hard pack and lit up with a disposable lighter. She blew out smoke and said, "You're a cop, right?"

Barnes shook his head. He searched the room with his eyes.

"PI?"

"No," Barnes said. "Where is it?"

"Where's what?"

He looked at Terri. "The machine."

"No way, pal," she said. She side-nodded to the dead body on the bed. "It's mine now."

Barnes didn't bother to pull the .45. He simply lifted his arm and pointed at it.

Terri remained still, her cigarette trembling between two fingers on her left hand. "Please. I need it."

"I only want to borrow it."

She sighed out a breath of smoke. Her knees worked madly up and down like a seamstress. "It's no use to you. It's almost out."

"Serum?" Barnes said.

She nodded.

"Who's your supplier?"

She gestured toward dead Daryl. "Duh."

"You shouldn't bite the hand that feeds," Barnes said.

"What about the hand that *beats*?" Terri replied.

"So what, then?" Barnes said. "You kill him, and since then you've been sitting in here using the machine to *be* him?"

She shivered for a moment and then looked at Barnes like he was from another planet. "I made her be me, asshole." The pimp's voice. "She needed me inside her at all times, dig?"

Barnes nodded. "Okay, I'll make you a deal. My room for whatever you've got left."

"Your room?" Back to Terri. "What's that gonna do for me?"

"You really want to be around when the cops finally get a whiff of Daryl here?"

Terri puffed on her smoke and put on the act of someone thinking things over. "I guess not."

"Then where is it?"

She sighed and pointed at the television.

"That's the TV," Barnes said. "Try again."

"You're so smart, eh, Mr. Clean?" Terri said. She lipped her cigarette and stood, walked over to the television and pulled the glass front off.

Inside was a machine. She tossed the glass on the unoccupied bed and wheeled the TV stand away from the wall, unplugged the machine, and guided it toward Barnes.

He stopped her at the doorway and peeked out to make sure no one was around. They wheeled the stand down the concrete sidewalk to his room. Once inside, they moved Barnes's TV out of the way and plugged in the machine. As it warmed up and found the motel's Wi-Fi signal, Barnes checked the serum bottle. "Looks like only enough for one go."

"Like I said."

Barnes checked the IV needle, crusty with old blood. The thought of sticking it into his vein churned his guts. "Got any fresh needles?"

"Be right back."

Terri left Barnes's room and headed back down to 114. He sat down on the bed, stared at the machine inside the gutted television. The red LED pulsed its slow beat. Barnes picked up his pint and finished it in one go.

"She's so much. Like Mom." The breathless voice.

"Who are you?" Barnes thought.

"Shhh," the voice replied.

Barnes chuckled.

New lights appeared in the room. Red and blue spraying across the ceiling from where the drapes failed to reach. Barnes went to the window and peeked out through the blinds. Two uniforms were hopping out of a cruiser and moving quickly toward 114 just as Terri was coming out.

"Freeze!"

"Hold it right there, honey. Hands up."

Terri put her hands over her head. Barnes could see she held a hermetically sealed, clean machine needle in her left hand.

"Turn around," a cop said. "Hands against the wall. Wait, what do you got there? Place it on the windowsill. Slowly."

Terri turned away from the uniforms. From directly behind they couldn't see her eyes. She placed the needle on the sill and looked up to catch Barnes's gaze.

He shook his head.

Daryl smirked.

The cops cuffed her and pressed her against the bricks. One of them picked up the needle. "What's this, huh?" he said. "Where's the machine?"

"Beats me," Daryl said, eyes still locked on Barnes.

The cop pointed into the motel room. "That Daryl in there?"

She blinked and shivered again, turned back into Terri. "I never touched him," she said. "I found him like that."

"Right," the cop said. He set the needle back on the windowsill and grabbed her purse. "Hundred bucks says I find a peashooter."

While the cop searched her purse, Barnes showed Terri the Bible with the gun inside. Her eyes thinned down to slits. He set the Bible down and made a gesture like the squeeze of a hypodermic needle and then pointed to himself.

Terri rolled her eyes.

The purse search came up empty. "Don't worry," the cop said, dropping the bag on the concrete, "we'll find it."

The second cop came out of the room, flashlight held up near his face, the black length of it extending back over his shoulder. "By the tattoos it's definitely Daryl. No doubt they were running a machine op, but it's gone."

"Where is it?" the first cop said to Terri. He put a hand on her shoulder, ready to spin her around. Terri took on Daryl's boxer stance. She leaned in toward the bricks, resisting the cop's pull just before he yanked her backward. She spun and shouldered him right in the chest. Well played, like he pulled her too hard and it wasn't her fault. The cop staggered back to find his balance. Terri backed against the windowsill, wrists cuffed behind her back, and picked up the needle. "Please," she said, backing down the sidewalk toward Barnes's Room 112, "don't hurt me."

Both cops drew down on her. "Not another step."

Terri was just this side of the door to Room 113. She released the needle behind her back. It bounced off her calf toward Barnes in 112, still ten feet from his door.

"Come on back here, honey," the first cop said.

Terri walked back toward them. "You scared me."

"Sure I did," the cop said. He started reciting her rights.

Barnes took off the holstered .45 and came out of his room. "What's the trouble out here?"

The second cop put his flashlight beam on Barnes. "Go back to your room, sir."

Barnes continued forward, shielding his eyes. "What's happening? I can't see."

"Get back in your fucking room, citizen!"

Barnes pulled a pratfall over a nearby parking block, landing on the concrete in front of Room 113. His hand deftly covering the needle as he went down.

"Jesus Christ," the second cop said. He lowered his flashlight beam.

"Go help him up," the first cop said.

"I'm fine," Barnes said. He stood and dusted himself off. "Sorry to bother you boys. Just a little confused is all. Maybe a little drunk."

"Go sleep it off," the first cop said as he loaded Terri into the back of the squad car.

11

It took three tries, but Barnes finally found the right vein. His forearm drizzled blood from the near misses. He pressed the IV needle's butterfly-shaped sticky pad down to his skin to hold it in place. He applied the suction cups to his temples and pulled out the machine's keyboard tray. Nothing about this homemade machine had ever been legal. There was no option for CogNet, no med card slide reader. You could ride illegally on the Echo Ring or nothing. He repeated the search Dawn had used at Ziti's—Adrian Flaherty, and then Detroit for hook-in location and Detroit for memory—and found the same three files on the peer-to-peer network. Each record showed the same IP address Dawn had written down.

He'd already ridden the Franklin file, leaving ColdCase and FiveLives. He checked the serum bottle. Enough for one ride.

ColdCase.

Barnes looked up to find his own image on the blank TV that'd been pushed across the room to make space for the machine. The man in the glass—bald, and with suction cups on his temples—looked like an experiment, a lab rat. Blood on his arm and his hands. His eyes, sunken and bleak. Not just an experiment but a prisoner, just like the many men he'd arrested and sent to the clink. They entered the place as ordinary as you please, some still sporting the tough guy act they carried through their trials and convictions, others scared out of their skulls, yet all still pretty much resembling their regular selves. Six months later they were clean-shaven and tattooed. Scarred, broken, and reborn.

These were the obvious physical signs. The more astute eye saw that the prisoner had been forcibly divorced from his soul, that he was reduced to a being who thought of nothing more than survival. Food was merely fuel. Muscles were stringy, rangy, and powerful. Teeth were now weapons, as were hands and feet. Eyes were for predation.

It was the same with munkies, who were prisoners in their own right. Just like meth-heads, crackheads, and all the junkies before them. A cell need not have walls, only the power to reduce its inmate to an animal.

Barnes smiled at himself on the television. The rounded nature of the old model's thick glass stretched his face ridiculously. He picked up the Gideon Bible, dumped Terri's .22 out onto the nearby bed, and bit down on the Bible's binding. He pressed "Enter" on the keyboard to load the file and twisted a knob from "Idle" to "Transmit." The machine clicked and hissed. The cold serum flooded his veins. He closed his eyes and lay back on the bed.

His body arched, head to heels.

The Vitruvian Man test pattern.

Please Stand By.

"Prepare for transmission."

Adrian Flaherty was staring at himself in a mirror. His skin was pale, and purple bags rimmed his eyes. He was in a restaurant bathroom. The door was closing as a restaurant patron left. The sounds of people outside—talking, eating, laughing—went mute when the door fell shut.

Flaherty sported a Mohawk tucked beneath a Detroit Tigers baseball cap. Red, circular lines peeked out where the machine's suction cups had recently been applied. Barnes's head felt hot, his body quickened by adrenaline. Flaherty cleared his throat and began speaking.

"I am a homicide detective with the Detroit police, First Precinct. I'm about to begin a personal surveillance on a man I have come to associate with something called the Madrox Project. This is not a sanctioned assignment, but I have reason to believe this man may be interfering with my investigation of the Eddie Able killer, possibly as part of a cover-up. For anyone who finds this memory, if the Eddie Able case hasn't been solved by the time you're here with me, please do what you can to bring information from this surveillance to the Detroit police, Homicide division."

Flaherty swallowed, adjusted his hat brim low to his eyes, and turned up his collar. He left the bathroom and entered the dining area of a small restaurant. Barnes's mouth watered with the scents of burgers and onions. The place was packed to the gills. He sidled by a waitress and filtered through a maze of tables. As he neared a wall of booths, he reached into his jacket pocket and gripped a small metal object. He kept his eyes away from the restaurant patrons. As he passed a particular booth he used the back like a walking stick and left the metal object, a tiny microphone, wedged between the vinyl cushion and the wood.

Flaherty crossed back through the tables and took a seat in a booth of his own. Barnes looked down to see bread crumbs on a white plate, plus the yellow streaks of mustard and some onions and chili from what remained of two coney dogs and seasoned curly fries. Next to the plate was a brown bell-shaped coffee mug, nearly full. Flaherty hunched low in the booth and moved up against the plate glass that served as the diner's outer wall. He put in a set of earbuds and focused his eyes on a couple sitting in the booth where he'd left his microphone.

The man was Dr. Hill, and sitting across from him was Jessica.

Barnes curled up on the motel bed like he'd been gut-shot. Around the Bible between his teeth he said, "No."

The first sound through the earbuds was Jessica's laughter. She threw back her head and slapped the table, tumbling silverware and drawing the eyes of other diners. Her hair was tied back, and she wore a loose-fitting sweater over a T-shirt and blue jeans. Her big blue eyes sparkled over her pixie nose and full lips.

Barnes felt pain in the back of his neck and shoulders. Nausea. His mind's eye turned over to a vision of himself standing up, walking across the diner, and dragging Dr. Hill out of that goddamn booth by his hair.

Once Jessica composed herself she looked into Dr. Hill's eyes, the smile still on her face, that small scar buried in her right eyebrow. She reached across the table and took the doctor's hand. On her left ring finger she brazenly wore her wedding band, her engagement ring inside of it, closer to her heart, the golden prongs gripping at an empty spot where a solitaire diamond had once been. What'd happened to it?

Dr. Hill gripped her hand in his own. The microphone picked up his sigh.

"Uh-oh," Jessica said. "Fun's over, isn't it?"

Dr. Hill hung his head, looked off.

"Tell me," Jessica said, piling her second hand on top of those already clasped. "It's the project, isn't it?"

Dr. Hill nodded.

"What happened?"

"Those kids," Dr. Hill said. "You know? The ones who escaped?"

Jessica nodded.

"It's almost like they felt bad for him," Dr. Hill said. "I mean, here they were, trapped in some basement set up like a funhouse, brought there by a drug dealer posing as a policeman, and *they* felt bad?"

"Stockholm syndrome?" Jessica said.

"Maybe," Dr. Hill said, "but they weren't with him for that long. Not like the others."

Jessica nodded thoughtfully.

"We put them on the machine," Dr. Hill said, "recorded their memories."

The waitress arrived at the couple's table. She was carrying a cup of soup and what looked like half a tuna melt, undoubtedly Jessica's order, plus a club sandwich with house chips and a pickle spear. The sight of the sandwich nearly made Barnes puke. Dr. Hill hadn't only stolen his wife but his favorite lunch.

Flaherty whispered to himself while the waitress served Dr. Hill and Jessica their food. "File name Eddie Doe One. That's Michael Doe, not his real name. Eddie Doe Two is Amy Doe. Also not her real name. They're two of only three to survive the 'funhouse' in the basement of 1613 Caulfield Avenue in Detroit, soundproofed with acoustic panels as well as noise insulation foam. The *others* he mentions are the victims that didn't survive. The cold case files revealed a photo album full of their pictures. Their remains were found buried in the home's backyard or in the earthen floor of the unfinished basement beneath the porch. Nine missing persons cases have been closed as a result of DNA matching. Michael and Amy both attest that, after several hours locked in the basement of 1613 Caulfield Avenue, a man dressed in an Eddie Able costume entered the room with Tyrell Diggs at his side."

"You know," Dr. Hill said, interrupting Flaherty's flow. The waitress had gone. "We started the project specifically to help solve this case."

"Bullshit," Flaherty whispered.

"To get him back on track," Dr. Hill said. "It's been on the book for decades. This guy, whoever he is, has been kidnapping and killing kids nearly as long as we've been alive."

The couple fell into silence. Jessica picked at her sandwich.

"Thirty years ago," Flaherty whispered, "there were two full-time Eddie Able costume rental operations running in Detroit, along with a handful of sole proprietorships. Twenty-seven known Eddie Able costumes in metro area circulation. Michael Doe described his Eddie Able as a doctor, while Amy Doe described hers as a plumber. Of the sole proprietorships, all of which possessed only one version of the Eddie Able costume, none had Eddie as a doctor or a plumber. Mostly they were the more common firemen and policemen versions. Of the two full-time rental operations, only an operation called Sparky Time Amusements had both a doctor and a plumber version."

"You're going to catch him," Jessica said. Again she reached out and gripped Dr. Hill's hand. "He won't hurt any more kids."

Barnes's sickness increased. His body overheated. Here was Jessica with another man, which was bad enough on its own, but she was back to her old self. No grim look on her face, no stress or worry. With Dr. Hill she was the girl he'd fallen in love with.

Was this the explanation for her erratic behavior? She found someone else, someone not so screwed up?

"That's just it," Dr. Hill said. "We were getting close, and then Flaherty started to fall apart. I wonder if we've made things worse."

"Some good has come out of it," Jessica said, "right?"

Flaherty whispered, "Each living Eddie Able costume renter from the years surrounding the abductions of Michael and Amy Doe was questioned by police. Particular attention was paid to those who rented both the doctor and plumber versions, as well as those who rented on multiple occasions. None of the costume renters were proven to be the Eddie Able in the basement of 1613 Caulfield Avenue. However, no employees, nor the owner of Sparky Time Amusements, were ever investigated. Inexplicably, their names have been redacted from the case files."

"I can't help but think," Dr. Hill said, "that we're risking his life."

"You can't compare the project to kidnapping and murdering children," Jessica said. "You're doing it for the right reason."

A waitress appeared at Flaherty's table, blocking his line of sight. She held out a glass coffee carafe. "Warm-up, hon?"

"No," Flaherty said gruffly.

The waitress lifted one eyebrow. "Okay then," she said, holding the *O* syllable. "I'll just leave you with this." She placed the bill on the table and walked off.

Flaherty refocused on Dr. Hill and Jessica.

"You've made progress, haven't you?" Jessica said.

Dr. Hill nodded. "In that regard, the project is showing promise, though we suspect he's onto us. He wrote 'Madrox' in one of his reports, plus there's some evidence missing."

Flaherty patted his chest pocket. Something small and rectangular in there. A cassette tape.

"Why would he steal evidence?" Jessica said.

"He's confused," Dr. Hill said. He pushed his food away, untouched. "Can we go?"

Jessica nodded. "Yeah."

Dr. Hill signaled for the waitress to bring the check. When he brought his hand back down, Jessica took it once again. She pulled him across the table and leaned forward into him, kissed him on the lips. "You know how much I love you, right?"

Darkness and silence.

"End of transmission."

The Vitruvian Man test pattern.

Please Stand By.

12

Barnes jiggled the serum bottle. Empty. He dropped it on the motel room floor and let his head fall into his hands. For a moment he just sat still, fighting back the whispers in his mind, the visions of Jessica with Dr. Hill. Her happiness.

You know how much I love you, right?

Tears pushed at the corners of his eyes. It was his fault, wasn't it? Had to be. His actions had somehow brought them together. Maybe she'd sought out psychiatric help for her messed-up husband, found the good doc on Google, decided she was the one who needed attention. Hell, maybe he'd introduced the two of them himself. He tried to recall Dr. Hill's face at a police get-together, maybe one of Darrow's barbecues, but nothing came to mind. Lost time? Blackouts?

Barnes peeled the suction cups off his temples and dropped them. They knocked mutely against the carpet. Next was the syringe. He slid it out of the vein in his right elbow. When the needle came free, a squirt of blood mixed with serum shot out. He thumbed the wound closed and held it with pressure.

When the bleeding stopped, Barnes left the motel room.

The morning sun fried his eyes. He stood still for a moment, letting them adjust. He felt like a rebar rod had been knocked over his head. Once he could see properly, he found there was crime scene tape dangling from one side of the open door to 114, a coroner's van waiting in the lot. The detectives must have come through while Barnes was on the machine. Cleanup time. The scent of death still hung in the air. It was worse than last night, in a way. Worse now that his sense of smell wasn't dimmed by alcohol.

The scent put Barnes in mind of Keisel Street, a cul-de-sac of three project apartment buildings on Detroit's southwest side, otherwise known as Machine City, otherwise known as Hell. When they were working together, he and Franklin had been called to one of the three buildings seemingly every month. He recalled one of his and Franklin's most unpleasant visits. They had moved toward the crime scene down a dingy hallway where the overhead fluorescent lights blinked and zapped over the bodies of dead june bugs and curled spiders. A large woman with a heaving chest alternately cried in pain and screamed some sort of garbled revenge outside an open apartment door while two uniforms pinned her against a wall to keep her from entering the crime scene. The uniforms' faces were pinched, their posture stiff due to the stench coming from inside the apartment.

It's unique, the scent of human death. The kind of scent that, even if you've never smelled it before, you know precisely what it is. You're made more acutely aware of your own mortality. You're forced to acknowledge the way of all flesh.

Barnes and Franklin stepped over the threshold as the wailing woman clutched at them through the locked arms of her captors. Her legs flailed as she snarled and grunted with the effort. Her yellow eyes were bloodshot from whatever toxin coursed through her system. Somewhere deeper in the building would be her apartment unit, inside of which there'd be a lineup of kids, small to large, like unstacked Russian dolls, taking care of each other while Mom shot up, snorted, or fucked her dignity into the ground.

The lone apartment window and sliding glass door had been covered over with a sheet and comforter respectively, leaving the bed bare. The mattress was soaked through with sweat, and black strands of hair lay on the crusty pillow. Stare at the bed long enough and you could see the contour of a body, like a sleeping ghost. Lie down and you might take on someone else's nightmares.

The furniture looked like props, the kind of stuff you'd put near Chris Farley for a fall-and-smash gag. One lamp wore a shade, the other did not. Dust particles swirled around the bare bulb. Drywall tape looped down from the ceiling with jagged paint along the sides, like band-saw blades with busted teeth. The bathroom door was framed in faux walnut. Bluebottle flies zipped in and out of the crack in the slightly ajar door. Franklin, his hands now in latex gloves, pushed the door open.

Both detectives recoiled. In the bathroom were the remains of a man, a munky who'd been killed for a reason that would likely never be known. Nor would his killer's identity. When the detectives arrived he had been dead for weeks, his body decayed to the point where it appeared to have liquefied into the bathroom floor, leaving only bones and bluebottles behind. There was a bullet hole in the back of his skull.

Barnes shook off the memory as he walked down the block to the liquor store at the corner, took $500 out of the ATM, and brought a fifth of Jack Daniel's plus a box of Band-Aids to the cashier.

"You're bleeding," the clerk commented as he rang up Barnes's purchases. He was standing behind inch-thick bulletproof glass. The goods and money had to be transferred between them like the case files between Hannibal Lecter and Clarice.

Barnes nodded and pushed two twenties under the glass.

"Guess that's what these are for, eh?" the clerk said, holding up the Band-Aids. He smiled, revealing two rows of summer teeth—some're here, some're there. Barnes hadn't noticed until now that his Band-Aids were branded for kids, Eddie Able in his doctor's getup. Antibacterial. The impulse-buy snack cakes near the counter were branded as Eddie Able as well. Each wrapper made up his facial features with a winking eye, while the yellow cake inside filled out the color of his hair.

Wouldn't it be bliss *if you never got old, like me?*

"Serum?" Barnes said to the clerk, raising his eyebrows in question.

"You're kidding, brotha," the clerk said, shaking his head. "You're kidding." He pushed Barnes's change under the glass.

Barnes collected his items and left. He stopped just outside the door to pour some Jack Daniel's over his bloody forearm. He dried off and bandaged his wounds in Eddie Able imagery. When it was done, he applied a healthy dose of the Jack Daniel's to his insides as well. He walked back down the street and went to the motel office of the Fleabag. Three of the walls were plate glass, floor to ceiling, and the other was concrete block. A tall U-shaped counter made up the service desk. The door behind it was halfway open. The counter's front panels were cheap laminate down to the floor. A TV was on in the back room, a low-rate comedy on the screen.

Barnes rang the steel bell on the counter.

The TV was paused. A chair squawked and a man emerged from the back fronted by the scent of yeast. He wore a nondescript T-shirt that he'd sweated down to a different color. His face was unshaven, but beneath a Michigan Wolverines hat his temples were bald. The needle tracks at his elbows confirmed his munky status.

"I'd like a couple more nights," Barnes said.

"Hey, man," the guy said, sitting down on a high stool that creaked beneath this weight, "we do by the hour. Told you that when you showed up. You already owe me fifty."

Barnes put $150 on the counter between them. "Two more nights." He nodded over his shoulder toward the coroner's van and the crime scene tape on the door of 114, all of which could be seen across the parking lot through the office's plate glass. "I think your clientele will be running a little thin for a couple days." He tapped the money with this finger. "Might be the best offer you get."

The man sighed and pulled the money across the counter.

"You know where I can get some serum?" Barnes said.

"Nope."

"What's your name?"

The guy looked up from his money. He leaned forward, laid his left elbow on the counter, and dropped his right arm beneath the Formica countertop. "Jerry."

"Listen to me, Jerry," Barnes said. "I'm in dire need of serum." He gestured toward Jerry's head, his clean-shaven skin. "Seems like you know the score. If you could help me out, I'd very much appreciate it."

His right hand still beneath the counter, Jerry held up the bills he'd just collected with his left hand. "This is me helping you out, bub."

"Hey now," Barnes said. "Big fella. I'm asking politely."

Jerry smiled. "And I'm refusing politely."

Barnes sighed. He pulled back his jacket to reveal the .45.

The sound of a clicking gun hammer was Jerry's response. It'd come from under the counter, where he undoubtedly had a shotgun hanging on a hook, Old West faro dealer–style, the serious end pointed out. It'd rip through the laminate panels and make mince of Barnes's thighs.

"You were saying?" Jerry said, his face slack beneath his dark-blue hat.

Barnes's body shivered. He closed his eyes and allowed the vibration to emanate from his chest out to his extremities. He swallowed and clenched his jaw. When the shivering was over he felt cold, but calm. "Go ahead," he said to Jerry. "Pull the trigger."

"Excuse me?"

Barnes made a bored rotating-hand gesture. "Get it over with, Jer. Pull the trigger."

"Look, man," Jerry said, "I—"

Barnes leaned over the counter, put his face right up to Jerry's. "Just . . . for God's sake . . . just do it."

Jerry screwed up his face. "What's wrong with you?"

Barnes batted the brim of Jerry's block M hat. It spun a quarter turn but stayed on his head. "Come on, big man."

Jerry sneered. "Hey, don't make me—"

Barnes slapped the hat again, knocking it off to reveal a salt-and-pepper buzz cut covering the splotchy skin on Jerry's head, the suction rings on his temples.

Jerry put up his hands. "Yo! What the fuck?"

Barnes slapped Jerry's bald head.

Jerry spun on his stool to dodge the next blow. Barnes pulled his Glock and placed it on the countertop, spun it until the barrel was pointed at Jerry. "Serum."

"I . . . I only know of one place," Jerry said from behind his hands.

"Where?"

"Dude," Jerry said, "you don't want to go there."

"Where?"

"Machine City."

"Who?"

"I don't know his name," Jerry said. "Some skinny white guy."

Barnes sat in his truck sipping bad coffee between belts of Jack Daniel's. He was parked at a twenty-four-hour gas station on Keisel Street, just a couple of blocks down from the projects at the cul-de-sac. Since leaving the motel he'd spent hours talking to street kids in the area, seeing who might have info on a skinny white serum dealer. The best he got were shrugs, the worst, threats. *Eat a dick, cracker. Step off, bitch! Why don't you go find Little Cher, asshole?*

He'd been ready to give up, but the gas-station attendant who'd sold him his coffee and talked into his chest with a nearly unintelligible accent seemed to recall a guy who called himself Verbatim coming in and out of the store now and again. Said he heard him mention "munky juice" once or twice on his cell. Said the afternoon clerk, a girl named Sharon, might know more.

So Barnes parked and waited.

His cell phone rang.

UNKNOWN.

He connected the call and said, "Since you won't tell me your name, I'm gonna call you Shadow."

"I like it. Where are you?"

"Wouldn't you like to know?"

"I want to help. I thought we. Established that."

"You're doing a shit job. I'm on Keisel Street. Machine City."

"Rough place."

Two munkies were fighting over what looked like a Snickers bar on the other side of the parking lot. Tug-of-war. They were kicking at each other, both so thin they might have been two scarecrows hopped down from their crosses. Their clothes were torn, barely covering their frames. Into the phone, Barnes said, "They say we're all God's children."

"No. Religion," Shadow said. "Or politics. Among friends."

"So what, we're friends now?"

There was a pause on the line, and then, "What do you. Believe in. Barnes?"

"I believe in what I see. What I can touch. What's real."

"You don't. Believe there's. A higher. Power up there. Looking down at us?"

"If so, he's not seeing much."

"You want to save. This world?" Shadow said.

"I want to help where I can. Take scum like you off the streets. Keep you from hurting people."

"You want. To play God. Then?"

"No," Barnes said. "That would be you. You're playing God with a man's life as we speak. A little girl's life, too."

"But you have. The power. To save him."

Barnes didn't reply. He'd looked up to find a young black woman walking across the gas-station lot. She strode like a runway model past the pumps and under the rain guards. Her hair was tied up in two little tufts on either side of her head, revealing high cheekbones and color-ful eyes. She wore a puffy red jacket with a furry collar and blue jeans.

"My mother," Shadow said, bringing Barnes back to the phone call. "Was a maid. When I was a boy. She used to. Drag me. To the homes. She would clean. I'd sit all day. While she scrubbed away. Other people's filth."

Barnes watched the woman enter the store as he spun the decoder ring on his finger. He said, "What company did she work for?"

Shadow chuckled weakly. "I remember," he said. "There was a house. She cleaned for free. Pro bono. One of your lawyers. Would say. She cleaned it. For free. Because the man. That lived there. Was con-fined. To a wheelchair. ALS. He was nearly. Incapable. Of taking care. Of himself. Much less his home."

"Sounds like a bad deal," Barnes said.

"Whenever. We were there. My mother. Jerked him off. He grunted. Eyelids fluttering. Until he came. On her hand. She didn't know I. Was watching."

"All that for free?" Barnes said. "Sounds like Mom was a saint."

"She was a whore. That man stank. Of feces. And there were bed-sores. On his legs. And arms. His body slumped at. Impossible. Angles in that chair. But his eyes. Detective. His eyes were alive. Like shining rubies. Darting. This way and that. Fully aware of. Everything. Around him. Fully aware but. Incapable. Of convincing. His body to move. 'They pleaded so.' My mother would say. 'His eyes. They pleaded so.'"

"Now you're going to tell me that God loved this man," Barnes said, "and that he sent your mother to help him."

"No. I'm going to tell you. Detective. That he didn't want. That from her. He didn't want. Her to touch him. She did it. For herself. She jerked him off. Because she could. Because it displayed. Her power over him. More power than. Had she hit him. Than had she. Stolen from him. Than had she. Charged him for. Her services. I'm going to tell you. Detective. That before. I killed him. I cut out his eyes. And dropped them. Into a bucket of paint. I'm going. To tell you. That he sat still. The entire time. His jaw working. Mutely. Up and down. Because his wasteland. Of a body. Couldn't even. Produce a scream."

The imagery sickened Barnes. His mouth watered and his guts churned. He closed his eyes and tried to stay calm, but his body trembled uncontrollably. He gripped the oh-shit handle with his available hand until the movement stopped.

"Is Adrian Flaherty suffering?" Barnes said. "Or did he just get too close?"

"You. Tell me."

Barnes offered no reply.

"Your friend's clock. Is ticking."

The line went dead.

The Iranian gas-station attendant walked out of the convenience store and hurried to a beat-up Toyota parked in the alley beyond. The vehicle struggled to a start, belched a cloud of blue smoke, backed out, and sped away.

Barnes called Franklin. He got voice mail. "I hope you put that trace on my line, 'cause I just got another call from our guy. He said his mother was a maid and more than likely a hooker. Maybe look into any of the Eddie Able cold case suspects whose mothers were maids." He ended the call and got out of his car, spilling the dregs of his coffee on the pavement. He tossed the cup into an overflowing trash can seated next to two rusted-out *Detroit News* newspaper boxes. The headline behind the foggy plexiglass read, WHERE'S LITTLE CHER? The gas-station doors opened automatically. An electronic bell dinged as he crossed the threshold.

The young black woman was behind the glass now, her chin resting on the butt of her right hand, elbow propped on the countertop. Her fingernails were polished but unpainted. Framed in useless trinkets and the lotto tickets taped to the glass, she looked like the reflection from a teenage girl's bedroom mirror. As Barnes approached he saw she was writing notes with a ballpoint pen, left-handed. There was an open textbook nearby. He rapped the countertop with his knuckles. "Whatchya studying?"

She looked up and said, "Calculus." Her eyes flashed to the bulk in his armpit and then back to his face. She raised an eyebrow.

"You're Sharon?"

Now both eyebrows came up. She reared back.

"The guy that just left," Barnes said, thumbing toward the automatic doors, "he gave me your name."

She relaxed, pursed her lips, tapped the countertop with her pen. "I am going to kick his Allah-worshipping ass."

Barnes smiled. "He said you might be able to help me out. I'm looking for a guy. Calls himself Verbatim?"

Sharon regarded Barnes for a moment and then said, "I want you to look at something." She pointed at her book.

Barnes looked down at the text. Through the thick, scratched glass the words might as well have been hieroglyphics, the formulas no better than chaos.

"Looks difficult," Sharon said, "doesn't it?"

"Sure does."

"And yet here you are, breaking my concentration when I have a test tomorrow."

Barnes harrumphed.

She watched and waited.

"I'm sorry," Barnes said. "I'll be quick. Verbatim?"

Sharon shook her head no.

"He's not in trouble. I need some, uh . . ."

She impatiently tapped her pen on her book.

"I think he lives in the buildings just up the street."

"Sounds like you already know where he is then."

"I don't know which building, or which unit."

"So stick around a bit. Maybe he'll show."

Barnes smiled. "You'd like that, wouldn't you?"

Sharon dropped her eyes back to her textbook, started back on her notes. "Puh-lease."

"Yep," Barnes said, speaking out into the empty store as if an audience were there. "Extremely handsome white guy just hanging around the gas station for hours, eating all the cheese puffs, drinking up all the Mountain Dew." He checked with her, found she wasn't looking. "Yes, ladies and gentlemen, I've got Mountain Dew money for days."

She kept her eyes down and shook her head. He could sense she was struggling to contain a smile.

"I might even buy some of these here"—he pulled a small rolled tube, like a miniature scroll, from a box on the counter and read what was printed on the side—"uh, Magic Horoscopes."

Sharon raised her eyes but not her head. "You're a Libra?"

Barnes spun the tube to see Libra printed on the opposite side. "Nah, I think I'm a Taurus."

She stopped writing and pulled up. "You don't know your astrological sign?"

He slid the horoscope scroll back into its box. "Who wants to be a couple fish or a set of scales? Or how about Cancer? Screw that. I'm a Taurus, like it or lump it."

"That means you're reliable and practical," Sharon said, and then she frowned. "And stubborn."

Barnes smiled wanly.

Sharon sighed. "I know Verbatim. He comes in here now and then. Big fan of the Tornados." She flashed her eyes at a set of coagulating taco-slash-burrito concoctions in the nearby food warmer. They were spinning on steel tubes next to several hot dogs that brought skin disease to mind. "I don't want to see him taken downtown."

Barnes drew a cross over his heart.

Sharon ripped off a strip of paper from her notebook. She wrote on it and then slid it through the money slot.

He read what she'd written:

Building C, Unit 37.

"Thank you," Barnes said. He placed a twenty-dollar bill in the money exchanger, grabbed two Tornados, bagged them in one of the wax-paper bags next to the warmer, and headed toward the doors. They slid open as he approached. The electronic bell dinged.

13

The three apartment buildings on Keisel Street were eighteen-story neoclassical structures plagued by graffiti, a collection of gang symbols, racial slurs, and threats in low and high places where you couldn't make sense of how the artist got them there. The projects were a black eye on Detroit's already battered face, part of what every hater pointed to when they wanted to bust the city's balls. Not that the state wasn't busting its own. Barnes had once seen a *Visit Michigan!* postcard depicting the dilapidated and abandoned Michigan Central Station as a tourist attraction.

Barnes walked down the third-floor hall in building C. An ammonia scent wafted over that of mildew. The tiles below were worn pale green, and the concrete walls, painted a lifeless gray, were scratched and scuffed from the move-ins and move-outs. The overhead lights gave everything a fluorescent hue.

Loud bass-driven music thumped as Barnes moved past the steel-reinforced door of Unit 34. Definitely disturbance of the peace. He stopped and kicked the door a few times. "Keep it down!"

No response from inside. Dude was probably passed out in there. A few more kicks. "Police!"

"Thought you weren't a policeman anymore." The familiar voice.

"Shhh."

No one came to the door.

Barnes walked on. He banged on the door to 37. It opened after a minute or so. Standing in the doorway was a gaunt, middle-aged white guy sporting a patchy beard and clad in a camouflage tank top and gray sweatpants. His eyes were bleary, and he had the hard lines and sunken cheeks of a heroin addict. The apartment smelled of Band-Aids. It couldn't have been that long since he'd cooked up.

"Verbatim?"

"Huh?"

"Are you Verbatim?"

"Duh," the guy said. He thumbed his chest. "Josh."

"I'm looking for Verbatim."

"That's what he's calling himself now?"

"Seems that way."

"The little twerp showed up a few weeks ago like he owns the place."

"May I come in?"

"What are you, the head vampire?" Josh said. He left the door open and walked back into the apartment's small living room, the ass of his threadbare sweatpants sagging low.

Barnes stepped inside and closed the door behind him. Josh sat down in a sweaty, busted-up microfiber recliner. He yanked a lever to kick up the footrest, *sproing-click-clack*. Everything in the apartment was trampled and strewn, as if the place were a giant blender and someone had just pressed the "Pulse" button. The television had on a rerun of *Two and a Half Men*. A woman lay curled up on a cheap love seat, the crooks of her arms bruised and possibly infected, her feet sticking out from beneath a red-and-white striped afghan, her toenails painted pink.

A heroin kit was on the end table, plain as day.

"He's in his room," Josh said, his dead eyes now locked on the television.

Barnes stepped down the only hallway toward the bedrooms in the back. There were two doors, one open, one closed. He knocked lightly on the closed door.

He heard two heel thumps hitting the floor and then the door flew open. A tall, skinny boy appeared. He loosely resembled Josh in the other room.

"What's up?" the kid said.

"I'm looking for some—"

"Who let you in?"

Barnes pointed over his shoulder. "Guy in the other room. Josh."

The kid squinted. "What do you want?"

"I'm looking for some serum."

"I don't sell serum," the kid said. "Have a nice day." He started to close the door.

"Wait," Barnes said, sticking out his foot to stop the closing door. He showed the kid his cash.

The kid opened the door back up. He leaned against the doorjamb and crossed his arms over his chest. He looked Barnes up and down, stopping momentarily on the spot where the Glock hung. "Let's see your badge."

"I'm not a cop."

"And this ain't a memory shop," the kid said, but he didn't move.

"What's it gonna take?"

"You ever seen me before?" the kid said.

Barnes shook his head.

"How'd you know where to find me?"

Barnes sighed. "We gonna make a deal or what?"

The kid stared at Barnes for a moment, his eyes boring into Barnes's own.

Barnes reached inside his jacket and pulled out the two Tornados tucked in the wax-paper bag. He proffered them like cigars.

A smile broke across the kid's face. He stepped back and held the door open.

Barnes entered the room. It had the furnishings of a prison cell—a twin mattress on a steel frame, a small wooden chair next to a nightstand, and a rickety bookshelf. He approached the far wall, coated corner to corner in posters for old 4-H rodeos. The posters spanned back through the years and covered different towns in different states, a variety of colors. Barnes moved closer to examine one that depicted a man riding a bucking bull, and underneath the image, Go Rodeo! The event was to be held from September 26 to October 1, 1982, at the state fairgrounds in Hastings, Nebraska.

"My gramps collected them," Verbatim said, indicating the posters. "Gave them to me before he passed. He was a deacon. They were all rolled up in one of those cardboard tubes with endcaps. Thought it was silly to keep them hidden like that, ya know? So I put them up."

Barnes nodded. There was something about the posters that spoke to the nomad inside him, called for him to rip up the roots of a stationary life, to go out into the world and get lost. He moved toward the bookshelf to find a collection of Hardy Boys and Choose Your Own Adventure paperbacks, plus some classics: *Catcher in the Rye, 1984, What's Eating Gilbert Grape.*

"You like to read?" Barnes asked.

"Reading is fundamental. Don't you know?"

"Once a kid starts to read . . . ," Barnes said, bemused.

". . . the world is an open book," Verbatim completed.

"What are you, like eighteen?"

"Have a seat," Verbatim said, gesturing toward the lone chair in the room. "What is it you said you need?"

"You know what I need."

"Right." Verbatim sat down on the edge of his mattress, reached down between his legs, and produced a full bottle of serum from beneath the bed. "My own mix. Better than the original."

"How's that?" Barnes said, noting the black rectangular shape of a machine lurking beneath the bed.

"Just trust me, man."

"No," Barnes said.

Verbatim cracked a smile.

Barnes didn't smile back.

"Okay," Verbatim said. "You know how, like, when you crumple up a piece of paper, no matter what you do after that, I mean, even if you flatten it and take an iron to it or something, it can't ever be the same again?"

Barnes nodded.

"That's what it's like when you put someone else's memories inside your head, only the piece of paper is your brain. This stuff here"—he held out the bottle—"won't leave so many crinkles."

"How do you know this?"

"It's just chemistry," Verbatim said.

"How much?"

"Two hundred."

Barnes handed him the money.

"Are you looking to be," Verbatim said, handing Barnes the bottle, "or not to be?"

"Come again?" Barnes said.

"Be someone else," Verbatim added, "or just not be you?"

"What's the difference?"

Verbatim looked off. His knee rocketed up and down. "Did you smell the ammonia in the hallway?"

"Yes."

"Couple hours ago a crackhead a few doors down poured ammonia all over her baby's face. They say the kid will be blind if he lives at all. Just two months old."

"Jesus."

"She said the kid was crying for no reason, but that's bullshit. He was probably hungry, and she was trying to sleep off the dope. Out of her mind. Too lazy to feed him, so she doused him with ammonia. Hear that music from 34? That's her boyfriend in there. After the cops took her away, he cranked up the volume. A guy like that is looking *not* to be, know what I mean?"

"Then I guess I'm looking to be," Barnes said.

The door to the bedroom burst open, startling Barnes. He reached toward the .45 inside his jacket but stopped short. There was a .38 Special in his face. The gun shook wildly in Josh's hand.

Barnes showed open palms.

Verbatim rolled his eyes. "What are you doing, Dad?"

"Sandy says he's a cop," Josh said, eyes wild.

"I know he's a cop," Verbatim said. He gave Barnes a sidelong glance. "Everyone in this building knows he's a cop. But he's a munky, too. No offense."

"None taken," Barnes said, "but I'm not a cop anymore."

"Shut up," Josh said. "Sandy says you're the cop who—"

"Yeah," Barnes said, cutting him off. "I'm the cop who caught Calavera."

"He's a fucking hero, okay?" Verbatim said. "Quit screwing around."

"Your wallet," Josh said. "Hand it over."

Barnes sighed. He looked past the barrel, past Josh's hands, and past the track marks on the man's arms to find his eyes. "I got about a hundred bucks, but I won't give it to you, so you're going to have to shoot me."

"I will," Josh said, cocking back the hammer on his revolver.

"Likely no one will hear the sound," Barnes said, "particularly considering the music in 34. And even if they do hear, they probably won't care."

"That's right," Josh said, "now hand it over."

"Do you have a decent mop?"

"What?" Josh said.

Verbatim smiled.

"Shooting me," Barns said, "puts my brains all over the walls and drops my body right here on the floor. That means cleanup. From the looks of the place I'm guessing you don't have a good mop, which'll run you about twenty bucks. Plus, you'll need a bucket, which is another fifteen, and then legitimate cleaning supplies, which'll be another ten to twenty depending on the stains. Already that's what, forty-five, fifty bucks? And unless you're planning on rolling me up in a rug you don't have, you're going to need to chop up my body and put me in heavy-duty garbage bags, which'll be another ten for the bags and maybe thirty for the cleaver. You gotta get a sharp one, or you'll be at me all day. You'll need towels, too. A lot of them. Probably twenty bucks' worth. All totaled, we're talking at least the hundred bucks you shot me for, maybe more, just to get my rotting body out of this shithole unit."

Verbatim bit the back of his hand to stem the laughter.

"The fuck you talking about?" Josh said.

Barnes sighed. He pretended to do sign language with one of his upturned hands while he said, "Killing me isn't worth the money."

Verbatim burst out laughing.

Josh turned the gun on his son. "Why are you laughing?"

In a flash Barnes snatched away Josh's gun and had the poor sap in a wristlock, down on his knees. Barnes slipped the .38 into the back of his waist, beneath his jacket.

"Hey, man," Josh said, wincing in pain from the wristlock, "I wasn't really gonna—"

Barnes cranked his wrist.

"Ow! Come on. That hurts."

Barnes produced his .45. He placed it firmly against Josh's forehead. The addict's eyes crossed as he looked at the barrel.

"Look at me," Barnes said.

Josh looked at him.

"You know those little fish," Barnes said, "that attach themselves to sharks?"

"Remoras," Verbatim said from behind.

"That's right," Barnes said. "Your son's a smart kid, Josh. You should listen to him more often." He increased the pressure of the wristlock. "Ask me why."

"Why?" Josh said through gritted teeth.

"Because he's the shark in this little family, and you're a remora. Understand?"

Josh closed his eyes and nodded, forehead still against the gun barrel.

Barnes released the man's wrist and holstered his gun. "Stay here a minute," he said. "Verbatim. Come with me." He walked down the hallway toward the front door of the unit. The woman on the couch hadn't moved. He walked out into the building's hallway and held the door open behind him.

Verbatim appeared in the open doorway.

"What's your real name, kid?"

"Robbie," Verbatim said, "or Robert, I guess, but people call me Ver—"

Barnes shook his head.

The kid smirked and looked down.

Barnes held up the bottle of serum. "How do I know it'll work, Robert?"

The kid looked up and held Barnes's gaze. "I guarantee it. Why did you lie?"

Scott J. Holliday

Barnes shook his head. "I didn't—"

"Yes you did," Verbatim said. "You're a cop. Why'd you say you weren't?"

"I'm not."

"But you're trying to find Little Cher, aren't you?"

Barnes gave the kid his dad's .38. "Keep it away from him. He'll just shoot his dick off."

14

The machine was still in the motel room at the Fleabag, inside that hollowed-out television, still plugged in. The LED light pulsed. Barnes connected the serum bottle, picked up the suction cups, and set them on the bed. He disconnected the needle and took it into the bathroom along with his fifth of Jack Daniel's. He cleansed the steel with the alcohol, careful not to prick his fingertips. When it was done he drank from the bottle.

"Eddie Doe One." The familiar voice.

"Shhh. I know."

He went back to the machine, attached the needle, and pulled out the keyboard tray. He typed "EddieDoeOne" into the machine's search field. One file returned from the Echo Ring.

Barnes closed his eyes. For a moment he just sat still, savoring the darkness, the silence. When they were first dating, Jessica, who was teaching fourth grade, told him she'd sometimes stand outside the classroom door with her eyes closed before going in. She'd just savor that moment of quiet. "It's the only peace I get for the rest of the day," she'd say. And then her face would come alive with that heartbreaking smile. The smile she was now sharing with Dr. Hill.

Barnes picked up the needle. He found an empty spot between the colorful Band-Aids and tapped his vein. He applied the suction cups to his temples and bit down on the spine of the Gideon Bible. He pressed "Enter," twisted the knob from "Idle" to "Transmit," closed his eyes, and lay back on the bed.

Click.

Hiss.

His body arched.

The Vitruvian Man test pattern.

Please Stand By.

"Prepare for transmission."

On a pixelated video screen the Insane Warrior pounded Dynamite Tommy over the back with his forearm. He then threw Tommy off the ropes, clotheslined him, and pinned him.

Michael Doe was playing the wrestling arcade game *Mania Challenge* but was no good. The match was over. The machine had won.

Michael stepped away from the cabinet and Barnes looked around at a room full of toys and games. The smell of new carpet. Arcade cabinets lined the near wall, pinballs along the far wall, a ping-pong table in the center of the room. Dollhouses were stacked in a corner flanked by action figures all over the floor. A steel door across from the arcade cabinets sealed the room. It was dead-bolted.

Michael walked across the space and plopped down into a red bean-bag chair. He picked up two He-Man action figures—Mer-Man and Skeletor—and began pitting them against each other in a fight. One of Mer-Man's interchangeable arms was the wrong color. Orange, so it must have come from Beast Man. The shoulder socket was loose from too many switches and it popped off while Barnes played with it. His wrists hurt from where Michael had been handcuffed. He pulled back his shirtsleeve to reveal red raw skin, threw down the action figures, and folded his arms over his chest.

A sound brought Michael to his feet. He turned toward the door and watched the keyhole spin as the dead bolt was unlocked. Barnes stepped backward, away from the door, until he bumped up against a pinball machine. A man entered the room. The same man who had picked Michael up in his fake police car, posing as an officer, telling him his parents needed him to come home. Michael jammed his hands into his armpits.

The man held the door open and stepped aside.

A large-as-life Eddie Able with a fiberglass head leaped into the room and threw his white-gloved hands to his hips. He was dressed as a doctor, complete with stethoscope and white coat. His eyes were big and blacked out. He had the trademark blond hair in a permanent curl, button nose, and a dimpled chin.

Michael began to shake.

Eddie pumped something in his left hand. Something clicked inside the glove. When he stopped, a recorded childlike voice from within the head said, "I'm Eddie, and I'm able!"

Barnes's bladder felt tickly, his throat dry.

The figure pumped its left hand again.

"Let's play!"

Eddie moved like a mime. He gestured theatrically toward the arcade cabinets and then toward the pinballs, the action figures, and the board games on the shelves, offering Michael his choices.

Michael said, "I want to go home."

The figure stood up straight. It pumped its left hand again. The recorded voice said, "Being friends is twice as nice!" Eddie once again gestured around the room, repeating Michael's choices.

Barnes reluctantly pointed to *Mania Challenge*.

Eddie rapidly pumped his left fist. When he stopped, the recorded voice sounded off, "Yippee!" Eddie clapped his thick gloves together before his fiberglass visage. He gestured with a big wave for Michael to come over.

Michael made his way to the arcade cabinet.

Scott J. Holliday

Eddie performed a bow and offered Michael the first player side of the game. Barnes obliged and Eddie, towering over young Michael, took the second player side.

Dynamite Tommy versus Hurricane Joe.

The match started, and Eddie Able proved to be as inexperienced as Michael. Barnes felt frustrated to play a match with such little strategy. Punches were missed, headlocks were overturned, clotheslines whiffed, and spin kicks were off by a mile. His mental reactions were quicker and more advanced than Michael's unchangeable physical responses.

Luckily, Eddie Able was just plain horrible.

Eventually, Michael, as Dynamite Tommy, pinned Hurricane Joe.

Eddie pumped his left hand several times. When the clicking stopped, the tinny voice within the head said, "I'm sad." He rubbed his thick white fists at the corners of his eyes to mimic crying.

Michael said, "Please, can I go home now?"

Eddie shook his big head no. He leaned in close to Michael and put a finger to his lips. "Shhh." He gestured again to *Mania Challenge*, asking for a rematch.

Michael shook his head.

Eddie pumped his hand a few times and then stopped. The voice said, "Let's play!" He gestured toward the board game shelves.

Michael nodded.

As they turned away from the game, Barnes noted that Tyrell Diggs had stationed himself on a stool near the bolted door. The man's eyes were half-open. His body sagged. Exhausted. Had Michael not kicked and beaten the door for the first half hour of being in the room, he might not have noticed that the keyhole on this side of the dead bolt was still turned perpendicular to the floor.

Unlocked.

Michael ran to the board game shelves and pulled out Connect Four. He showed the box to Eddie. Eddie rapidly clapped his hands for a second and then began pumping his fist. Barnes started toward

130

the gaming table with Connect Four. When Eddie's clicking stopped, the recorded voice said, "Mommy doesn't love you anymore, but I do!"

Michael stopped.

Eddie performed a finger snap, as if to say *darn it*, and started pumping again. This time, when the clicking stopped, the voice said, "I'm Eddie, and I'm able!"

Michael situated the vertical board game on a small table. He set it up so he would be looking over Eddie's shoulder at Tyrell Diggs while they played.

The game began. Michael dropped a yellow token into the center slot.

With his thick white gloves, Eddie struggled to pick up a red token from the table. Once he got one, he moved the token toward the game, but it fell before he could slot it. The token bounced off the table and onto the floor, where it rolled toward the pinball machines.

"Goddammit," Eddie said, pounding the table and using his real voice, not a recording. He sounded like a hissing snake.

Tyrell's eyes opened at the noise. He looked around sleepily.

"I'll get it," Michael said. He hopped up and ran across the room, found the token under a pinball machine. He brought it back and handed it to Eddie. "See? It's okay."

Eddie pumped his left fist a few times. When he stopped, the tinny voice said, "I love you!"

Barnes sat down at the game.

Eddie played his token, blocking Michael's lateral move along the bottom row.

Michael dropped a token.

Eddie, now challenged to pick up another token, held up a finger in the triumph of a great idea. He placed the thick finger on a token and slid it across the table until it dropped into his opposite hand. He held both hands high, like a boxer who'd just won a fight.

"Smart," Michael said.

Eddie fingered his fiberglass temple and nodded.

Scott J. Holliday

Michael looked past him to see that Tyrell Diggs's eyes had once again fallen closed.

Eddie slotted his token, blocking Michael's move again.

Michael picked up a token and said, "Watch this." He placed the token on the table like a football on a tee. He then flicked the token across the room. It landed near the pinball machines and rolled under.

Eddie mimicked laughter by throwing both hands over his fiberglass smile and tittering about.

"I'll get it," Michael said. He hopped up and moved across the room, quickly but quietly. He crawled under the pinballs to search for the object. As Barnes moved beneath the machines, he heard a light bump from behind, something thumping down on the indoor/outdoor carpet.

Michael spotted his token, deep beneath the shadows of the pinballs. He belly-crawled toward it. From behind he heard a faint noise: *cli-cli-cli-cli-click.*

Michael wrapped his fingers around the token. When he picked it up, he also got something else, something the token had been covering. He sat up and separated the two items, examined the new one. A tooth. It was covered by a single brace and a little twist of wire that'd been snapped off.

The clicking sound stopped, followed by a creak from a poorly oiled hinge.

Michael came out from beneath the pinball machines with the token and the tooth. Eddie was standing over him, a pistol in his right hand, now gloveless.

White male, Barnes thought.

The safe on the wall was open, the discarded puffy white glove resting halfway inside. Eddie's chair was tipped over, the cause of the thumping sound Michael had heard. Tyrell Diggs murmured, half-asleep.

132

Eddie pumped his still-gloved left hand. No other part of him moved. When the clicking stopped, the recorded voice said, "Eddie doesn't like tricks."

Michael held out the token. "I found it."

The huge fiberglass head tilted to one side, curious. Eddie pumped his hand. "Being friends is twice as nice!"

"Yeah," Michael said.

Eddie pumped again, once. "Being friends is twice as nice!"

Michael nodded, still holding out the token. "Twice as nice." His opposite hand shook so badly that he dropped the tooth. It fell to the carpet.

Eddie looked down. For a moment the figure just stared at the tooth, gun in hand, but then it began pumping, pumping, pumping its opposite hand. Just when it seemed like the clicking would never stop, it did. Eddie brought the gun up and pointed it at Michael's face as the voice from within the fiberglass head said, "Wouldn't it be *bliss* if you never got old, like me?"

Barnes continued to hold out the token, his body rigid with fear. He smelled gun oil and burnt powder.

Eddie turned his big head to look at the token. He reached out tentatively with his white-gloved hand.

Michael dropped the token.

It rolled across the carpet.

Eddie followed the token's path with his pitch-black eyes.

Michael ducked beneath the gun and punched Eddie Able in the crotch.

The figure made a huff sound and dropped to its knees.

Michael ran for the door.

Tyrell Diggs was just picking up his sleepy head as Michael arrived and turned the door handle.

"Tyrell!" Eddie breathlessly screamed.

Scott J. Holliday

Diggs came alive, eyes wide. He reached out for Michael, but the boy slipped beneath his grasp and through the open door.

Michael grabbed the outer handle and yanked the door shut behind him, but it never clicked home. Instead there was a cracking sound and a howl of pain. Tyrell Diggs's forearm.

Barnes ran up the stairs. Through the kitchen and into the living room. People slept on beat-up couches, some on the floor. White powder on small mirrors. Needles and metal spoons on the coffee table.

"Hey, little man," a woman said, her voice dreamy.

Michael ran out the front door and down the block.

Darkness and silence.

"End of transmission."

The Vitruvian Man test pattern.

Please Stand By.

15

Barnes sat up in bed, his body coated in sweat. His lips were cracked and bleeding from biting the Bible. He spat the book onto the filthy mattress and rested his elbows on his knees. His breathing hitched as flashes of Eddie Able's fiberglass head rolled through his mind. He blinked and shook the visions off, but they kept coming, like bowling balls knocking down pins.

He stood but found he was unbalanced and had to sit back down. His legs trembled. Too many sounds. Too many visions. He cried out in the empty room. The sound was like feedback in his ears, but it helped. His breathing returned to normal. His body stopped shaking.

Eddie had been a white male and still young at the time of Michael Doe's abduction, maybe early twenties, judging by the look of his hands. His voice had that same weakness as Shadow's, the same as the breathless voice inside his head, that same inability to string words into sentences.

How could this person be inside me?

Barnes stood, steadying himself with the stand on which the gutted TV and machine rested. He wheeled the whole thing with him into the bathroom and sat down on the toilet, the IV still in his arm, the suction cups still on his temples. The concentration of his piss was so dark it came out like fire.

The motel room's grimy tub was inviting. Barnes imagined himself in it, lying faceup, the water over his ears. A sensory deprivation chamber. He could just lie there for days, draining the cooled water and refilling it. So warm. So red.

He closed his eyes to the vision, rubbed his wrists.

"Don't think like that." A new voice from within. The kid. Michael Doe.

"Shhh."

Barnes wheeled his IV dance partner back to the bed. He stationed the TV stand near the head and pulled out the keyboard tray. He reached out to begin tapping the keys, but his phone rang, stopping him. He pushed the tray back in, picked up the phone, and connected the call. "Barnes."

"How's it going, buddy?" Franklin said.

"Well," Barnes said, "it's an overcast day in Detroit, and I'm sitting in a shitty motel room that rents by the hour."

"You should call Robin Leach," Franklin said.

"I did," Barnes said. "He's on his way."

Franklin laughed.

"What was it that doctor of yours said?" Barnes said.

"Dr. Hill?"

"Yeah. How does he help?"

"He marginalizes the other voices," Franklin said. "Gives you a bigger slice of the pie. You really should—"

"How?"

"Shit, I don't know," Franklin said. "Better to ask the doc yourself."

"I've done it before," Barnes said. "After Calavera, I beat the voices on my own."

"Even a blind squirrel," Franklin said. He paused, and then continued. "Your mysterious caller. You sure you want to know?"

"Of course," Barnes said.

"No one."

"What's that?"

"No one but me has called your number in days."

Barnes sighed.

"You need help, bud."

Barnes disconnected the call. He tossed the cell phone aside and dropped his head into his hands. From the corner of his eye he could see the Gideon Bible. The spine looked like it'd been attacked by a dog. He flipped the book open. The pages came to rest in the book of Jonah. Barnes recalled the Sunday school story about the prophet being swallowed by a whale. According to the scripture, Jonah lived in the whale's belly for three days before it barfed him back onshore so he could preach the word of God. Barnes recalled the cartoon imagery the church had provided: Jonah inside the whale, sitting near a campfire inside the belly of a beast. Absurd. In reality his bones would have been instantly crushed, he'd suffocate and die within minutes, if not seconds, and later he'd be shat out into an endless ocean. Barnes smirked to imagine his Sunday school teacher clapping the Bible closed and saying, "The truth is, kids, Jonah would have been whale shit."

He began to chuckle. The laughter grew from within, like a storm cloud in his belly, in his lungs. He erupted with it, found himself slapping his knees and hooting. He laughed until he choked, until he was crying. His body jerked with each howl. Tears streamed down his face, dripped onto his ankles and the dampened carpet below.

When it was done, he called Jessica.

The call was connected, but Jessica didn't say anything.

"Is that you, baby?" Barnes said, still smiling.

"What do you want?" she said.

"I miss you."

No reply.

"Remember how things used to be?"

"Yes, I remember," she said. "Do you?"

"Of course." His eyes found the pulsing red LED of the machine. "I want us to be like that again."

"It doesn't matter what you want," Jessica said. "Isn't that right? It only matters what that machine wants."

"To hell with the machine." As the words left his mouth he placed a hand on the machine's hard plastic top, felt the vibration of its cooling fan. "It's not the machine, okay? It's . . . Look, a man's life is at stake. A little girl. Am I supposed to just let them die when I could stop it?"

"You can't stop it."

"What's that supposed to mean?"

"Whatever you want it to mean." She hung up.

Barnes whipped the phone across the room. It smacked against the drywall and fell behind the second bed. He pulled out the machine's keyboard tray and typed "EddieDoeTwo." One file returned. He tapped the "Enter" key to load the file, reached for the knob to begin transmission.

His phone rang.

Barnes crawled across the second bed and reached over the edge. He found the phone and checked the caller ID.

UNKNOWN.

Barnes connected the call and said, "Fuck you," into the mouthpiece.

"Tsk, tsk," Shadow said. "Again with the. Vulgar language."

"You're not real," Barnes said. "I'm talking to myself right now."

"We're back. To this now?" Shadow said.

"You don't sound like him."

"Who am I. Supposed to. Sound like?"

"You know damn well who," Barnes said.

Silence on the line, and then, "But I. Helped you. Didn't I?"

"Listen to him." The familiar voice.

"Shhh."

"How are we. Doing," Shadow said. "On our little. Project, anyway? Where did we. Leave off?"

"You. Are. Not. Real."

"What did you. Discover about. Ricky's code?"

"What?" Barnes said. "Who cares about my brother's riddle? I'm trying to save a little girl."

"She's dead!" Shadow said. "Don't mention. Her again!"

Barnes pulled the phone away from his ear, angled the mic toward his mouth. "And you are not real!"

"Adrian Flaherty," Shadow said. His voice sounded thin from the earpiece at a distance. "May disagree. With you. I'm sure I will feel. Very real. To him. When I carve out. His lungs."

Barnes shook his head. He put the phone back to his ear. "I'm arguing with myself. This is so stupid."

"Don't double. Your trouble," Shadow said. "What does. It mean?"

"What?"

"Your brother's words. Right? Don't double. Your trouble. I've got thoughts."

Barnes rubbed a hand over the bristles on his head, unsure how to respond.

"You're. Supposed to solve. The riddle," Shadow said. "But don't double. Your trouble. What were the. Decoder ring. Numbers. That made up. Shadow?"

Barnes found Ricky's note on the opposite bed. He read the numbers he'd written down. "Nineteen, eight, one, four, fifteen, twenty-three."

"How does. It read," Shadow said. "If you don't. Translate. The letters. That make. Double numbers?"

Barnes wrote it down, and then read the results aloud. "S-eight-one-four-O-W."

"And what was it. Ricky said. To Freddie. About the menu?"

"So crazy that you brought that menu," Barnes said, staring off. "Oh, shit."

"What?"

"It's a license plate," Barnes said. "S-eight-one-four-O-W. One of the plates under the resin counter at Mancino's. Jesus. We saw it every weekend for years, ate breakfast on it every Saturday morning. It's a Maine plate."

"Huzzah," Shadow said.

Barnes smiled. "How could you know these things if you weren't in my head?"

"I know nothing," Shadow said. "I simply. Played detective. Took the time. To think about. The clues. You were the one. Who figured it out."

"I don't buy that," Barnes said. He took the phone away from his ear and was about to disconnect the call.

"Detective!"

Barnes put the phone back to his ear.

"It was Franklin," Shadow said. "Wasn't it? He told you. There were no. Incoming calls. From me. Yes?"

Barnes said nothing.

"Oh. Poor Barnesy. Let me clue. You in. On a little secret. Just between. You and I." He took a long, slow intake of breath and then struggled to say a complete sentence. "William Franklin is telling you lies."

It'd grown late. Luckily, Mancino's was a twenty-four-hour joint. Barnes sat in his truck in the parking lot, watching through the plate glass as diner patrons went in and came out, cooks hard at work behind the counter, waitresses pouring coffee and gleefully throwing their heads back in response to customer quips. His spot at the counter was taken, so the thing to do was wait. The scents invaded his vehicle. Burgers, onions, fries.

Melodian and Brittanian protesters were stationed outside of the Three Aces Memory Shop across the street. They walked a pill-shaped circuit on the sidewalk out front, each holding a handmade sign—THE MACHINE IS GOD'S WRATH, SERUM = POISON, YOU ARE NOT BRAD PITT! A nuisance to memory men trying to make an honest buck. Shop owners were part of the good side, the side aiding people with med cards, people whose reality was truly worth escaping, but these nuts didn't know any better. To them any machine was a tool of the devil and a sign of the apocalypse. Any shared memory was a sin.

One of the protesters, a Melodian who had clearly called it quits for the evening, was inside Mancino's enjoying what looked like a burger and fries. His sign was propped next to him in his booth, the words facing down. His sideburn bangs dangled down toward his food.

Barnes's attention was pulled back across the street. A man, likely the shop owner, had come out of Three Aces and started screaming something at the protesters. Barnes couldn't make out his words. The protesters screamed back, jabbing their signs at him from the sidewalk. So long as they stayed on that concrete strip they were on public property, allowed to be there. But move in the shopkeeper's direction and it was trespassing. The memory man reared back and hurled an object at the protesters. Maybe a rock? It fell harmlessly between them and bounced out into the street. One of the Brittanians turned around and waggled her ass. Or maybe it was *his* ass. Hard to tell.

Barnes turned on the truck radio and adjusted the volume. A low hum like static came forth. He reached for the tuner but stopped when the speakers sounded off:

"Nine-one-one. What's your emergency?"

There was a cassette in the old truck's player.

"It's Georgie," a woman said, her voice frantic and wavering. "He didn't come home from school. He's got yearbook, but after that he always comes right home. In an hour it'll be dark and . . . and . . ."

Barnes pressed the "Eject" button. The cassette popped out. It was labeled CASE #572486-627. He pushed the cassette back in.

"Calm down, ma'am. Can you tell me your name?"

"My name's Alice. I . . . wait. Hold on."

In the background there was the sound of a door hinge creaking. It was light, tinny sound, followed by the sound of the latch clicking. Then there was a bang, presumably the phone clapping down on the counter or a table as the sound was followed by quick footsteps. The woman's voice could now be heard at a distance from the phone. "Where have you been? You had us frightened to death!"

"I'm sorry, Mom," a boy said. He seemed out of breath.

"Young man, you are in very deep trouble. March straight to your room right now. I'll send your father to come talk to you."

"But Mom—"

"No buts! March!"

Then came the sound of footsteps, first against a hard floor and then muted against carpet. A moment later the woman came back to the phone. "It's okay. He's home now. My God, I'm so embarrassed."

"That's quite all right, ma'am. Happy to be of service."

"Goodbye."

Just before the call was disconnected, the creaking door hinge could be heard again, and the woman pulled an intake of breath. The tape played a dial tone for several seconds before it stopped and ejected itself.

Barnes turned off the radio.

He called Franklin's phone. Got voice mail. "This shit isn't funny," Barnes said into the cell. "Planting this evidence tape in my truck? Why are you doing this, Billy? Why are you—" His body tremored uncontrollably. His mouth stayed open to say more, but he found himself unable to speak. Didn't know what to say. He disconnected the call and set the phone down.

His spot at the diner counter opened up. He got out of the truck and went to the front door. Nostalgia cracked like a whip. Barnes was twelve years old again coming through that door. He passed the dusty gumball machine, the drop-a-quarter scale and horoscope, and the empty newspaper rack on his way into the dining area. He stepped off the outdoor rug onto brown, square tiles and damp-darkened grout. A diner was as close as a wayward soul could get to coming home without actually walking over their own threshold. A place as much for the down-and-out as the well-to-do. No judgment, no remorse, no bullshit.

Barnes plopped down on what was once his customary stool. The only difference from twenty-five years before was a duct tape repair job on the cushion. He smirked to consider that his own bony ass had been part of wearing it out. He plucked up a menu from the vertical stand before him.

Yeah, the prices had definitely changed.

"Coffee?"

The waitress standing before him was middle-aged with hawkish features and a little too much eyeliner. Her brunette hair was tied up behind her head and seemingly held in place with a pencil. Her name tag read PALOMA. She tilted a coffeepot toward Barnes's overturned cup. He flipped it over to accept what she was offering.

"Know what you want?" she said.

"Club. Sandwich." The breathless voice.

"Fuck you."

"Excuse me?" the waitress said, her face screwed up into shock.

Barnes closed his eyes and put two shaky fingers to each temple, rubbing to no avail. He opened his eyes and looked at the waitress. "I'm sorry," he said, and pointed to his head. "It's this thing I got. Sometimes I say things I don't mean."

"Oh my God," she said. She set down the carafe and laid a hand on his arm. "You have Tourette's? My cousin has that. He can't stop saying 'That's a classic' and . . ." She leaned in close and whispered, "'Fuckface,' over and over again. It's pretty much all he says."

Barnes smirked and nodded. "I know how he feels."

"I don't judge," Paloma said. She poised her pen over her notepad. "I just take orders."

"Two eggs," Barnes said, "over medium, sausage, and rye toast."

"Hash browns?"

"Nah."

Paloma called out to the back as she walked away. "I got two chicks flipped medium, side of fingers, and fake-bakes on fifteen."

A cook called out, "No micks?"

"No micks," the waitress replied.

The system hadn't changed since Barnes was a boy. No micks meant no potatoes. Had he ordered white toast instead of rye, she would have asked for sunburns instead of fake-bakes. Had he ordered wheat toast, she would have asked for suntans. Rye toast was fake-bakes because it was already brown before it met the heat.

Barnes picked up his cup and spun on his stool. He took in the sights and sounds, the clinking silverware, the rattling ice, the hot slurps of low-octane coffee. Truckers and students, munkies and families. The tabletop jukeboxes of long ago had been replaced with framed photos of local high school football teams and cheerleading squads extending back through the years. At a nearby booth was a picture of the squad from twenty years back. The girls all sported big hair and wide smiles with fists on hips. At that same table a man dug into a slice of apple pie with ice cream on top. The scene jogged Barnes's memory. His first date with Jessica, or second, according to her logic. They'd gone to a diner in Brush Park and had apple pie with a slice of American cheese baked on top. The food had been amazing. *She* had been amazing. She'd cracked him up with how much she hated the Grand Canyon. Her smile that night had been magical. He could still pick up her scent, somewhere in his mind, as though she were there with him now.

"She doesn't love you." The familiar voice.

"Here you are, hon," the waitress said.

Barnes turned back to the counter as she set down a heavy plate and refilled his cup. The sausage was cooked crispy brown, as was the toast, and the eggs looked perfect for dipping. The scents made him salivate, but he recalled his mission and moved the plate aside. Beneath his breakfast and beneath the resin that had trapped it for so many years was the Maine license plate he'd come to see. S81 4OW. The plate depicted a black-capped chickadee on an evergreen branch, a pine cone dangling beneath the bird's feet. The subscripted state motto was VACATIONLAND.

Barnes dropped a twenty on the counter and ran out of the diner.

16

The battered old sign at Vacationland had a subscript:

A LAND OF FUN . . . FOR EVERYONE!

Barnes stood before the rotting remains of a wooden split-rail fence. He overlooked what resembled a postapocalyptic putt-putt golf course. A fiberglass gorilla stared down from the eighteenth hole, its features pale and worn from years of weathering. Cavities appeared at the shoulders and feet, strands of fiberglass-like hair protruding into the black holes. It was the same with the T. rex on the seventh hole and the windmill on the twelfth, which had a noticeable lean. Barnes recalled that if you aimed just right you could shoot your ball between the base of the windmill and the turf, where it would get caught and be lost for good. Ricky once reached inside the gap to retrieve his ball and said he could feel a bunch in there. The boys surmised it was cheaper for Vacationland to buy more balls than fix the problem.

Beyond the putt-putt course there was an abandoned go-kart track, rusted-out batting cages, and the skeletal remains of a bungee trampoline. The dilapidated building at the edge of the putt-putt course once held Vacationland's video arcade. The arcade's interior was always warm, always smelled of fresh popcorn and pizza. Whenever they had enough bottle-return money, Johnny and Ricky rode their BMX bikes to Vacationland to spend the afternoon. They played *Pac-Man* and *Journey* and *Galaga* until their money was almost up, and with their last two quarters they faced off on *Mania Challenge*.

Vacationland had finally closed its doors several years back. Home entertainment systems had not only grown capable of replacing the arcade games but the putt-putt, go-karts, and batting cages, too. The place had been up for sale for around a decade before they finally padlocked it. Barnes recalled that the offering started confidently: a couple of inconspicuous FOR SALE signs in the smaller windows, something to lure in a big spender. After a few weeks there were a couple more signs in the windows, then some around the putt-putt course and at the batting cages. Vacationland's owners finally resorted to a Realtor sign out front, but to no avail.

The place still seemed to be for sale. The Realtor sign was still there, though coated in graffiti. The FOR SALE signs in the arcade windows might still be up, too, if they hadn't been shattered and pushed in.

An emaciated couch sat in the center of the Vacationland parking lot. Two hooded figures in baggy jeans perched like vultures on the furniture's back. Their stark white sneakers rested on ruined cushions. Barnes could recall a dozen arrests he'd made at that couch.

His cell buzzed.

A text message from UNKNOWN. He read it.

Go balls out.

Barnes turned in a circle, checking the nearby cars and alleys, certain he was being watched. Surely a voice in his mind couldn't produce a text message, could it?

He checked the phone again. The message was still there.

Barnes looked up at the tilted windmill on the putt-putt course. The blades were gone now, but miraculously the base still stood. He hopped over the split-rail fence and started toward the windmill, marginally aware that one of the two figures on the couch rose to his movement and started across the lot in his direction.

Barnes continued forward.

The dealer called out, "Fuck you doing here, boss?"

Barnes moved toward the windmill, stepping over the shredded remains of green outdoor turf and rubber tee mats.

"Hey, man," the dealer said, "golf course is closed." He hopped over the fence on a course to intercept Barnes before he reached the windmill.

Barnes stepped past a fiberglass pelican whose mouth used to hold putt-putt scorecards. The top beak was broken off now, and the mouth was filled with leaves, cigarette butts, and used hypodermic needles.

The dealer appeared in front of Barnes with his hand up. A young Asian man with a scar above his left eye. His pants sagged ridiculously, exposing the full ass of his underwear.

"Just playing through," Barnes said with a smirk.

The dealer lifted his hoodie to reveal a knife tucked into his waist. The handle was mother-of-pearl. "Well, I ain't playing at all."

"What's the problem?" Barnes said. "I can't walk across here?"

"This here Yakuza territory."

Some years back it'd been White Wolf territory, and before that the Latin Lords. The couch stayed the same through the regime changes. The Iron Throne.

"What do you want?" Barnes said.

"Your soul," the kid said. He removed the blade from his waist and brandished it. "And it won't come cheap."

"Damn," Barnes said, smiling, "that was pretty good."

The kid blinked, tilted his head.

Barnes pulled back his jacket and exposed the hilt of the gun. "No, I'm not five-o or poe-poe or whatever little phrase you've got, okay? I'm just a—"

"You're a pig?"

"No. But I'm *Falling Down*, understand? Michael Douglas–style."

"Michael who?"

"You don't know Michael Douglas?"

"Nah, man," the kid said. "I ain't a sack of old balls like you."

"What are you, seventeen?" Barnes said.

The kid rolled his eyes.

"Let me guess. You grew up on the skids south of Chinatown, your mother was Japanese, your father was a white dude, maybe, but you've never met him. Or maybe he's the one who gave you that scar. Either way, you dropped out of school because some gang-lord told you Yakuza means 'gangster' and your skin tone and eye shape make you family. And now here you are selling dope, wielding a blade, and rocking a bad attitude in the name of *family*."

"You don't know me, motherfucker."

"But I do," Barnes said. "I grew up the same way."

"Bullshit."

"Really," Barnes said. "I used to be a Japanese kid, too."

At first the kid's eyebrows collided, but then a big smile grew on his face. He chuckled. "Sure you did."

"Yakuza doesn't mean gangster," Barnes said, "no matter what your gang-lord says. It means 'bad hand.' Eight-nine-three. The worst hand you can be dealt."

"What are you looking for here, boss?"

"I just want to look under that windmill over there," Barnes said. "I won't be a minute."

The kid stepped aside and gestured for Barnes to pass.

Barnes went to the windmill. He knelt beside it, opposite the lean, and tried to pry it up. The mill wouldn't budge.

"Hey, kid," Barnes said. "Help me out, will ya?"

The kid checked with his mate back on the couch, who was talking with an addict in a tank top and a pair of Pistons shorts, preoccupied with a drug deal. Dude must have been freezing.

The kid came over.

Scott J. Holliday

"Grab this edge right here," Barnes said, indicating the gap where the windmill rose away from the concrete course.

The kid pulled up his pants and gripped the windmill.

"On three," Barnes said. "One, two, three."

The windmill creaked, cracked, and finally toppled over.

"Whoa!" the kid said as colorful golf balls spread out at their feet. One of them actually rolled into the cup at the end of the course. "Hole in one, bitch!"

Barnes looked around inside the hollow windmill. On the near wall, at about the full length of a boy's arm, he saw a note held down with duct tape. Barnes reached in, removed the note, and pocketed it.

"What was that?" the kid said.

"A clue," Barnes said.

"I thought you weren't a pig?"

"Call it a scavenger hunt," Barnes said.

"Whatever you say, boss," the kid said. He made a pocket out of his loosely fitting hoodie, scooped up a few of the colored golf balls into the pocket, and ran back toward his partner on the couch. "Yo, man, check this shit out."

Barnes went back to his truck. He hopped into the cab, took a breath, and opened the note. It read:

Johnny,

I must really be dead. That's messed up. Give my G.I. Joes to Candy Harper, okay?

Here's your next riddle:

I come out in spring,

I make a loud crack.

I give stitches their wings,

While onlookers react.

Ricky

Candy Harper? Barnes vaguely recollected the name but couldn't connect it to a face.

He lifted his head and looked out across the Vacationland parking lot. The two drug dealers had taken off their shoes, dropped golf balls into their socks, and were swinging them around like ancient weapons, parrying in bare feet.

Barnes drove back to his motel room.

He sat down on the bed. The search result for EddieDoeTwo was still on the machine's small screen. He spun the decoder ring on his finger while he sat and thought.

I come out in spring.

What comes out in spring? Flowers? He could imagine a flower rising from parched soil and making cracks, but that didn't seem like Ricky's style.

I give stitches their wings?

No idea.

Barnes rubbed his temples. He looked again at the screen. EddieDoeTwo. Another child kidnapped. A girl in the memory this time. Amy Doe. Barnes felt pressure behind his eyes, a roiling in his guts. He felt alone. Trapped in a small place with the machine. His slaver.

It wasn't true, though. He could leave anytime. He could just walk out the door, go home, and try to fix his life . . . but could any of these kidnapped kids say the same? Certainly not those buried at that horrible house. Certainly not Cherry Daniels.

Barnes inserted the needle. He applied the suction cups. He bit the spine of the Gideon Bible, tapped "Enter," and turned the dial. The machine clicked and hissed. The serum flowed and his body seized. The Vitruvian Man test pattern appeared.

Barnes found himself walking down a sidewalk, his thumbs hooked into the straps of a heavy backpack. Amy turned her head to the sound of children playing. A little girl, no more than two or three, was chasing a slightly older boy through a nearby front yard. She was in diapers, he wore no shirt. They were laughing. Amy smiled. Despite the weight of her backpack, she began to skip down the sidewalk, purposefully stomping the cracks that break mothers' backs. She envisioned her mother yelping and falling to the ground from her perch above the powdered mirror on the coffee table, screaming for help but no one coming. The thought made Amy feel weightless.

A car pulled up beside. The engine idled as it kept her pace.

Barnes ignored the car.

"Hey, sweetie," a voice said.

Amy stopped. She looked. One of those old police cars. A man in the driver's seat.

"Where you headed?" Tyrell Diggs said.

"What's it to ya?" Amy said.

Diggs smiled. Big teeth. "Thought I might give you a lift home. Your parents are looking for you."

"No they're not," Amy said.

A dreamy smile came to Tyrell's face. "Aw," he said, "you remind me of my daughter."

"You have a daughter?"

"Of course," Tyrell said. "She's not as beautiful as you are."

"What an awful thing to say," Amy said, but her heart raced as Tyrell's eyes scanned her up and down. She lowered her head and rolled her ankle, felt those butterflies she'd been feeling of late, the sickness that came to her when boys looked at her. The terrible sweetness she felt when their eyes found her chest, which had sprouted over the summer, when their eyes found her tummy, her legs.

Diggs reached over and popped the passenger door open. "Get in. I'll take you back home."

"No," Amy said. "I'm running away."

"Why?"

"My parents are losers. All they do is drink beer and snort coke and watch Jerry Springer."

"Then let's run away together," Diggs said.

"Where?"

"Where would you like to go?"

"Seattle."

"Seattle, it is."

"What about your daughter?"

"What about her?"

"Won't she miss you?"

Diggs's smile faded. "I don't really have a daughter."

"Then why'd you say you did?"

"Because I like you."

The sweetness swam through Barnes's system. Amy's heart thumped in his chest. He scratched at her arms. "Don't lie anymore, okay?"

"Cross my heart," Diggs said, elaborately crossing his heart with long yellow fingernails.

Amy took off her backpack and got in the car. "How far away is Seattle?"

That big smile returned to Diggs's face. "Just look out there," he said, pointing outside of the car.

Barnes turned her head to look. The two kids she'd seen earlier were rounding a house and heading toward the backyard, the girl still chasing the boy.

"Do you see it?" Diggs said.

"I don't see anything."

Burlap dropped in front of Amy's eyes, startling her. She reached up and felt the material over her ears and over the top of her head. The scent of it. The scratchy feel.

The burlap suddenly cinched around her neck. Her scream was choked off by the bag.

Darkness and silence.

"End of transmission."

The Vitruvian Man test pattern.

Please Stand By.

17

Barnes lay still on the motel room bed, his eyes closed. He said, "Why did it stop?"

"I stopped it."

Barnes opened his eyes. Detective Franklin sat on the opposite bed, his elbows on his knees, his big hands clasped together. Dr. Hill stood in the far corner, leaning against the wall, his hands in his pockets, his horsehead cane propped against his hip.

Barnes glanced at the machine as he sat up. The dial had been turned back from "Transmit" to "Idle." He turned his body and set his feet on the floor. His vein was still tapped, the suction cups still attached. He checked the time on the nightstand alarm clock: 2:41 a.m.

"I'm sorry I got you into this," Franklin said.

"How'd you find me?"

Franklin flicked the badge that hung from a chain on his neck. It reverberated with a pinging sound as it swung back and forth. "Echo Ring. Led us right to this machine."

William Franklin is telling you lies.

"How come you're not looking for Flaherty?" Barnes said.

Franklin frowned. "You think we aren't trying?"

"You're here with me, aren't you?" Barnes said. He gestured to indicate the room as well as Dr. Hill. "You two are sitting on your asses when you could be out finding Flaherty and taking down this bastard that keeps calling me. You could be finding Cherry Daniels."

"Despite what you think," Franklin said, "we're round the clock on Little Cher's case right now. We got detectives digging into every one of her friendships, her relatives, even the people at *Starmonizers*. Uniforms have been canvassing her neighborhood for days."

Barnes looked off.

"And I've got you telling me about this mysterious caller who claims to have Flaherty, only no one's called your cell phone in days except me." Franklin looked at the nearly empty fifth of Jack Daniel's on the nightstand. He sighed. "We all thought you were good, but you're not. Even Jes—"

"Leave her out of this."

"Fine," Franklin said, "but what about the kid, huh?"

Barnes held his old partner's stare. "Why are you here?"

"Came to help you before it's too late."

"Before *what's* too late?"

"You're losing. Can't you see that?" Franklin tapped his temple. "The people inside are taking you over. Maybe they never left."

"I'm good."

Franklin shook his head. "You don't want supervision? Fine. You don't want professional help? Fine." He reached into his jacket pocket and slid out an envelope. "Maybe this will help you get your head on straight."

"What's that?" Barnes said. "Another vision quest from Freddie Cohen? No thanks."

Franklin handed the envelope over. "She asked me to deliver it if I found you."

Barnes opened the envelope. Inside there was an application for divorce. None of the fields were filled in, and there was no signature. He shook his head. "She's bluffing."

"No, she's not," Dr. Hill said.

"What the fuck do you know about it?" Barnes said. "Huh, prick?"

Dr. Hill popped off the wall, picked up his cane, and used it as he stepped toward Barnes.

Franklin held up a hand to Dr. Hill, stopping him.

"I don't want him here," Barnes said to Franklin. "Get him out of here before I kill him."

Franklin looked at Dr. Hill and nodded. The doctor rolled his eyes. He left the motel room on a gimpy leg, slamming the door shut behind him.

"What happened to him?" Barnes said.

"Don't worry about it," Franklin said.

"Whatever it was," Barnes said, "I hope it hurt."

Franklin sighed and rubbed his hands over his face and head. He looked off. "After Calavera, I heard you'd been shot. I thought I lost my partner."

"Lucky me," Barnes said. "I lived."

Franklin turned to face him. "You're an asshole."

"Tell me something I don't know."

"You're an asshole with no friends," Franklin said. "Figured I'd be the one to have to say some words at your funeral."

"Sorry I pulled through and screwed up your speech."

Franklin hesitated a moment, his eyes searching Barnes's face, his teeth gnawing at his lower lip. Finally, he said, "You still left. You quit on me."

Barnes dropped his eyes.

"Want to hear your eulogy?" Franklin said.

Barnes shrugged.

"Dumbass went and got himself killed. Amen."

Barnes harrumphed. He reached for the bottle of whiskey on the nightstand but stopped short. He drummed his fingers on the wood.

"LeeAnne left me," Franklin said. "Said she'd had enough of nights like this. Three a.m. and I'm in a shitbag motel room trying to figure out God knows what. Could be home. *Should* be home."

"I'm sorry," Barnes said. "I didn't know."

"Fuck your sorry," Franklin said. "I'm only telling you as a word of warning." He pointed at the divorce papers. "She's not bluffing. This shit doesn't end well even in the best of scenarios, and that kid doesn't need to grow up without a father."

"A divorce won't mean I'm not around. I can still be there."

"This fucking thing will be there," Franklin said. He kicked the TV stand holding up the machine. "Or you'll be up at Bracken with Watkins and Calavera, or Andy Kemp or Reyes or whoever the hell he is this week, being whoever the hell you are this week. Flaherty will be gone, and Cherry Daniels will be dead."

Barnes found the red pulsing eye of the machine. "I don't know what went wrong, Billy, between me and Jessica. She's not the same as she used to be."

"None of us are."

Barnes looked up. "What happened?"

"Nothing," Franklin said. "Everything?"

"Can I get her back?"

Franklin stood. "She said if I can get you supervised by Dr. Hill she'd at least try. She said if I can bring you back—the real, actual you, not some guy trading time with the voices in his head—she'll tear that paperwork up. Otherwise, you might want to start filling that shit out."

"I *am* the real me."

"Who are you trying to convince?" Franklin said. He started toward the motel room door.

"What do you know about Dr. Hill?" Barnes said.

"What's that supposed to mean?"

Barnes thought of that scene in the diner. Jessica and Dr. Hill. His guts tightened. "She was . . ." He shook his head.

"She was what?"

"Jessica was with him," Barnes said.

Franklin lifted an eyebrow.

"How long has it been going on?" Barnes said. He held out the divorce papers. "You must know."

"I know she hasn't been happy for some time," Franklin said. "You were all good, you know? You beat the voices and got your focus back. But I guess she feels like you're not the same anymore."

"I don't know what that means."

"And I don't know what else to tell you," Franklin said.

"She told him she loved him."

"I'll talk to him."

"Do more than that," Barnes said. "If I've got any shot, you've got to do more than that."

"I'll make sure he understands," Franklin said. He left the room.

Barnes folded up the divorce papers and stuffed them back into the envelope. He plucked the fifth off the nightstand and drank. His throat burned. His guts swam. He set down the bottle and waited for the numbing effect.

His cell phone rang.

UNKNOWN.

Barnes let it ring until it stopped.

The phone started ringing again.

Barnes snatched it up and spoke into the receiver, "Not now." Then he disconnected the call.

It started ringing again.

Barnes picked it up, put the phone to his ear.

"Hang up. Again," Shadow said. "And Flaherty. Bleeds."

"What do you want?"

"What have. You got?"

"Another riddle," Barnes said.

"Splendid. Let's hear it."

"The Madrox Project." The familiar voice.

"Shhh."

159

"I come out in spring," Barnes said. "I make a loud crack. I give stitches their wings, while onlookers react."

"It's from Ricky. Yes?"

"Cute," Barnes said. "Like you don't know."

"Hmm," Shadow said. "I come out in spring. What comes out. In spring?"

"All I've got so far is flowers," Barnes said. "But that's not Ricky."

"Okay," Shadow said. "What else?"

"I'm thinking about 'I give stitches their wings.' It's too odd a sentence. Makes me think the answer's in there somewhere."

"Ricky was ten. When he died. Yes?"

"You know he was."

"Complicated riddles. From such a. Young boy."

"He was smart."

"An old soul. You might say."

"Mom used to say that about him," Barnes said. He smiled. "'You've been here before, Ricky Barnes,' she'd say, and then she'd chuck his chin. He'd fall back in slow motion."

Shadow laughed. A sound not so breathless as his speaking voice. "Maybe he had. Been here before. Maybe he'll come back. Again."

"How's that?" Barnes said.

"If a soul can live. Two lives. Why not three. Or four? Why not. A hundred?"

Barnes sat up. "Why not five?"

"Sure," Shadow said. "Why not five? It's just as. Arbitrary as any. Other."

"I have to go," Barnes said.

"Did I help?"

"Yes," Barnes said.

The line went dead.

Barnes pulled out the machine's keyboard and typed in the same search criteria that Dawn from Ziti's had used: Flaherty as the keyword,

Detroit for hook-in location, and Detroit again for memory location. The same three files appeared. ColdCase, Franklin, and FiveLives.

"Don't." The familiar voice.

"Shhh."

Barnes selected the FiveLives file and tapped "Enter." He checked the needle in his arm, still there. He checked the suction cups. Everything was in order. He picked up the Gideon Bible, bit down, turned the machine's dial from "Idle" to "Transmit," and lay back.

A click and a hiss.

Barnes's eyes were closed. His tongue felt thick in his mouth. He ran it along his upper teeth, swallowed saliva. Nervous. He wrung his hands together. They felt as big as softballs and were covered with some kind of cloth. His nose found the tangy scent of old sweat.

His eyes opened. He could see, but his vision was hindered by something black. It was like he was looking through a screen or through . . .

. . . *Jesus.* He was looking through mesh.

Barnes was sitting in a stairway, a few steps up from a dead-bolted steel door. The air inside the fiberglass head was stifling. Sweat poured down his forehead and dripped off his nose. He stood and examined his white-gloved hands, looked down at his clown-size shoes. His legs were shaky. His heart thumped madly.

The door at the bottom of the stairs opened. Tyrell Diggs was there, smiling. He stepped back and pulled the door fully open. He bowed theatrically for Eddie Able's grand entrance into the funhouse.

Barnes walked down the steps, stopped for a moment on the landing, and then leaped into the basement. He made a show of it by spreading his arms and twirling. When the twirling stopped, he depressed a joy buzzer hidden in the glove on his left hand. The toy didn't buzz, as Barnes expected it might. It clicked and a speaker box inside the fiberglass head sounded off in an excited, childlike voice. "I'm Eddie, and I'm able!"

He clicked the buzzer twice.

"Let's play!"

Barnes looked down at a boy no more than ten years old, sitting with his legs out sideways on the indoor/outdoor carpet. His cheeks were awash with fresh tears following the tracks of those already fallen. His eyes were like those of a sullen dog. He wore a Transformers T-shirt and dirty blue jeans. Among the lights and sounds of the pinball machines and arcade games the boy seemed out of space and time. He could have been Ricky, could have been Richie, could have been any sad boy, ripped away from his family and held captive.

The boy said, "I don't want to play anymore."

Eddie clicked the joy buzzer. The speaker box sounded off again. "Being friends is twice as nice!"

The boy's head dropped. He said, "Please, mister. I want to go home now."

Barnes held back a cry. He willed his legs to step toward the boy, to lean down and scoop him up, to tell him it's going to be okay. But it was no use; the memory was immutable.

The man posing as Eddie Able licked his lips. Flakes of dry skin. The inside of the fiberglass head seemed to grow more stifling. His throat felt constricted. Eddie clicked the buzzer three times and the speaker box sounded off. "This is your home now."

"No!" the boy said, his eyes fierce. "I want to go home. I hate you!"

The man in the suit was perplexed and agonized by the boy's response. His mind had been filled with the sounds of laughter, a vision of him and the boy running in a green meadow beneath a cartoon-blue sky, a feeling of togetherness that can only be shared with a friend. No obligation. No contract. No force. Just two pals. He clicked the buzzer. The speaker box sounded off. "Buck up, little camper."

The kid stood up. More tears streamed down his face. He wiped them away defiantly. "I wish you were dead."

Barnes's chest ached. Eddie's shoulders slumped.

Echoes of different children's voices sounded off in the man's head, chanting, "Shitty pants, shitty pants, shitty, shitty, shitty pants." Barnes endured a memory, this man inside the Eddie Able outfit, just a kid, standing in an alley encircled by boys. Fire escapes overhead. Dumpsters against a chain-link fence. The stench of diarrhea. The warmth of it trailing down the backs of his legs, cooling as it neared his shoes. Two of the boys held stickball bats.

"Hey, shitty pants. Why don't you shit your pants again, huh?"

Laughter.

The boy's stomach gurgled. More diarrhea. Tears on his face.

"Look at him crying! What a pussy!"

More laughter.

"You know what we do to pants-shitters?" one of the boys said, brandishing his stickball bat. He could have been Freddie Cohen's brother. "We beat more shit out of them!"

Continued laughter as the bully stepped forward and brought the bat over his head. Barnes felt remnant points of pain on his skull and back as the man pushed the memory away. He walked in goofy shoes to the combination safe on the wall and dialed 19-1-4. He opened the safe and pulled out a handgun. He walked back over to the boy and pointed it at his face.

The boy pissed his blue jeans dark.

"Leo," Tyrell Diggs said from behind, "what are you doing?"

"Shut up," Leo said. His words came out of Barnes's mouth with difficulty, requiring all his lung power, all the strength of his diaphragm. He cocked back the hammer and lowered the barrel to the boy's chest.

"Mister," the boy said, "quit playing around. I'm scared."

Leo clicked the buzzer. The speaker box sounded off. "Wouldn't it be *bliss* if you never got old, like me?"

"What?"

A shot rang in Barnes's ears. He cried out in the motel room. His body trembled as he wept. He wanted free of the memory, free of the machine, but there was no escape.

Leo's gloved hand shook wildly, still holding the gun. The scent of burnt cordite had filled up the room.

"Jesus Christ," Tyrell said. "What the fuck have you done?"

Leo wheeled on Tyrell and pointed the gun.

Tyrell put up his hands.

"Clean it up," Leo struggled to say. "Double. Your pay."

Tyrell Diggs hesitated for a moment but then bobbed his head.

Leo put the gun back in the safe, closed it, and spun the lock. He gestured toward the basement door. "Let me out."

Tyrell produced his keys. His hands trembled so much he struggled to get the right one into the keyhole, but eventually he finished the task.

Barnes walked out of the basement on weak legs. He started up the stairs but fell to his knees and turned to sit on the steps. Leo reached up and took off the fiberglass head. Barnes felt the cool of the basement air, smelled the cordite emerging from the room below, the scents of piss and blood. Leo rubbed his gloved hands over his face. Echoes of laughter still in his mind. His head ached. His imagined meadow was empty now. The grass had turned brown, the sky gray.

Barnes screamed, "Let me go!"

A vision emerged in Leo's mind. A room in an apartment. Scents of old carpet, cigarette smoke, and booze. A woman in a navy-blue-and-white maid's outfit, the skirt cut short and low at the chest. She was slightly overweight, but shapely. Early forties. Shotgun makeup. She blinked slowly and leaned against a yellow stove in the kitchen.

Mom.

"What are you looking at?" the woman said, her speech slurred.

"Nothing, Mom," Leo said in his memory. He was looking down upon her, taller than she was. When he moved his underwear crinkled. Adult diapers.

"What?" Mom said. She angrily gripped her crotch through her outfit. "You want some of this, too?"

Leo shook his head.

She smirked and staggered forward. "Not old enough for that, are you, boy?"

Leo shook his head.

"You're a fuckin' midget, huh?" She reached up and rapped her knuckles on the top of his head. "Up here?"

"Don't. Do that. Mom."

"Every swingin' dick on the block has had a piece of this," Mom said, gripping her crotch again, rubbing it horribly. "But not you, though, huh? Just a boy. Don't you wish?"

"Stay home. Today. Mom."

"And do what?" She gripped his cheek and shook his face. "Watch cartoons wif my wittle baby boy?"

"I'm not. A baby!" Piss trickled out of Leo's penis. The wetness was soaked up by his diapers. His sphincter tightened. Heat there.

"Who do you think pays the rent around here, huh? Who puts food on the table?" She thumbed her chest. "Me."

Barnes closed his eyes as she reached for her crotch again. Leo clutched at his pant legs with sweaty palms. Tears pressured at the backs of his eyes.

"This!" she said. "*This* is what pays for you to sit in your diapers all day and play with your dolls and games. This is what pays for your little sewing kits and gadgets. Open your eyes, you little maggot. Open them!"

Leo opened his eyes. Tears rolled down his cheeks. She had pulled up her skirt to reveal her womanhood, brown and furry with gray hair. His stomach tightened. Bile rose in his throat. He swallowed it down.

"No diapers here, huh?" she sneered. "God, if only you'd slipped out early. Don't I wish?"

"I'm sorry. Mom."

"I'm sorry. Mom," she repeated in a mocking tone as she pulled down her skirt to cover herself. "What's *sorry* gonna get me? Grow up and get a job, ya fuckin' bed-wetter. You got no friends, no skills, no spine. Goddammit!"

"I'm sorry," Leo said through gritted teeth. His jaw was clenched so hard it clicked and shot pain down through his neck.

The vision died and everything went blank and silent. Barnes stayed under the machine's spell. He was paralyzed in darkness for what felt like minutes, and then he was back in the stairwell, fiberglass head back on, looking out through the black mesh. The door at the bottom of the stairs opened again, just as before, and Tyrell Diggs was there, just as before.

No. What's wrong? There must be a glitch.

Leo stood, just as before. Nervous. His heart thumped madly. Diggs stepped back and opened the door with a similar flourish, but not quite the same as the first time. He was wearing different clothes. Leo leaped into the room and did his twirl. He clicked the buzzer in his left hand. The speaker box sounded off. "I'm Eddie, and I'm able!"

He clicked the buzzer again.

"Let's play!"

Barnes found he was looking down at a little girl, not the boy from before.

Not a glitch. Not the same memory.

The girl's face, just as the boy's, was awash with tears. Her clothes were dirty. She'd been there awhile.

Terror set in when Barnes recalled the memory's file name. FiveLives.

A binge.

The man named Leo, posing inside the Eddie Able costume, went through a conversation with the girl that was nearly identical to the one he'd had with the previous boy. The result was the same. His internal wish the same. His painful memories the same. Echoes of bully laughter. The girl no longer wanted to play and stood up to him. Leo opened the safe, 19-1-4, retrieved the gun, aimed at the girl's chest, and clicked the buzzer.

"Wouldn't it be *bliss* if you never got old, like me?"

The girl screamed.

-Record skip-

Barnes was in the stairwell again. Sweating in the fiberglass head again. Nervous again.

Tyrell Diggs opened the door again.

Leo entered again, twirled again, clicked the buzzer again.

"I'm Eddie, and I'm able!"

"Let's play!"

A boy said no.

The safe was opened. 19-1-4.

"Wouldn't it be *bliss* if you never got old, like me?"

The boy screamed.

In the motel room Barnes sobbed through the echoes of gunshots. His body twitched on the bed. His hands clutched the filthy sheets. He silently said *no, no, no* around the Bible in his mouth.

-Record skip-

Barnes in the stairwell.

Sweating.

Nervous.

Tyrell opened the door.

Barnes entered.

Twirled.

Clicked the buzzer.

"I'm Eddie, and I'm able!"

A girl said no.

The safe. 19-1-4.

"Wouldn't it be *bliss* if you never got old, like me?"

A scream.

Barnes curled into a fetal position on the bed. His sobbing turned over to a soundless, open-mouthed wail as the Bible fell out. His face was an image of anguish.

-Record skip-

Barnes in the stairwell.

Diggs.

The door.

Enter.

Twirl.

Buzzer.

"I'm Eddie, and I'm able!"

No.

19-1-4.

"Wouldn't it be *bliss* if you never got old, like me?"

Barnes laughed hysterically on the bed, screaming, "Yes, yes, yes!"

Darkness and silence.

"End of transmission."

The Vitruvian Man test pattern.

Please Stand By.

18

Sweat trickled off Barnes's face and chest, down his arms and back as he sat up slowly. He peeled the suction cups from his temples and yanked the needle from his arm. Blood spurted from his elbow. He absently clamped his hand over the hole and bent forward over his knees, rocking. Continued echoes of gunshots in his mind. The bodies of children fell through his thoughts in a repeating loop—all of them with startled looks on their faces.

Barnes struggled up to his feet. He gripped the fifth of Jack Daniel's by the neck and walked into the bathroom, his arm drizzling blood over Eddie Able Band-Aids. He set the bottle in the sink, fell to the toilet, and barfed. Three heaves and he was empty, three jolts of sour bile. His body curled and cringed for more, but that was it.

He stood up shaky, picked up the fifth and smashed it against the sink, brought a shard of glass up to the pulsing jugular vein in his neck.

"No." Leo's voice.

"Fuck you."

"Don't!" The familiar voice.

"Shhh."

"Don't fail him."

A vision from Freddie Cohen's memory came to Barnes's mind. Ricky standing at the top of that ridge. His smile, his eyes.

"I've already failed him," Barnes said. He pressed the glass into his neck, felt the skin begin to yield, but a new vision stopped him.

Adrian Flaherty, his face in the restaurant bathroom mirror staring back intently. His suspicion of Dr. Hill and the mysterious Madrox Project.

"You can still save her." The familiar voice.

"No. I can't go back on that machine."

"You know his name."

"Leo."

Barnes dropped what remained of the bottle. It shattered on the bathroom floor. He stepped around the glass and back out into the motel room. He wiped off the blood and bandaged his arm. He pocketed his phone and put on his holster and jacket, picked up the machine, lifted it over his head, and slammed it on the floor. The red LED went blank for a moment but then returned to pulsing. Barnes stomped the machine until the plastic shattered, exposing circuitry and wires. He stomped and stomped, his heel cracking and pulverizing the machine's artificial heart until, finally, the LED light faded out.

He left the motel room and went to his truck.

He pulled out of the parking lot and drove without direction or destination. It was morning again. The sun was bright and hurt his eyes. He slowed to a stop at the edge of what was once a city playground and threw the gearshift into park. The weeds had overtaken the place now. The jungle gyms had become wilted, rusted things. A merry-go-round was turned over on its head. At the nearby baseball diamond, once covered in minced gravel but now lost to weeds and discarded appliances, a man and his son practiced grounders.

"Keep that glove down," the man said as he tossed a baseball into the air. He swung a wooden bat at the ball, shooting it toward the boy, who was standing out by what was once third base.

Barnes smiled wearily at the scene, his vision blurry from tears not yet fallen. A shiver started in his guts and overtook his body, his mind. He closed his eyes, sending the tears down his cheeks, and waited until the feeling passed, until he went numb. His mouth still tasted of bile. He grabbed a piece of gum from the pack in the visor and popped it in.

His salivary glands ached with the fruity sweetness. He settled into his seat, fiddling idly with the decoder ring on his finger.

19-1-4.

Barnes turned the ring to 19. *S.* 1 was clearly *A*, and 4 was *D*.

SAD.

"Are you sad, Leo?"

No reply.

The crack of the bat made Barnes look up. The kid fielded another grounder and fired the ball to the backstop behind his father.

"Good one!" the man said. He tossed another ball into the air. Barnes watched the ball rise, stop, and fall back down. White leather and red stitches.

I come out in spring.

Baseball season starts in spring.

I make a loud crack.

The bat cracks the ball.

I give stitches their wings.

The bat sends the stitched ball flying.

While onlookers react.

The audience cheers.

The crack of the . . . *bat.*

Barnes turned the decoder ring to *B*, then *A*, and then *T*.

2-1-20.

2120?

He took out Ricky's note and read.

Give my G.I. Joes to Candy Harper, okay?

A foggy memory bloomed in his mind—a girl's eyes, her figure, her flat belly. Barnes's cheeks grew hot as his mind traveled back to a pair of hips barely covered by a cheerleader's skirt, her perfect legs. He recalled a thigh being pierced with a needle.

Insulin?

Barnes bumped his temple with the meat of this palm. This girl . . . who was she? A cheerleader. That much he knew.

Yeah, that much he knew.

He threw the truck in drive and stomped the accelerator.

Barnes pulled back into the parking lot at Mancino's. The morning rush was at a lull, which merely meant he wouldn't have to wait in line for a seat; otherwise, the place was nearly packed. He dropped out of the truck and went inside the diner, walked past the hostess waiting to seat customers.

Most of the booths were taken, but Barnes found one along the far wall that was empty. He slid across the padded seat to the framed picture of a high school cheerleading team. None of the faces looked familiar. He scanned the names listed below the photo but didn't find Candy Harper.

"Sir, can I help you find a seat?" A voice from across the diner.

Barnes didn't respond. He moved to another empty booth but never sat down. The photo was of a football team. Barnes hopped up onto the table to get a high-level view of the other photos at the other booths.

"Hey," the same voice said. "What the hell are you doing?"

Barnes looked down to find the shift manager—Gordon, according to his silver name tag—staring up at him. The man had thick glasses and short sleeves, a red tie.

"Just gimme a sec," Barnes said.

"No!" Gordon said. "Get down from there, now!"

Barnes ignored Gordon and scanned the photos in the booths. All of the other patrons' eyes were on him, their faces dismayed, mouths hanging open. Scrambled eggs quivered on forks. None of the photos seemed to jog his—*Wait, there it was.*

172

Barnes hopped down from the table.

"Sir, I'll kindly ask you to leave this establish—"

"Shut up," Barnes said, stepping past the man.

Gordon threw a hand to his chest like an insulted debutante.

Barnes continued toward the booth. A trucker sat alone, enjoying a plate of bacon and eggs over easy, white toast. He wore a black vest and had old, faded tattoos down to his wrists. He watched cautiously as Barnes approached.

"Sorry," Barnes said when he reached the man's table, "I just need to take a look at the photo at the end of your booth."

The man glanced at the photo and then back at Barnes. "Be my guest."

Barnes sat down and slid across to the image. He scanned the girls' faces until one jogged his memory. Pretty, blonde hair, wide smile. He scanned down to the bottom to read, *Third row, from left to right, Jill Hainsley, Becky Ward, Candy Harper.* His memory was jogged again . . . 2120 . . . what was it?

A hand came down on his shoulder, gripped his jacket, tugged at him.

Barnes looked up to see Gordon, the shift manager, gritting his teeth as he tried to yank him out of the booth.

"Hold on," Barnes said.

"No," Gordon said, sending spittle out from his lips, "you need to leave. I'll call the police."

Barnes employed a trick so many suspects had employed against him during arrests—just pull up your legs and let your detainer try to drag your entire body weight. It was virtually impossible.

The trucker across the booth chewed his food and sipped his coffee. *2120,* Barnes thought. *Candy Harper . . . 2120 . . .*

"Fairchild Avenue." The familiar voice.

At the sound of the voice Barnes's body chilled and he clenched his jaw. He blinked rapidly as his body absorbed a wave of nausea. When it was over he put his feet down and slid out of the booth. Gordon, who was employing so much pressure to pull him out, spilled over into the booth across the way. To the seated trucker Barnes said, "Thank you."

The trucker saluted with his coffee cup as Barnes turned and left. He tracked across the parking lot toward his vehicle. As he reached into his pocket for the keys he heard a female voice.

"Good night, sweet prince."

He turned his head in time to see a yellow Taser reach out from behind a red Chevy Aveo. The hand that held the weapon was tattooed with a spiderweb. He heard a buzzing sound as a crack of lightning flashed across his vision, and then there was only blackness.

19

Barnes awakened with a start. He was lying on his back. He tried to sit up but found he was strapped down to a padded table. His head thumped painfully. A damp, earthy scent. He looked around to discover he was in the basement at Ziti's Sub and Grub. A needle in his arm, suction cups attached to his head. Dawn sat on a chair in the corner, relaxed and smiling, red lipstick vivid against her white teeth. Her yellow Taser was tucked in her waist. Barnes's gun and shoulder holster hung from a hook on the wall near her head.

She tilted her head and called out, "He's up!"

"What the hell's going on?" Barnes said. He struggled against his restraints.

"You'll see," she said. She crossed her legs, and her foot did a little dance on the hinge of her ankle.

Harrison entered the room. His apron was gone. Whatever semblance of a friendly demeanor he'd once had was gone, too. He was no longer a blue-collar guy making subs and scratching out a living at his takeout restaurant, but a brash, intense individual of obvious status. Trailing behind him was a woman Barnes vaguely recognized. She was disheveled and had an addict's eyes. Circles had been shaved into her temples. Skinny. Veiny arms. The "after" picture in an antismoking campaign.

Harrison closed the door behind the woman, locking the four of them in the room.

"What's this about?" Barnes said.

Harrison offered the disheveled woman a folding metal chair. She took it and sat down, put her purse on her knees. Harrison took his own chair, scratching the legs loudly against the floor as he dragged it next to Barnes's table. He sat down and leaned in close to Barnes's face. "How you doin', big fella?"

"Been better," Barnes said.

Harrison smiled and sat back in his chair. He crossed his arms over his chest. His right knee rocketed up and down.

"Is this about Raphael?" Barnes said. "I mean, Danny? I told you, I don't know any—"

"No," Harrison said.

"Then what?"

Harrison gestured toward the disheveled woman. "Recognize her?"

Barnes looked the woman over for a second time. He knew her but couldn't place from where.

"That's Little Cher's mom," Harrison said. "Hannah Daniels. The woman who gave birth to such an angelic voice. You know Little Cher took fourth place on *Starmonizers*? Should have gotten first. She was robbed." He smiled at Hannah. "Say hello to Detective Barnes, Ms. Daniels."

The woman nodded curtly at Barnes.

"I'm not a detective anymore," Barnes said to Harrison.

"The cops refused to put her on the machine," Harrison said, continuing as though Barnes hadn't spoken. "So she came to us."

Barnes turned to Hannah Daniels. "If you have something the police could use, you need to tell them. These people can't help you."

"I just want my daughter back," Hannah said quietly.

"She already told the police all she knows," Dawn added. "It's *those* people who can't help her."

"What does this have to do with me?" Barnes said.

"Hannah," Dawn replied, "was a little, shall we say, *inebriated* the day Cherry was abducted."

176

Hannah Daniels covered her eyes with a bony hand.

"It's okay, honey," Dawn said. She leaned forward and laid a hand on Hannah's shoulder. "We all make mistakes."

"She spent up all Little Cher's money on booze and dope," Harrison said. "Spent the poor girl's auto show retainer as soon as the check cleared."

Hannah's shoulders heaved as she began sobbing.

Barnes tried to wriggle out of his restraints, but it was no use. "Let me free."

Harrison stared strangely at Barnes. "Don't you want to help Little Cher?"

"Let me free," Barnes said, "or—"

"Or what?" Harrison spat. His eyes grew fierce. He clenched his fists, looked like an MMA fighter ready to charge across the octagon. Maybe somewhere in his mind he was.

"Your kind no longer believes the machine will help," Dawn said. "So we hooked Hannah in to see what she might recall"—she drew back a lock of Hannah's stringy hair—"despite spending the afternoon on a bender with her junkie boyfriend. Unfortunately there was nothing of value on her memory pull." She winked at Barnes. For the first time he noted the fresh red rings on her bald temples.

"Who are you people?" he said, though he was fairly certain he knew the answer.

Harrison shivered. It was almost imperceptible, but definitely there. He appeared more philosophical when he said, "That's a slippery question."

"No, it's not."

"Depends on your perspective," Harrison said.

"The Sect of Shifting Sands."

Harrison examined his fingernails.

"Do not aid them." The familiar voice.

"Shhh."

"You can't help her," Barnes said.

"That's why you're here," Harrison said.

"What do you want from me?" Barnes said.

Harrison shivered again, and again his visage changed. His voice took on a womanly tone. "You've been working Little Cher's case."

"Don't put me in her memory," Barnes said. "I won't see anything Dawn couldn't."

"Oh, you poor thing," Harrison said. "You don't understand, do you?"

"You're Gabriel Messina," Barnes said. "The Shivering Man."

"Little ol' me?" Harrison said, a hand to his chest in denial, but his smile betrayed him.

"I won't ride her memory," Barnes said.

"No need to go there," Harrison said, waving his hand dismissively. "As you say, Dawn has already gone through all that mess. Nothing new to see."

"Then what?"

Harrison patted the machine like it was an obedient dog. "It records, too, you know? You have memories, don't you, sweetie?"

"Nothing of value to thi—" Barnes stopped, then the realization struck him. "Oh God, no. Please, don't."

Harrison took hold of Barnes's hand, squeezed it reassuringly. "Hannah will be fine riding your memories, Detective. I'm certain of it."

Barnes turned to Hannah Daniels. "You don't want to do this."

"She needs to know what happened to her kid," Dawn said. "You've seen things. You know things."

"The Sect of Shifting Sands will save that little girl," Harrison said. "The *machine* will save her."

"Listen to me," Barnes said to Hannah. "This monster who took your daughter, you don't want his thoughts in your head. The things he's done. You don't want to know."

"Hold on now," Harrison said. "You have the perpetrator *in mind*? The man who took Little Cher?"

"No," Barnes said. "I mean, the police have a suspect, but—"

Harrison reached out with a pinkie extended and flipped the machine's dial from "Idle" to "Record."

A click and a hiss.

Barnes closed his eyes. He fought thoughts of Leo, of that Eddie Able mask, of FiveLives, but he was fighting the purple dinosaur. Flashes of children falling, the sound of Leo's breathless voice, his horrible mother, that fiberglass head, the heat and sweat from within . . .

Barnes stopped fighting the visions. Instead he concentrated on Ricky up on that ridge and smiling down at Freddie Cohen. He thought of Jessica, too. Flashes of the brilliant moments they'd shared. Laughing hysterically in a diner. Over what? He couldn't recall. Did it matter? The way she tucked a lock of hair behind her ear, and how it always fell back out. The two of them at Ricky's grave, his hand in hers. She'd made him throw salt over his shoulder, said it was salt in the face of the demon standing behind him.

Ricky again. He'd set up little green army men around the living room in an expansive tactical formation, but Johnny came through pretending to be Godzilla and knocked everything down. God, how Ricky cried over that. Or the time they both got BB guns for Christmas. Ricky had put the barrel of his gun right up to Johnny's toe and pulled the trigger, cracking the bone.

Back to Jessica. Older now. She'd just given birth. They were riding home from the hospital and stopped at a red light. She and the baby were in the back. She reached up and put her hand on his shoulder, looked at him in the rearview mirror, eyes hopeful and nervous. He'd gripped her hand and held it until the light turned green.

Back to Ricky. His revenge for Johnny's Godzilla tactic was to reset the Nintendo right in the middle of a five-hour *Metal Gear* session.

Johnny howled with rage and chased him out of the trailer and into the woods.

Barnes settled into his memories, immersed himself in the nostalgia, in the good things that defined his oftentimes dismal existence. It felt right to dwell there. It felt fine.

The machine stopped recording.

Barnes opened his eyes to find Dawn standing over him, smiling happily as her tongue traced her upper teeth. She waggled the Taser before his eyes and pressed the button. Electricity arced from one post to the other.

"Good night, sweet prince."

20

The back of a pickup truck is no place for a nap. Barnes woke up with his head against the toolbox in the back, his neck kinked at an angle. He sat up blinking and rubbed his head. His body was fried. Maybe literally. But he smiled. They'd get nothing from his memory pull. If anything, Hannah Daniels would feel his happiness instead of Leo's horror.

He struggled over the side of the bed wall and landed on his knees on the concrete below. The truck was still parked at Mancino's. He leaned against the vehicle to stabilize himself as he stood up.

Across the street, in front of Three Aces, remained two protesters. They sat on the curb, their signs over their knees, sharing a cigarette. The one on the left was a Melodian, the other a Brittanian complete with pigtails and a plaid backpack. If only these nuts knew where Gabriel Messina was hiding. In plain sight, as it were.

Barnes got into the truck, started it, and drove away. He fought the urge to drive right back to Ziti's, knock some teeth from Messina's head, and drag Hannah Daniels out of their misguided captivity. The woman was a mess and the Sect was making matters worse, offering the machine as a beacon of hope. There was only suffering for Hannah, only pain until her daughter was found safe. Worse if she wasn't. He needed to get in front of this investigation, find Flaherty, find Cherry, and unplug all these people from more damage. Dealing with Messina could wait.

He pulled up to Candy Harper's childhood home at 2120 Fairchild Avenue. The tiny house was situated up against the train tracks at

Calvary Junction, where suburbia began giving way to the expanse of Whitehall Forest. The roads here were gravel. The grass at 2120 hadn't been mowed in weeks. The hedge out front had overtaken the concrete porch and was reaching for the house itself. Sun-bleached paint flaked away from the T1-11 siding.

Barnes picked up Zandar and Destro, got out of his truck, went to the front door, and knocked on the screen. The flimsy aluminum rattled under his knuckles.

A teenage girl opened the door. She had light brown eyes and blonde hair. A black BTBAM T-shirt was cut and tied in a knot above her belly, and her jeans were cut so short the white front pockets peeked out against her thighs. Memories came rushing back. Barnes had to blink to ensure he wasn't looking at the Candy Harper of his youth but undeniably the woman's daughter. The scent from inside the house was Chef Boyardee and stale cigarette smoke. Barnes recalled Candy as a girl younger than the one who stood before him running off to the gas station at Calvary Junction to buy her mother's Viceroys.

The girl said, "Momma told you not to come around anymore. You people got shit in your ears, or what?"

"Excuse me?" Barnes said.

"You're one of them Jehovahs, right?"

"No."

"Okay then, whaddya want?"

"Is your mother home?"

"You know my momma?"

"Candy Harper," Barnes said. The name felt both familiar and strange coming out of his mouth.

"She's Candy, all right, but she goes by Smith now."

"Is she home?"

"Course she is. Where else would she be?"

"Could I come in and talk with her?"

The girl looked at the two G.I. Joe action figures in Barnes's hand. "You bringing her those?"

Barnes nodded.

"Then I guess she'll want to see you." She pushed open the door. "Come on in."

Barnes stepped into the house, which was run-down and unkempt. He pulled a double take. The furniture was the same as when he was a boy, at least thirty years old now, undoubtedly more. The cushions on the couch were as thin as sheets, the material torn to expose stuffing the color of chicken fat. Two-by-fours had breached the arms in various places. The cheap wood was browned and smoothed by human touch. The art on the walls was the same as he remembered—three separate paintings of nothing more than colorful strokes resembling tangled yarn. He recalled Candy telling him and Ricky that her grandfather had painted them and that they were abstracts. Barnes couldn't make sense of them, then or now.

"I ain't seen you before," the girl said as she led him down the hallway toward the back bedrooms where the cigarette smoke scent grew stronger. "How do you know Momma?"

"We're old friends," Barnes said.

"Then you might want to brace yourself, mister."

"How's that?"

"She ain't like she used to be."

When Barnes and Ricky were boys, Candy Harper was their queen. A tall girl, plus she was a couple of years older with the female shape to go with her maturity. She wore too-short shorts, just like her daughter, and during the summer she ran around in nothing else but a bikini top. Barnes grew flush, recalling he used to masturbate to a vision of Candy smiling at him while pulling the string on that bikini top, her breasts finally popping loose after days of threatening to. Mom used to say she felt sorry for the poor girl, that she'd end up twirling on a pole. Barnes hadn't known what twirling on a pole meant, but he understood that it was probably improper and probably something worth considering.

Everyone thought Candy was dumb. She ran around with two boys younger than she was, her ass hanging out of her shorts, playing with their G.I. Joe action figures while she practically ignored the boys and girls her own age. Her G.I. Joe collection shamed what Johnny and Ricky had. She kept the figures in their packaging and never actually opened them. The boys couldn't understand that. Ricky once said, "Why have them if you don't play with them?"

Candy, sitting with her legs hugged up to her chest and her arms wrapped around her knees, said, "They'll be worth money someday."

Ricky said, "Well, they ain't worth shit right now."

Candy smirked and looked off, nibbled at her wrist. "Mr. Price says each one is worth a hand job, and a blow job gets me five."

The boys exchanged a wide-eyed glance. Johnny was marginally sure what a hand job meant, but a blow job? Good God. The words, spoken through a mouthful of her own skin, reddened his cheeks and dampened his palms.

"She's in here," Candy's daughter said. She pushed open the door to the home's master bedroom.

The person in the bed was a skeleton image of what Candy Harper had once been. She was lying on her side in silk pajamas that had fallen down her hip to reveal the bony frame below. The skin sagged down and then sloped back up toward her ribs before her pajamas covered her again. Her face was almost literally a skull, her lips pulled back to reveal her teeth and gums, her eyes dropped deep into eye sockets, glinting like pinballs. Her hair was thin blonde wisps, and a tracheostomy tube had been placed in her throat. A cat sprawled on the bed next to her. The animal was fat, its tail curling and moving languidly.

The room was stuffy. An oscillating fan turned in the far corner, pushing the scents of cat piss and cigarette smoke around the space. A box of Marlboro Mediums lay on the nightstand, plus a yellow plastic lighter. The walls were lined with shelving units to the ceiling, each one meticulously stacked with G.I. Joe action figures, all still in their packaging, including the skin-color-changing Zartan, the Baroness, Duke, and Cover Girl, who came with a tank. With so many duplicates the shelves looked like they were factions from different armies. Barnes found the Destro shelf. He smirked. She had more than he could count.

"Momma," the girl said, "you got a visitor."

Candy picked up her head. She blinked.

"Don't move too much," the girl said. "She'll lose you."

"Who is it?" Candy said, holding a finger on the end of her trach tube to give strength to her brittle voice. Her eyes moved back and forth across the area where Barnes stood.

"It's John Barnes," he said.

A smile came to Candy's face. "Little Johnny Barnes?"

"Hello, Candy."

"To what do I owe such a pleasure?"

"Don't make her talk too much," the girl said. "She's got cancer in her throat."

Barnes nodded.

Candy waved her daughter off with a skeletal hand.

"You need some water?" the girl said.

Candy closed her eyes and shook her head. The girl looked at Barnes by way of asking the same question.

"Thank you," he said. "I'm fine."

The girl left the room.

"Have a seat, Johnny," Candy said, "if you haven't already. My eyes aren't what they once were. This goddamn diabetes. I only get shapes these days. Soon I'll be totally blind. Edgar does my looking for me."

At the sound of its name the cat lifted its head and looked at Candy, who reached out and dragged a hand across its back. The cat turned to watch Barnes take a seat on a kitchen chair next to the bed, gripping the nearby dresser to ease himself down. The action figures in his hand clacked against the wood.

"What's that?" Candy said, turning an ear to the sound.

"Oh, these?" Barnes said. "Couple of G.I. Joes. I found them recently, and I . . ." He stopped when a strange smile came to Candy's face. Water welled up in the red lines around her sunken eyes.

Barnes said, "What is it?"

"You come here looking for a hand job, Johnny Barnes?"

Barnes's cheeks, already flush, grew enflamed. His palms got sweaty. He rubbed his off hand against his leg, felt a tear welling in his own eye, soreness in his throat. He held up the two action figures so that Candy might see them more clearly. "I wish I had three more."

Candy looked curiously at the figures for a moment, trying to find focus, and then the mathematical realization struck her. She laughed as heartily as her frail body would allow.

Barnes laughed, too.

Edgar's tail swayed like seaweed.

Candy put her finger to her trach tube and said, "Did you ever wonder why I used to hang around with you two boys?"

"I have always wondered that," Barnes said.

"People used to say I was nuts to be running with a couple of boys years younger than me, but you know what you boys had that the rest of them didn't?"

Barnes shook his head. "No."

"Humility. Your cheeks got red when you saw me the way I was, barely dressed all the time, flaunting what I had." She smirked and took a beat, moved her head to find him again. "Please tell me they're red right now."

"They are."

"Yeah. You got quiet and coy, just like now."

"We had our thoughts," Barnes said.

"But you kept them to yourselves," Candy said. "That's what mattered."

Barnes nodded.

"That Ricky, though," Candy said, "he would have made his move one day. Of that I was sure. The little scoundrel. I can't say I wouldn't have let him. No offense, Johnny."

"None taken."

A train hurled by on the tracks just outside the window. The floor rumbled, the house's old bones creaked, and the G.I. Joe shelves rattled, but everything stayed in place. Edgar never took his eyes off Barnes.

"So what brings you here, Mr. Barnes," Candy said, "all grown up and probably a cop?"

"Used to be," Barnes said.

"Knew you would," Candy said. "Detective even, right?"

"Yeah."

"Of course. What brings you, honey?"

"Well," Barnes said, fiddling with the action figures in his hands, "did Ricky ever tell you about a time capsule he was—" He stopped when Candy held up her hand.

"Say no more," she said. "I know what you came here for. Been waiting all these years to give it."

"Give what?" Barnes said.

"Ricky's riddle. I can't remember it for shit, but your brother made me write it down. I still have it." She wiped at her nose with the back of her hand. "Last time I ever saw him."

"Where is it?" Barnes said.

Candy pointed at the dresser next to Barnes, which was covered in trinkets and figurines, bangles and bracelets. Situated in the center was a pink-and-silver jewelry box. Barnes opened the lid. A ballerina popped up and wobbled around on a spring. The music box played the theme to *Swan Lake* in plinking notes.

Candy smiled and swayed to the music. "Lift up the tray."

Barnes gripped a pink velvet tray filled with rings and necklaces embedded with ruby-colored stones. Beneath the tray were folded pieces of paper that looked like notes passed in high school.

"The green one," Candy said.

Barnes pushed aside some of the notes to find a folded sheet that was pale green. He removed it from the box and unfolded the paper.

"Read it to me," Candy said.

The handwriting was not Ricky's but clearly that of a girl. Barnes read out loud what was written.

"The runner-up and who's next, three threes and two dozen. My age minus one, midnight's younger cousin."

Candy nodded as he read, smiled knowingly. When he was done, she said, "Take it with you, Johnny Barnes, but before you do, circle 'my.'"

"What's that?"

"Circle 'my.' Ricky stressed 'my' when he made me write it down. *My* age minus one. *My* age. He wouldn't tell me why."

"But I'll bet he smirked," Barnes said, finishing up the circle around *my*.

"You're goddamn right he did," Candy said. "And he winked at me. Made me want to smack him one good."

Barnes chuckled. "You and me both."

Candy's off hand returned to Edgar's back. The cat closed its eyes to her touch. Candy blindly regarded the cat for a moment and then said, "You ever hear that question marks are based on cat's tails?"

"No," Barnes said. "I never heard that."

"If you watch a cat from behind when he's getting into something, watch his little butthole and tail curling, it looks like a question mark."

Barnes smirked.

"Exclamation marks, too," Candy said. "Soon as they get excited, up goes that tail, straight as can be. Pow!"

Barnes looked at Edgar. The cat dropped its head onto the bed and purred, turned its belly to Candy's touch.

188

"There was too much in that brother of yours," Candy said. "Too much life. Too much knowledge. Too much . . . light." She took her hand away from the cat and reached out aimlessly toward Barnes. "Too much for one little body to hold."

Barnes hesitated but eventually took her frail hand.

She gripped his hand and squeezed. "I know you took responsibility for Ricky dying. Maybe you still do. Hell, it's twenty-five years later and you're chasing his riddle."

Barnes breathed out through his nose.

"Your little brother was never long for this world, Detective Barnes. Had it not been that train that took him, it would have been something else. The world just reached up and stole him the same way a kid steals something from a candy store, not knowing it's wrong. The world just sees something bright, something that shines, and takes it. That's all."

"I guess so," Barnes said.

She patted his hand. "Go on and solve that riddle, Johnny. Go and find that last bit of shine."

21

"His name is Leo," Barnes said into his phone. He was sitting in his truck in Candy's driveway, talking to Franklin.

"How do you know that?" Franklin said.

"What does it matter?" Barnes said. "I just know. Were any of the sole proprietors or independent costume renters from the case files named Leo or Leon? Maybe Leonardo?"

"I can check," Franklin said.

"While you're at it," Barnes said, "why were the owners of Sparky Time Amusements redacted from the files?"

Franklin sighed. "You're going on Flaherty's theory now, huh? You spent some time with him on the machine and, let me guess, you're looking for info on something called the Madrox Project?"

"What is it?" Barnes said.

"What is *what*?"

"The Madrox Project."

"Get that bullshit out of your head," Franklin said. "Flaherty theorized a cover-up. He thought some cop went off the reservation, got dressed up as Eddie Able, and sliced up an entire family—the unnamed third boy that escaped Caulfield Avenue, plus his mother and father."

"Georgie and Alice," Barnes said. "The 911 call."

"Yeah, well, I guess you'd know about that now, too. Flaherty wanted to expose what he called the Madrox Project, so he started sniffing around the precinct and with Internal Affairs, got himself into a kettle of water with Captain Darrow. That's when he started using the machine daily."

"I don't understand."

"The dude thought using the machine was making him a better detective. Thought it was expanding his brain power or something."

"Come on."

"Who do you think redacted those files?" Franklin said. "Flaherty himself. He decided there was a cover-up, and no one could convince him otherwise, so he created one."

"Bullshit."

"What's bullshit?" Franklin said. "The idea that a cop dressed up as a life-size doll and killed the family who just happened to own Sparky Time Amusements, putting himself on the hook for everything that went down at 1613 Caulfield Av? Or that Adrian Flaherty was a shit detective and a munky so desperate for a case to solve he made up his own?"

"They were the owners?" Barnes said.

"Huh?"

"You just said that the family, Georgie and Alice's family, were the owners of Sparky Time Amusements."

A flash of memory ran through Barnes's mind: the six-foot Eddie Able across the river from young Freddie Cohen, the one with blood on his gloves, the one with blood on his lips after he gestured for Freddie to *shhh*.

"Brother," Franklin said, "let me take you to Dr. Hill."

"Don't put me in a room with that asshole," Barnes said.

Franklin offered no reply.

"Which is it, Billy?" Barnes said.

"Which is what?"

"Is Adrian Flaherty a thorough detective, like you once had me believe, or is he a shit detective making up his own cases?"

There was a long pause on the line, and then, "I don't know."

Barnes disconnected the call. He pulled away from Candy's house and drove home. He idled up the driveway and killed the engine. For a moment he just sat and stared at the house while the engine cooled and ticked. His stare was broken when a coyote poked its head out from behind his detached garage. It eyed his truck for a second and then dashed off through the yard and down the street, using the sidewalk like an animal path.

Barnes got out of the cab. He went back behind the garage to find the garbage cans toppled over, the trash strewn. He cleaned up the mess and put the lids back on the cans. The back entry door to the garage was cracked open. He went inside. It smelled of concrete cleaner and cat litter. Jessica's car was parked in the far spot. The near side was overrun with what looked like a kit for a wooden jungle gym: weatherproofed four-by-fours, bolts, and chains for swings. Next to that was a snap line, a circular saw, and a square. A toolbox lay on the floor, a framing hammer thrown in over the collection of socket wrenches and hexagonal heads, boxes of screws, boxes of nails.

Barnes grabbed a broom, swept some bent nails and sawdust into a pan, and tossed the debris away. He started packing away the toolbox but stopped when he heard a sound. He looked up to find Richie in the doorway.

"Hey, Dynamite," Barnes said.

"Heard your truck," the boy said. "Whatcha doing?"

"Just cleaning up," Barnes said.

"You ever gonna finish that thing?"

"Someday, bud."

"Where have you been?"

"I got pulled in by a case."

Richie looked down. He toed at the concrete floor beneath his feet. A morning sunbeam lit up his shoulder and crossed him like a sash.

"What's on your mind?" Barnes said.

The boy looked up. "You don't like my hair this long, do you?"

"It's fine," Barnes said.

"Mom says you want me to cut it short so I can look like Ricky."

"So you can. Fail him again." The breathless voice.

"No," Barnes said. "I just—"

"Is that why Mom's drinking? Because of Ricky?"

"What do you mean?"

"Since you left she's just been sitting around the house drinking, acting funny."

"Where is she now?"

"Upstairs. She didn't get up today. I made my own cereal."

"That's good," Barnes said. He scooped the boy up into his arms and carried him out of the garage, pulling the door closed behind them. Richie wrapped his arms around his father and drove his face into Barnes's neck. The boy shuddered as he began to cry.

"It's okay, kid," Barnes said. "Everything's going to be okay."

They crossed the porch and entered the house. Barnes carried Richie up the stairs to his bedroom. He set him down on the bed. "Just stay here for a bit, okay? I'm going to talk with Mom."

Richie nodded. He lay on the bed and curled into a fetal position, gripping his pillow. Barnes pulled up the covers and offered a monkey bite. Richie reached out and bit back.

Barnes went down the hallway into the master bedroom. Jessica was inside, curled up in nearly the same position as Richie. Dust swirled around her in the morning light. Barnes sat on the edge of the bed near his wife's knees. An empty vodka bottle lay on the floor near the nightstand.

He placed a hand on Jessica's shoulder.

She didn't awaken. Didn't move. Her breathing was rhythmic and deep. He shook her lightly, but still she slept.

He removed his hand.

"I don't know what to say to you, Jess," Barnes said, speaking softly in the silent room. "I don't know what went wrong or how I can fix it." He sat quietly for a moment, and then said, "We were so happy. You used to smile and laugh. You used to . . ." His chest ached. His vision went blurry. "Where have you gone?"

Jessica murmured in her sleep. Barnes recalled the first time he'd heard her do that. He was lying awake in this same bed, back when this same room was undecorated. They had just moved in and didn't have two nickels to rub together. She'd fallen asleep quickly after an exhausting day, but he found sleep more difficult. He sat up in bed and stared at the blank walls, just that morning painted her choice of terra-cotta red. Some of the paint was still on his hands. He dug at the paint beneath his fingernails, thinking he couldn't believe his luck. To be with this woman, in this place, starting a life together. He didn't deserve it. Didn't deserve her. As these thoughts passed through his head she murmured in her sleep, just as she had a moment ago. Her words were unintelligible, but she looked happy, and he took it as reassurance that she felt as lucky as he did.

He wasn't so sure anymore.

His mind traveled back to the moment he'd left her in her apartment with all those police officers, the moment after Calavera had attacked. The killer had bound her wrists and ankles and painted her face like a death bride. Barnes saw her before she saw him, and he ran. He was afraid of the pain and misery he had escorted into her life. He was afraid the shit show that was his existence would infect hers, too.

But she came to him anyway.

He recalled the moment when she walked up the sidewalk toward his porch while he sat with his jackknife, scraping motor oil from beneath his fingernails. Funny, it seemed like paint in the memory now. That same terra-cotta red. It was the first decent day of spring and the air was still cold, though the sun warmed his skin. She approached with trepidation, her purse over her shoulder and tucked defensively high. She sat down next to him. He'd looked over and smiled.

She said, "I love you."

"I love you, too."

She'd rummaged through her purse and produced a pregnancy test, smiled uneasily, and showed it to him. "Two lines means we're a family."

"She would be happier without you." The familiar voice.

"Why?"

"She doesn't love you."

Barnes looked at Jessica, innocent in sleep, her hands tucked up beneath the pillow, her hair flowing back. As beautiful as she was on that first day of spring, and these days just as cold. Had her trepidation ever faded? Had she ever really believed in what they had?

"Shhh."

He placed the divorce papers on the nightstand, left the bedroom, and went down the stairs into the kitchen. He grabbed a beer from the fridge and went out onto the porch. He sat down on the steps and hung his head, the beer held loosely in his right hand, dangling in the space between his legs.

His phone rang.

Barnes set down the beer and picked up the phone.

UNKNOWN.

He connected the call and said, "Hello, Leo."

"Aw," Leo said. "No more. Shadow?"

"I'm going to find you."

"That's the same thing. Flaherty said. You're retracing. His steps, you know? So much easier. To just hook in. And ride his memories."

Barnes said nothing.

"What time. Is it?"

Barnes checked his watch. "Eleven a.m."

"You have. Until midnight."

"Or what?"

"Or I carve. Flaherty's face. Think he'd look good. As Eddie Able?"

The line went dead.

Barnes dialed Franklin.

"Where you at?" Franklin said.

"You got an address for Leo or what?" Barnes said.

"That's the least of your worries right now."

"What's that supposed to mean?"

"Got an anonymous call," Franklin said. "Some guy claims a cop showed up at his place, waving a gun around. Says you were trying to buy serum in Machine City."

Barnes offered no reply.

"You can't go around threatening people like that."

"So arrest me."

"I might."

"Look," Barnes said, "we don't have time to screw around. Leo just gave me a deadline. If we don't find Flaherty by midnight, he's dead. If this guy's got Little Cher, she may be dead, too."

"This guy that called from Machine City," Franklin said, "he sounded stressed."

"He's a heroin junkie," Barnes said. "He pointed a gun at me first by the way."

"He said to tell you the shark is in trouble. I guess that means something to you? Something I should know about?"

"It's Machine City," Barnes said. "What does it matter?"

"All right," Franklin said. "Meantime, I'm still running a background on this Leo character you've found. Leonardo Vance. We got an old address, but he's moved and left no forwarding. I got someone chasing it down as we speak. There's something else. This Leo, he's got a condition called dysarthria. It screws up his ability to speak. That sound like your guy?"

"Yes."

"According to our file," Franklin said, "he got knocked in the head when he was a kid. Some kids took a disliking to him with stickball bats. It messed up some of his motor functions. His mother, a hooker, dumped him sometime afterward. He was in and out of juvie for a while, no other family. A couple years later, right around the time Leo turned eighteen, his mother was allegedly killed by a john. Near as we can tell, Leo worked some odd jobs after that and then disappeared. The people he worked for say he seemed dumb because of the way he talked but that he was actually smart. They also said they didn't like having him around. Gave them the willies."

"That'd be him."

"Meet me at Roosevelt's at eight p.m. If we can locate him in the meantime, we'll go get him."

Barnes disconnected the call and went back into the house, back upstairs to Richie's room. The boy was lying in the same position as when Barnes had left him. "Hey, bud," Barnes said. Richie stirred, opened his eyes. "Grab your shoes. We're going for a ride."

Richie rolled off the bed and jammed his feet into a pair of small white sneakers next to the bed. On the side of each little shoe was a purple pony with rainbow-colored hair. The laces were loose with knots on the end so they wouldn't unravel. Richie pulled up the tongues, snatched a red jacket from a brass hook, and slid it on. "Where we going?"

"Gotta give your mom some time to sleep it off," Barnes said. "Can't leave you on your own."

"I can handle myself," Richie said.

Barnes smiled. "I know you can. Let's go anyway. We'll pick up a treat."

The kid's eyes brightened.
Barnes left a note on the kitchen table:

Jess,

Richie's with me. Went out for ice cream. We'll be back soon.

Love,
John

22

After a swing by Handi-Ice to pick up a mint chocolate chip sugar cone, Barnes pulled up to a curb in Brush Park.

"Why are we stopping?" Richie said between licks. He had worked the ice cream into a globe by rotating it across his tongue.

"Oh, you know," Barnes said, peeking through the windshield at the row housing unit on the other side of the street. Jessica's old apartment. "Just reminiscing."

"What's 'reminiscing' mean?"

"Remembering the past."

Richie looked out the window, looked up and down the street. It was noon, but the sky was overcast and everything that might be bright was muted. A middle-aged woman walked a Boston terrier on a leash. She wore a high school girl's outfit and pigtails in the fashion of a Brittanian. The dog scampered back and forth excitedly, testing the limits of the chain.

"Why here?" Richie asked.

Barnes pointed out the window. "Your mom used to live right there."

"Really?"

"Yep."

"Cool!"

Barnes fell into a trance staring at Jessica's old home. He'd loved her before he'd even met her, loved her from within Dale Wilson's memory, the janitor she passed in the halls of the elementary school at which she taught. Love by proxy, like loving a movie actress or a model. A silly thing until somehow that love is made real. She was a spirit to him, someone who filled him with light. Being with her was like being in an exotic place where things looked different, sounded different, smelled different. He couldn't stay broken with her, couldn't stay drunk, couldn't stay a munky. The fight to push out the voices was a fight to keep her love. There had been shouting matches within his mind, confusion and anger. He sometimes found himself coming into consciousness in unfamiliar places, waking up while walking, maybe in a mall, down an alley, out of a coffee shop. The surreal nature of his experiences led to madness. There were punched mirrors and bandaged hands, entire nights of sobbing in the corner, and daily screaming fits before, finally, recovery. The voices silenced. He'd won. He'd done the best he could. He was a good husband and father. He'd proved himself worthy of salvation.

What went wrong?

A man walked out the front of Jessica's old brownstone. Barnes focused on him and then pulled back when he noted Dr. Hill's limp and horsehead cane. "What the fuck?"

"Da-ad," Richie chided. "No cussing."

"Sorry," Barnes said, eyes on Dr. Hill as he moved down the sidewalk and managed his way into a car. The brake lights lit up as he started the engine and pulled into the flow of traffic.

"Where are we going now?" Richie said.

"Just gonna drive around for a bit, Dynamite," Barnes said.

Richie smiled. "Sure thing, Hurricane."

They tailed Dr. Hill as he made his way through the city. He started making illogical turns and backtracking, clearly aware they were on him. Eventually he turned into an empty parking lot in front of a shuttered Kmart. Barnes pulled past the lot and turned around at the next light, drove back. Dr. Hill had driven out into the center of the lot and parked his car. He was leaning against the back bumper with his arms folded, cane at his side.

Barnes turned into the lot and accelerated.

"What are we doing?" Richie said.

"Just settling a score," Barnes said. He stopped the car short of Dr. Hill's position and threw it into park. "Stay in the truck, okay?"

Richie nodded.

"You're pure crap at tailing," Dr. Hill said as Barnes got out of the cab. "Saw you the whole way."

Barnes closed the truck door and looked back to make sure the windows were up. He turned back to Dr. Hill. "You and I need to talk."

Dr. Hill smiled. "I'm glad you've come to your senses."

"It's not that kind of talk."

"Oh. Is it the kind of talk where I should 'put up my dukes'?" Dr. Hill brought up his fists and mimicked a boxer's dance while still leaning against the car. He threw a couple of jabs at the air.

"Kick his fuckin' ass." The familiar voice.

"Shhh."

"She's my wife," Barnes said.

Dr. Hill turned his head. "Huh?"

"Jessica," Barnes said. "Stay away from her."

Dr. Hill's face went pale, and then red. He closed his eyes and took a second to compose himself. A shamed smile came to his face. "How did you find out?"

Barnes tapped his temple. "The machine," he said. "Flaherty was onto you and this Madrox Project."

Dr. Hill nodded. "Suspected I was the mastermind behind it?"

"Something like that."

"Well, he was right." He turned up his hands at his sides.

"The Madrox Project," Barnes said. "What is it?"

"It's not good for you to know."

"It's less good for you not to tell me," Barnes said.

Dr. Hill smirked. "Okay. You're aware that Flaherty reopened the Eddie Able case?"

Barnes nodded.

"Being inside Franklin made him curious. He pulled the old files on Tyrell Diggs, found out he was involved with an unsolved case from thirty years ago. Still with me?"

"Yes."

"Case had gone cold," Dr. Hill said, "but not for lack of trying. This guy, he was just too good. No one could catch up with him, even though he's been at it for, what, thirty years? We started looking for alternative ways to nail him."

"And that's where you came in, huh?" Barnes said.

"You could say that."

"For what?"

"That's confidential," Dr. Hill said.

"That's it?"

"That's all you get to know."

"No," Barnes said. "I need more."

Dr. Hill shrugged.

Barnes looked at the cane near Dr. Hill's leg. "How about I knock that cane over your head a few times. Will that help?"

"You're gonna attack me in front of your kid?"

Barnes looked sidelong at the truck, Richie inside. "What were you doing at my wife's old apartment just now?"

"A little girl's life is at stake," Dr. Hill said. "An eyewitness has come forward, saying they saw an old-style police cruiser in the neighborhood on the day Little Cher was taken."

"Like Diggs," Barnes said.

"Just like Diggs."

"Only Diggs ain't around anymore," Barnes said, "thanks to Detective Franklin."

"Seems our guy may be operating on his own now. Little Cher's a celebrity, which means we're getting public pressure to put the witness on the machine. In this case we absolutely would, but we don't have one."

"What does this have to do with my wife's old apartment?"

"Nothing," Dr. Hill said. "It's just this situation is more important than that, and we need you focused on what matters most."

"Little Cher," Barnes said.

"And Flaherty."

"Eddie Able."

Dr. Hill nodded. "We believe he's been selling his memories to select buyers on the Echo Ring, sick-minded people who love that sort of thing. We're fairly certain Flaherty entrapped him, found the location of the machine he used, and tracked that down, too, but—"

"He went missing," Barnes said.

"Bingo."

Barnes started back toward the truck. "I'll find him. After that, we'll talk."

23

Jessica was sitting on the porch steps when Barnes pulled up to the curb in front of his home. He parked the vehicle and killed the engine. Both he and Richie looked at Jessica through the windshield.

She waved to them, his note in her hand.

"Don't be hard on her," Richie said.

"I won't."

They got out.

Richie ran up the sidewalk and hopped into his mother's arms as she stood up. She hugged him fiercely. "I'm so sorry," she said. Her voice was muffled because her lips were buried in the boy's hair.

"It's okay, Mom."

She set him down and squatted to look him in the eye. Tears threatened at her lower eyelids. "I will *never* do that again."

"I know," Richie said. Then he leaned close to his mother and whispered something in her ear.

Jessica nodded at whatever the boy said. She pulled back and regarded him. "Go inside now, okay?"

Richie smiled. He opened the screen door, ran through, and let it slam shut behind him.

"Thank you for the note," Jessica said.

Barnes nodded.

"I'm sorry for what I've done," Jessica said. "It was irresponsible and dangerous."

"We all make mistakes."

"It's just . . . this whole thing, it's been difficult. You, back on that machine, back in that horrible world." She looked away in pain, shook her head.

"What did he say to you?" Barnes said.

"Who?" Jessica said.

"Richie. Just now."

She closed her eyes, took a breath, and said, "Don't be so hard on him."

Barnes smirked. "That's all?"

"Come inside. I want to show you something."

Barnes followed her into the house, past the stairs, and into the den, which held a computer desk with a Mac Mini and monitor, keyboard, and mouse. Jessica sat down in a spare chair and gestured for Barnes to sit in the computer chair. He started to peel off his jacket.

Jessica gasped at the Band-Aids on his arms, the dry blood.

Barnes slid the jacket back on. "Sorry."

"Bring up the *Detroit News*," Jessica said.

Barnes sat down. He moved the mouse and the monitor lit up. He went to a browser and typed in the URL for the *Detroit News*. The main headline read, LITTLE CHER STILL MISSING, COPS REFUSE MACHINE.

"That's who you're trying to save," Jessica said. "That's who matters right now, okay?"

"They think I can help them," Barnes said, "by finding Flaherty."

Jessica hung her head. Tears rolled down her cheeks. Barnes reached out to her, but she stood up and backed away. "Then find him."

"I'm trying," Barnes said.

"Try harder," she said angrily and left the room.

Barnes turned back to the computer monitor. He read more of the article, which stated that the police had discovered an eyewitness but wouldn't use the machine to record the witness's memories. The story went on to discuss particulars of the legal battle a few years back that had ended with the machine's use for investigations and recreation rendered illegal. The reporter felt the police should break the law to save the girl.

Barnes was about to shut down the browser when the familiar voice sounded off in his mind.

"The IP address."

"What?"

"Look it up."

Barnes searched his pockets to find the IP address he'd written down at Ziti's, the address of the peer-to-peer Echo Ring computer where the ColdCase, Franklin, and FiveLives files were stored.

64.199.1.7

Slowly, and with growing trepidation, he typed a new URL into the browser—http://www.whatismyip.com.

The browser reloaded and a page appeared. Among the various ads and blinking buttons competing for space on the screen was his computer's IP address—*64.199.1.7.*

Barnes opened the Finder app. He searched for Echo Ring and found a folder. He double-clicked the folder, but it was password protected.

"Madrox." The familiar voice.

Barnes typed in "Madrox."

The folder opened. Three files were inside:

ColdCase.

FiveLives.

Franklin.

24

Barnes drove down Keisel Street. He pulled up to building C and parked. People were everywhere. Most sat on stoops over ground-floor patios made up of brick pavers. Some sat in lawn chairs on the concrete that passed as the courtyard commons. The rest were on the move, clad in colorful shirts, oversize shorts, and untied sneakers. Baseball caps were turned backward, the brims level straight. Bottles in brown paper bags. Drug dealers and their prey. Deals were being made beneath rimless backboards. Shouting could be heard, both near and far. Little kids chased each other around the grounds, slipping in and out between the buildings in bare feet. A woman in green shower shoes staggered past the front bumper of Barnes's truck, a handbag in the crook of her arm, her head wobbling in a drugged-out state. She hitched her long skirt as she stepped up the curb onto the sidewalk.

Barnes got out of the truck. He weaved through the crowd to the doors of building C. Someone had freshly spray-painted a gang symbol on the door. *White Wolves.* The paint's scent wafted as he pushed through and entered the stairwell. His steps echoed on the mesh steel steps as he climbed to the third floor where the paint scent turned over to the tang of ammonia.

He opened the hallway door to find a man standing there in a striped tank top and pair of cargo shorts, looking at his own reflection in the scratched plexiglass that covered the fire hose. His skin was so pale it resembled Elmer's glue. He pointed a finger aggressively into his own chest. "You talking to me?"

Barnes started past him, but the man spun on him, reached out and grabbed his arm.

"What are you doing here, pal?" the man said.

Barnes looked down at the man's spindly hand clutching his bicep. "Just passing through."

"This is a private residence," the man said, squeezing Barnes's arm. "How'd you get in he—" He blinked, shook his head, regarded Barnes again. "How'd you get in he—" He blinked again.

Barnes raised an eyebrow.

"Who are you?" the man said.

"I might ask you the same question," Barnes said.

The man's eyes shifted to the envelope sticking out from Barnes's inner jacket pocket. He smirked. "I see. You want an autograph." He let go of Barnes's arm and grabbed the letter, pulled a Sharpie from his own pocket. "Who should I make it out to?"

"Freddie Cohen," Barnes said.

The man turned around and placed the letter against the plexiglass. He said "To Freddie C" as he wrote, and then finished the signature with a flourish. He turned around and slapped the letter against Barnes's chest. He winked. "Next time, just ask."

Barnes checked the letter as the man walked away. The autograph was mostly a scribble, but he made out Robert De Niro. "Hey, Bobby," he said.

The man stopped at the stairway door, his hand on the knob. He looked back at Barnes, gave him that famous De Niro squint, that bemused frown.

"Thanks."

"Forget about it."

De Niro left. The hallway was quiet now. Barnes pulled his weapon and approached Unit 37 slowly, stepping on the balls of his feet. He put an ear to the door and listened. The TV was on. Muffled canned laughter. He tested the door, found it unlocked. He opened it slowly and peeked through. Josh was passed out in his recliner. Sandy looked like she hadn't moved since the last time he'd been there. The heroin kit was over by her now.

Barnes moved past them and down the hallway. He came to Verbatim's door and knocked lightly. For a moment there was no sound, but then Barnes heard shuffling feet. He readied his gun and stood back away from the door, against the wall. It opened slowly, only a crack. Verbatim's eye appeared, searching. When he found Barnes, he said, "You coming in?"

Barnes didn't move. "Your dad called the precinct. Said you were in trouble."

"He didn't call," Verbatim said. "It was me."

"Why?"

"Wanted to talk to you."

"About what?"

"Come in."

"Who's in there with you?"

"No one. I swear." He opened the door more fully, showing Barnes the room was empty.

"Don't. Go in." The breathless voice.

"Shhh."

Barnes examined the empty room, tried to see beneath the bed from the hallway. All seemed clear.

Verbatim backed away from the door. He sat down on the edge of the bed and waited.

Barnes entered the room and closed the door behind him. After a final scan he holstered his gun and said, "I'm on an important case. If you're in trouble, you—"

"I'm not the one in trouble," Verbatim said. "You are."

Barnes tilted his head. "How's that?"

"It's better if you see for yourself." Verbatim reached under the bed with two hands. He gripped the machine and slid it out.

Barnes closed his eyes and fought back the shiver. He won the battle with the sick feeling rising from his guts, remaining himself.

"You know that cop, Flaherty?" Verbatim said. He set the machine on the nightstand, plugged a keyboard into a USB port along the side.

"What about him?"

"You need to see what he's been up to."

"How do you know Flaherty?"

"I don't. I guess he used to come around here to fill his quota by making busts." Verbatim unwrapped a new IV tube. "My mom said he was a munky and that a guy down the hall sold him a lot of shitty serum, sold him time on the machine until one day Flaherty decides he's gonna bust the guy instead. I would say he's a bastard for that, but the vacancy helped me reestablish my own game. My dad told you I just got back a few weeks ago? Yeah, well, I got back from six months served. Use to have a tidy little operation running in Redford, now I'm back in with the Needle-Dum and Needle-Dee until I get enough saved."

"What does this have to do with me?" Barnes said.

Verbatim held up the machine's suction cups. "You need to see for yourself."

A pain worked its way from one side of Barnes's head to the other. An image of a falling boy. A bullet hole to the chest. A falling girl. Another bullet hole. The gunshots. Over and over. The blood. The empty meadow. Again he started to tremble but bit it back and focused. "No."

"Was I right about the case you're on?" Verbatim said. "Cherry Daniels?"

"What does it matter?"

"I'd just like to know."

"Your guy, Flaherty," Barnes said. "He's gone missing."

"Just gone, right? Into thin air?"

"How do you know that?"

"Just a hunch, based on some files I found."

"I've checked the Ring for Flaherty's files," Barnes said. "I've already been him."

"That's funny," Verbatim said, "'cause he sure spent a lot of time being you."

"What's that supposed to mean?"

"Don't you know?" Verbatim said. "Your memory is a classic on the Ring. You busting Calavera, getting shot, nearly dying. People love it. Especially the salt in the wounds. I hear it hurts like a mofo."

Barnes stood there, dumbstruck.

"It seems Flaherty rode your file all the time," Verbatim said, "according to the people around here that knew him." He gestured toward Barnes with the suction cups.

"What memory is this?" Barnes said.

"A binge I made. I think it will help you."

"A binge of what?"

"Flaherty's memories."

"I told you," Barnes said. "I already rode his files."

"Not this," Verbatim said. "You would never have found this."

"Why not?"

Verbatim sighed. "Okay, look . . . the Echo Ring is illegal as shit, but it's kind of like streaming free movies or whatever. Everyone does it and no one seems to care. Too many people to bust, housewives and kids and shit, so the police just leave it alone. But the real hard stuff? The kind of memories they'll kick down your door about? That all goes down on Sickle Web. If you're not a hacker, you'll never get in."

"And you're a hacker?"

Verbatim breathed on his knuckles and then rubbed them on his shirt. "Your boy Flaherty put his files on the Echo Ring. That was as much as he was going to do to make sure they'd be found someday, but someone—I swear it wasn't me—hacked his machine and stole some of his files, deleted the original copies."

"Why would someone do that?"

Verbatim gestured again with the suction cups. "The guy in this binge had plenty of reason."

"Why would he put the files on this Sickle Web?"

"It's like a secret society where crazies go to show off, the sick shit they've done. No sense having it unless you can . . . I don't know, preen?"

Barnes paused. He watched Verbatim for a moment and then asked, "Why would you go to all this trouble to help me?"

"I'm not helping you," Verbatim said. "I'm helping Little Cher."

Barnes ruminated, suspecting a trap. No. The kid was being honest. "How long is the binge?"

"Fifteen minutes."

Barnes peeled off his jacket and sat down on the bed.

"Been a fun couple of days, huh?" Verbatim said, indicating the Eddie Able Band-Aids and dry blood on Barnes's arms.

"A riot," Barnes said.

Verbatim ran his fingers along Barnes's temple. "Gotta take you down a bit," he said. He grabbed a can of shaving cream and a blue disposable razor.

Barnes closed his eyes as Verbatim coated his head with shaving cream. The scent hurled him back to his days as a detective, when he was on the machine almost daily. It'd cost him so much. But he'd saved lives. He'd done some good.

Hadn't he?

After the shave, Verbatim toweled off Barnes's head and applied the suction cups. "Go ahead and lay back," he said, pulling up a chair. He unwrapped a clean needle and attached it to the tube. With expert-level finesse he slid the needle into an open spot on Barnes's right arm, successfully tapping the vein.

Barnes spat out his gum and caught it in his left hand. "Got a bit?"

"I figured you for a grinder."

"A grinder?"

"Tooth grinder," Verbatim said. He clacked his teeth together. "No bit."

"Who on earth would do that?"

"Aren't you a member of the Sect?"

"No."

"Not yet," Verbatim said.

Barnes put the gum back in his mouth.

Verbatim typed on the machine's keyboard and tapped the "Enter" key. "You ready?"

"Can you sing?" Barnes said.

Verbatim said, "Nope," and turned the dial.

Click.

Hiss.

Barnes's body arched.

Darkness and silence.

25

A blue dot pulsed on a computer screen, around it a map of Detroit. The dot centered on the northeast corner of Tillman and Selden Streets, northwest of Corktown.

"Got you, son of a bitch," Flaherty said.

-Record skip-

Flaherty was in an unmarked sedan. He drove slowly down a darkened city block past burned-out basements and abandoned homes. He parked at the curb, eyes locked on a dilapidated white house sitting alone in a field at the end of the block. The house's upstairs windows were all blacked out, but the basement windows were emitting weak, colorful streams of light around wooden planks. The street sign at the corner was sheared off at the base. Sections of the sidewalk were missing, and a fire hydrant was unplugged but dry, its mouth like an open sore.

Flaherty got out of the car and lightly clicked the door closed. The sounds of vehicles moving down the nearby I-96 freeway nearly drowned out the chirring crickets. The air had that wrong-side-of-the-tracks smell, something like decaying drywall and rust. Flaherty drew his .45 Glock and clicked off the safety. Barnes felt soothed by the gun in his hand.

Flaherty moved across the street and started up the sidewalk.

-Record skip-

Flaherty stood on the porch of the house. The structure leaned to one side and Barnes had to counter-lean to keep his balance. There was no storm door, and the front door had the same diamond-shaped window of the Masterson trailer of Barnes's youth. He blinked away a vision of Ted Nugent staring out crazily, fought the urge to ring the doorbell and run. The door's cheap veneer peeled down in curls that rattled like leaves when Flaherty knocked.

No answer.

"Open up," Flaherty said. "Police!"

No response.

Flaherty clicked on a long metal flashlight, held it overhand-style and kicked in the door. The mildew scent was instant and fierce. Before him was a clogged vein of a path that weaved through the foyer toward the kitchen. Walls of stacked magazines and newspapers to the ceiling. No doubt there were entryways to rooms on either side, but the stacks blocked them off. Flaherty moved through, flashlight in one hand, Glock in the other. Creaky floorboards. He passed the legs and heads of dolls stuffed between the magazines and papers, piles of circuit boards, notebooks, and clear plastic cups with pools of molded juice.

"Police!" Flaherty said. "Anyone in the house step out into the open, now!"

The house remained silent.

He made his way into the kitchen and pulled the string on a light over the table. Moths and flies lifted from unseen places and converged toward the light. They whirled around the bare bulb as Barnes backed up and assessed the scene. The table was overrun with stacks of half-eaten TV dinners, some crawling with maggots. The sink was filled to overflowing with red pots, yellow-and-green plates, and grimy silverware. The cupboard knobs were haloed by decades of dirt.

Flaherty pulled open a door opposite the refrigerator, revealing a stairwell leading down to the basement.

-Record skip-

Light sliced from beneath the door at the bottom of the steps. The mildew scent was stronger here. Flaherty took shorter breaths. He turned the brass door handle slowly, found it unlocked. The dead bolt above, however, stopped the door from opening. Barnes eased the brass handle back to its original position, took a quiet step back, and kicked the door. There was a crack, but the door held.

Flaherty kicked it again, splintering the doorjamb, but again the door held.

A third kick and the door was open. Barnes looked at a room lined with pinball and arcade games. They provided the only light, like a thousand eyes blinking out of the darkness in red and green and blue. Bleeps and bloops, laser sounds and explosions. The room smelled of human feces.

"I know you're here," Flaherty said, moving his flashlight beam across the space. The light failed to reveal a human form. Flaherty spun around the open door, weapon aimed. No one there. He moved deeper into the room. Tucked between two pinballs was a padded table. Next to it, a machine. He moved closer to the table, sweeping back and forth with his gun to cover the shadowed corners.

A shuffling sound pulled Flaherty's eyes, flashlight, and weapon up to the dingy drop ceiling. A tile above the padded table was missing. The flashlight beam exposed the lead pipes and cobwebs hiding beyond the asbestos tiles.

Barnes backed up against the arcade games for a better shooting angle. "Come down from there."

More shuffling noises above. Hard to tell where the movement came from. Flaherty moved to the center of the room, flashlight still aimed at the missing tile. "Come down from there, now!"

A body dropped down from the ceiling behind him, landing half-way up the stairs.

Flaherty spun. He fired rapidly, strobe-lighting the room with gun blasts.

But the man had already escaped.

Barnes ran up the steps to find the door to the kitchen closed and locked. He fired at the handle until the mechanism broke apart.

-Record skip-

Flaherty ran across the open field behind the house, chasing a silhouette in the distance. The man was running toward the embankment at I-96.

"Freeze!" Barnes called.

The man kept running. Staggering, actually. He had the gait of an injured or elderly man. He reached the barrier at the freeway and toppled over it.

Flaherty chased until he arrived at the barrier. The man tumbled down the slope and skidded to a stop at the freeway shoulder. The passing cars blew his loose-fitting clothing and Mohawk mane around.

"Don't move!" Flaherty called down.

The man ran across the lanes.

Barnes cringed as the southbound cars and trucks, all doing seventy or more, barreled down on him. He narrowly escaped getting hit in the first lane, found a lucky blank spot at the second, but was sure to die in the third lane before reaching the opposite shoulder. A blue sedan would never be able to stop in time.

The sedan swerved into the open middle lane, laying on its horn.

The man paused at the concrete divider. He looked back. Even from a distance Barnes could see he had soft, babylike features that came across as terrifying on a grown man. He was well into his forties, maybe fifty. His eyes had the faraway stare of a sociopath, his lips stuck in a mocking, nearly flat grin.

The man flipped over the barrier to find the northbound lanes were empty. A stumbling sprint across the freeway and he was scrambling up the slope on the other side. Flaherty took aim and fired, but a handgun at such a distance couldn't find the mark.

The man made the top of the embankment, toppled over the last barrier, and disappeared.

-Record skip-

Flaherty was back in the funhouse basement. He stared down at the machine, its red eye pulsating in the darkness. He reached out, but stopped. Instead he got out his cell phone, opened the contacts list, and held his thumb over DISPATCH.

"Goddammit," he said, and then put the phone away. He unplugged the machine, wrapped up the wires, and took it up the stairs and out to his car. He put it in the trunk, slammed the lid closed, and got in the driver's side. He picked up the car radio and pressed the "Call" button. "Dispatch, this is Detective Adrian Flaherty, badge 5-3-9-0."

"Go ahead, 5-3-9-0."

"Can you run a records check on a house? Address is 25487 Selden in Detroit."

"One moment."

Flaherty ran a hand over his head while he waited. Barnes felt that the Mohawk was trimmed short. He noted the small sting in Flaherty's elbow pit, felt the presence of a cotton ball and Band-Aid there.

The radio crackled when dispatch came back. "The home is abandoned. Last known owner was a Martha Diggs, deceased."

Flaherty sighed. "Son named Tyrell?"

"Let me see . . . ," the dispatcher said. "Yes."

"Electricity's on in the house," Flaherty said. "How's that possible?"

"You'd have to check with DTE on that one," the dispatcher said. "Though I'd venture it's due to a broken meter. My cousin's got a broken meter, and she hasn't paid an electric bill in eight years."

-Record skip-

Flaherty parked at the curb near the First Precinct. For a moment he just sat and watched the comings and goings of officers, detectives, and civilians. He imagined himself walking into the building with the machine under his arm, turning it in for evidence, and then . . . what? Someone would take the ride, wouldn't they? Someone would examine the evidence that could help track down Eddie Able.

Someone *else*.

Flaherty pulled into the lot and parked his unmarked. He popped the trunk, pulled out the machine, and walked away from the precinct to the employee lot where his truck was waiting.

Darkness and silence.

"End of transmission."

The Vitruvian Man test pattern.

Please Stand By.

26

Barnes woke up slowly, blinking.

A noise.

His cell ringing.

He patted his pockets, found he was under a blanket. He sat up. Verbatim was gone. The room was nearly dark. Weak light from the streetlamps filtered through the horizontal blinds over the small window. He peeled off the blanket. He felt rested, alert, vital. The needle had been removed from his arm, the suction cups removed from his temples. His arm was bandaged, the dry blood cleaned away.

The machine was gone.

Barnes reached for his jacket on the nightstand, found his phone in a pocket. The caller ID was Franklin. The time was 8:03 p.m.

Shit. He'd slept for hours.

He connected the call.

"Where the fuck are you?" Franklin said.

Barnes sighed heavily, still shaking off sleep. His gum was flavorless and dry. He spat it out. "You got an address on this Leo or what?"

"You were supposed to meet me at Roosevelt's."

"When?"

"Now."

"I'll be there in a minute."

Barnes disconnected the call and picked up his jacket. The wax paper that'd once held Verbatim's Tornados had been underneath. It fell and floated to the floor. He left the bedroom and found his way back through the apartment. Sandy still hadn't moved. Josh was standing in the kitchen, a pot boiling in front of him on the stove. He looked up as Barnes neared the front door.

"Robbie left," Josh said.

Barnes nodded. He turned the doorknob and started opening the door.

"He told me to tell you something," Josh said.

Barnes stopped, looked at the heroin addict.

"Let Flaherty be."

"Say what?" Barnes said.

"He said, 'Let Flaherty be,' and then something else."

Barnes tilted back his head in question.

Josh said, "Gabriel Messina says 'Hello.'"

Barnes left. He walked down the ammonia hallway, took the stairs down to the ground floor, and exited building C into the commons. It was raining again. The activity outside was reduced to a lull. Dealers were home for dinner, drying off, maybe catching a rerun on the tube before crawling back out into the night.

His passenger-side window had been shattered. The interior of the truck was soaked. A muddy brick paver had landed on the seat, square bits of glass everywhere. Barnes shook his head as he brushed glass off the driver's seat and hopped in. He threw the brick paver out the passenger window and brushed more glass off the items in the passenger side—the Twinkie, Rufus, and *Giant-Size Fantastic Four*, number four.

"*The Madrox Project.*" The familiar voice.

"*Shhh.*"

Barnes drove away.

The parking lot at Roosevelt's was half-full, a far sight better than most days. Barnes found a spot near the middle of the pack and walked into the bar, his shoulders hunched against the downpour. A few faces turned his way as he entered, the bartender included. He found Franklin and Dr. Hill were sitting in the same booth as before. He slid into the seat across from them.

A man slid in next to him, locking him in the booth.

The man had been sitting at the bar when Barnes had walked in. No doubt a beat cop in plain clothes. The place was likely crawling with them. The half-full parking lot should have been a giveaway. Barnes sized up his new booth partner. A tough customer, to be sure, but in a moment he'd be cradling a broken nose.

"Leo's address," Barnes said to Franklin. "You got it?"

Franklin frowned. "Yes, I do, but—"

"Let's have it."

"You're not a detective," Franklin said. "What are you going to do, go kick in his door?"

Barnes felt the weight of the Glock in his armpit, reminding him he had options. If they thought he was packing, they would have frisked him, right?

"Don't worry about Leo," Franklin said. "We're going to take him down, and it's all thanks to you. I'm sorry you had to go through all this, but it's helped us locate a serial killer. You're a hero. Now you need to get healthy."

Barnes looked at Dr. Hill. "How can you make me healthy?"

"We'll systematically remove each life presence in your mind."

Barnes chuckled. "Life presence?"

"They may seem only like voices to you," Dr. Hill said, "but they're fully developed personalities that have taken root in your mind and grown over time."

"I kicked them all out already," Barnes said. "After Calavera, one at a time, on my own."

"Some may still be there," Dr. Hill said. "If what Detective Franklin tells me is true, Calavera, himself, may still be there."

Barnes looked down at the table. He stared at it for a moment, studying the wood grain, tapping a finger. He shifted his eyes to the nearby wall, covered in black-and-white photos of Teddy Roosevelt smiling, riding horses, young and old, Rough Rider and president. Barnes watched his booth partners from the corner of his eye. Franklin and the beat cop were following his line of vision. Barnes moved his gaze up the wall to the TV behind Franklin and Dr. Hill, where a Tigers baseball game was in the bottom of the fifth, Tigers down 2–0, Cabrera up to bat with a man on third. Stock-ticking beneath the game was a headline . . . SINGING SENSATION CHERRY "LITTLE CHER" DANIELS IS STILL MISSING. POLICE ARE BAFFLED BUT REFUSE TO USE THE MACHINE, DESPITE HAVING A WITNESS . . . The lug sitting next to Barnes lifted his chin and tilted his head to see what he was staring at. Franklin turned his big body and looked back over his shoulder.

Dr. Hill kept his eyes on Barnes. He looked amused.

"I can see them, too," Barnes said, staring at the TV, "these life presences. Sometimes, if I think really hard, I—"

Barnes reached into his armpit and gripped his gun. As he drew the weapon and his arm recoiled, he cracked his elbow on the beat cop's nose. The cop spilled out of the booth, howling with his hands over his face. Barnes slid out with his weapon aimed at Dr. Hill. "Keep your dicks in your pants, boys!"

Franklin put his hand on his gun, but he was too late.

Barnes yanked Hill up from his seat and corralled him from behind with his arm around the doctor's throat. The horsehead cane fell and clacked the tiles. Half the bar patrons were suddenly standing. Plainclothes cops with their hands on the hilts of the guns in their holsters. A pissed-off flash mob.

"Stand down," Franklin said, addressing all the cops.

Barnes backed toward the restrooms with Dr. Hill in his grasp. "Billy," Barnes said. "Billy, I need that address."

Franklin emerged from the booth. He stood and straightened his tie as he faced Barnes and his hostage. He rubbed a hand down the lower half of his suit jacket. "You got me over a barrel here, Barnesy." The cops converged behind him.

"The address," Barnes said. He placed the muzzle of his gun against Dr. Hill's temple. The cops crowded closer. They sneered and moved in threatening ways.

"What are you going to do?" Franklin said, holding out his arms to keep all the cops at bay.

"I'm going to finish what I started," Barnes said. "What *you* started for me."

"You're stuck here," Franklin said. "They're already out there booting your truck."

"The fucking address!"

Franklin sighed. "I never meant for it to go this way."

"Yeah, no shit," Barnes said.

"6025 Troy Street," Franklin said. "Happy? Now put the gun down."

"Ferndale?"

Franklin nodded.

Barnes backed up and pulled Dr. Hill with him through the men's-room door. He spun the doctor around and pointed the gun between his eyes. To his credit, Dr. Hill didn't look scared. He leaned against a sink to steady himself without his cane.

Barnes held out his hand. "Keys."

Dr. Hill turned them over.

Barnes checked the car key logo. Ford.

"Which one?" Barnes said.

"Black Fusion," Dr. Hill said. "Edge of the lot."

"I don't want to kill you," Barnes said.

"I don't want to die."

"You really want to help me?"

"You need evaluation."

"I need to stop a killer," Barnes said.

"There're twenty cops in this bar who can stop him," Dr. Hill said. "You've done your part."

"You don't understand," Barnes said. "I need this collar. I need . . ." The gun trembled in his hand. He gritted his teeth and focused. "Just help me."

They held each other's gaze for a moment.

"I'll come back," Barnes said. "I swear. We'll talk."

Dr. Hill nodded.

Barnes turned his back on the doctor, climbed up on the sink, and pushed out the crank window near the ceiling. Rain dripped off the angled frame. He began squeezing through the window, legs first, and looked back at Dr. Hill.

The doctor turned toward the bathroom door and called out, "Franklin!"

As Barnes dropped to the asphalt below, he heard Franklin respond over the sound of the rain. "What is it?"

"He's got some demands."

Barnes crept along the back of the building and took a scan of the parking lot. A black Ford Fusion was parked away from the other vehicles. Barnes crouched and made a break for the car, used the key at the driver's door instead of the fob, and got inside. He turned off the automatic headlights and started the engine. Through the blurry windshield he saw two plainclothes officers exit the bar through the front door. They split paths and headed around behind the building, each from a different direction.

Barnes drove slowly past the parked cars toward the driveway. He passed his truck, which now had a yellow boot on the back tire. He pulled down the driveway, turned onto the street, and drove about a hundred feet before he gunned it. As he merged onto the expressway, north toward Ferndale, his phone rang.

UNKNOWN.

Barnes picked up the call, put the phone to his ear.

"Do you have. Another riddle?" Leo said.

"I do," Barnes said.

"Let's hear it."

Barnes propped his cell up with his shoulder. He drove with one hand while he got out Candy's green note and read Ricky's riddle. "The runner-up and who's next. Three threes and two dozen. My age minus one. Midnight's younger cousin."

"Tough one," Leo said. "What do you have. So far?"

"I think it's a reverse of the other two riddles," Barnes said. "I think he's trying to feed me numbers that can be decoded into a word."

"Sounds right."

"So if a runner-up is second place, that's two, and if who's next is third place, that's three. *B* and *C* on the decoder ring. I don't think there are any words that start with BC, so maybe it's meant to be twenty-three, which would be *W*."

"That's good. Logic."

"You know," Barnes said, "I really did think you were just a voice in my head."

Leo chuckled. "And now you're. Certain I'm not?"

"I'm certain."

There was a moment of silence on the line. Barnes pulled off the expressway into Ferndale. He slowed as he turned onto a side street.

Leo said, "Three threes. Is next, yes?"

"Yeah," Barnes said. "This is where it gets tough. Is that three threes, like three-three-three? Or is it thirty-three? Or maybe it's nine?"

"It's nine."

"Right," Barnes said, "because three-three-three would be CCC, and there's no thirty-third letter in the alphabet. So if it's nine on the decoder ring, it's *I*, which makes WI."

"And. Two dozen?"

"If it's meant to be twenty-four, that would make it X, according to the ring. WIX. I don't like that. But if it's twelve-twelve, that'd be LL, which gives us WILL."

"You really. Are a great. Detective," Leo said. "I'm sorry that you're. Going to lose. Flaherty."

"What makes you so sure?" Barnes said. He glanced at the clock on the dashboard: 9:12 p.m. "I still have a few hours."

"But you're. Not close," Leo said.

Barnes pulled onto Troy Street. He was on the 7000 block. He drove west and the numbers went down. "Maybe I'm right outside your door."

"Let me check," Leo said. "No. I don't see you."

Barnes pulled to the curb and parked in front of 6034 Troy, a few doors down and on the opposite side of the street from 6025. "Look again."

"Aw," Leo said. "Quit fucking. With me. If you were out there. You'd be. Kicking in the door."

Barnes disconnected the call and got out of the vehicle. He eased the door closed until it clicked. He crouched behind the cars and moved up the street until he was in front of 6025 Troy. The rain soaked through his clothing, made his movements heavy. He peeked over the top of a sedan parked on the street in front of the house. The lights were on, but the drapes were closed. There was no screen door. An aluminum awning covered a concrete porch. He pulled his gun, steadied his breathing, and ran across the yard.

Two steps up to the porch and he kicked in the door.

Barnes stepped into the living room sweeping his gun. The carpet was worn down to the crosshatch. A cheap couch sat on the far side of the room, plus a love seat, a little flat screen on a stump of an entertainment center, and generic prints on the walls. An end table held up a lamp with a stained shade. A second stain could be discerned on the wall behind the couch. Barnes moved quietly through the living room into the kitchen beyond. A cell phone sat next to a box of doughnuts on a kitchen table with chipped veneer and steel legs. The stove was clean, like it'd never been used. The refrigerator was a base model without magnets. The cupboards and Formica countertops, cheap. Apart from the worn-out carpet and stains on the walls, the place could have been a model.

Off the edge of the kitchen, two steps led down to a landing. Brass treads. The stairs turned from the landing and headed toward the basement. Opposite the basement stairs was an open door to the backyard.

Barnes moved through the door and found himself on a patio. The chain-link fence at the back of the yard was still shimmying from recent weight, raindrops flicking off it. Barnes ran across the yard and hopped the fence. He landed on the other side, the fence rattling behind him. A jungle gym here. Green plastic slide. Slick and wet. Yellow rope. He ran past it. Started down the driveway. The scent of food from inside the neighboring house. Corned beef. The *tink* of silverware against a plate as he passed beneath a window.

A shadow passed beneath a streetlamp.

Barnes chased it. He came out on the sidewalk. Saw the shadow up ahead and to his left.

"Freeze!"

The shadow didn't stop. It split two parked cars and dashed to the other side of the street. Barnes crossed, too, as the shadow ducked between the houses. Barnes followed, passed through an open fence gate, stomped through a puddle, crossed another backyard, scaled another fence, caught sight of the shadow as it moved between more houses.

Barnes chased. He came out on the next street.

No shadow.

Barnes scanned the street left to right, right to left.

A dog barked over the rain.

Barnes ran toward the sound. He came to the yard and slowed down. The dog was a yellow Lab barking up into a tree in a backyard. The gate was open. The homeowner appeared at the side door. A woman in pajamas and a pink robe. She said, "Moose, be quiet!"

"Ma'am," Barnes said.

"Oh Jesus!" the woman said. She clutched a hand to her chest.

"Police," Barnes said. He took a glance her way, saw her face had gone catatonic. "Please stay in your home."

Beyond the woman there was a man, presumably her husband, maybe her adult son, looking out the rain-soaked window into the yard. His hair was sweaty and plastered to his head. Hat hair. He wore a bulky Michigan State sweatshirt.

Barnes passed through the gate and approached the tree slowly, aiming his weapon up into the canopy.

"Don't move," he said, searching for a shadowed mass as he checked the dog's line of vision. He arrived beneath the tree to find a man sitting on a branch about ten feet off the ground. "Get down from there."

"Don't," the man said, breathing hard, "shoot."

27

Barnes dragged Leo through the back door at 6025 Troy. He pressed him up against the wall at the landing and pointed down the stairs. "What's down there, huh?"

Leo shook his head. "I don't know."

"Sure you don't," Barnes said. Now that they were in the light he examined Leo's face. Hard to say if it was the same man he'd seen in Flaherty's memory. He was in his forties, his face was soft and the eyes dark and beady, but he didn't seem to have that detached look. He started down the steps, dragging Leo by the hair. They arrived at the bottom of the staircase, where there was a door. Barnes tried the handle but found it locked. He slammed Leo against the door. "No funhouse in there, right?"

Leo's lips quivered. "I don't know. I'm telling you."

"Where's the key?" Barnes said.

Leo shook his head.

"Never mind," Barnes said. He drew his gun. "I've got my own." He blasted a hole in the doorknob and used Leo's body weight to shove the door open, sending the man to the floor, where he curled up into a ball.

The basement was dark. Barnes found a light switch and flicked it on.

There were no video games, no pinball machines, no toys. The floor was concrete, painted brown. The ceiling was open, exposing rafters, copper piping, PVC. No washer, no dryer, no utility sink. Just a blank space. Barnes shivered where he stood, closed his eyes, stood still for a moment while his guts went icy. He opened his eyes, went back to Leo and squatted next to him, his elbows on his thighs, his gun dangling in the space between his knees. Leo maneuvered his way up to a sitting position.

"Where is she?" Barnes said.

"Who?"

"You know damn well who."

Leo sighed. He looked at Barnes. "You want answers?"

"I want justice."

"There is no justice."

"No?" Barnes said. He placed his gun against Leo's temple. "Why don't we skip the electric chair and I'll deliver your justice here and now."

Leo closed his eyes. "Killing me is not justice."

"Where's the girl?"

"She's gone."

"Murdering people makes you feel better, doesn't it?"

"I'm no different than you. No different than any man who ever thought of killing."

"Bullshit," Barnes said.

"I have just been willing to act on my feelings."

"You kill kids."

"Why does the lion chase the smallest zebra?"

Barnes drove the weapon hard against Leo's head, forcing him to tilt. "Because it's easier, right? And all because they wouldn't play with you."

Leo nodded.

"No." The breathless voice. *"Because. They wanted. To leave."*

"How about it, then?" Barnes said. He applied pressure to the trigger. Felt its minimal resistance. "You ready to leave?"

"Why is it," Leo said, staring blankly, despite the barrel against his head, "you people equate long life with good life? All the good of life ends when you age. You spend your adult lives only wishing you could be young again."

"You don't get to decide what's good or bad," Barnes said.

"You stole my machine," Leo said, his eyes turning slowly to Barnes. "Where is it?"

There came the sound of footsteps charging through the house.

Barnes shook with coldness, closed his eyes, opened them, saw things differently. He looked at Leo. "Seems like you're speaking pretty well these days."

Leo just stared back.

Barnes rubbed his own shaved head. "Where's your Mohawk?"

Leo's Adam's apple traveled up and down.

Barnes brought up his pistol and dropped the hilt on Leo's head like a hammer. Leo fell sideways.

"Holy shit!" A uniformed officer appeared at the mouth of the stairway. "He shot him!"

"I didn't shoot him," Barnes said. "He's fine."

Two more uniformed officers appeared. All three came down the stairs. They began lifting the unconscious Leo to his feet. One placed him in cuffs. They helped him up the steps. Barnes noticed the price tag was still attached to the tag inside Leo's T-shirt, hanging behind his neck. Barnes followed the officers up, went into the living room, and threw back the drapes on the front window. No cruisers were outside, no gumball lights spinning. He turned back and examined the room—the stain on the lampshade, the stain on the wall behind the couch. He'd seen stains like that before. Stains that'd been soaked and scrubbed but were too stubborn to go away completely. Bloodstains.

One of the uniforms appeared in the kitchen doorway. He flicked back his hat and put his fists on his hips. "Good work, Barnes."

The officer's face was familiar. His hair was plastered down to his head beneath his hat. *Jesus.* He was the same man as in the house two streets over, the man in the MSU sweatshirt.

"Thanks," Barnes said. He looked past the officer to see Leo in handcuffs, sitting at the kitchen table, eating a doughnut with a lump on his head. Probably some convict getting time sliced off his sentence to pose as Barnes's target. The other two officers were leaning up against the counters with their arms crossed over their chests. Too casual.

"Good thing we got here when we did," the officer said.

"They've been here all along." The familiar voice.

"Yeah," Barnes said absently.

A memory came to Barnes with painful clarity. A memory within a memory from when he was on the machine as Billy Franklin. Franklin and his former partner, Watkins, were standing on a sidewalk outside a house. *This* house. 6025 Troy. Franklin said, "We're just gonna talk to him, that's all."

The memory faded, but Barnes knew the story of what happened next. As Franklin told it, "Watkins walked into the house with a .45 and blew a hole through Gerald Dawson's head. There are still bloodstains on the lampshade and on the wall behind the couch in that safe house in Ferndale."

Safe house.

The uniformed officer smiled at Barnes.

"Looks like my work is done here," Barnes said. He turned toward the door, which was still wide open from when he'd kicked it in.

"Hold up," the officer said, putting out a hand. "Aren't you going to wait for Franklin and them?"

"Nah," Barnes said. He kept moving.

"Wait," the officer said.

Barnes stopped. He looked back over his shoulder. The officer had unsnapped the button on the sidearm holster on his waist. His hand was hanging in the air above the gun.

"What is it?" Barnes said.

"Just . . . wait."

Barnes ran.

He heard "Son of a bitch!" from behind as he crossed the yard and slipped between two parked cars, heard the click and static of a police radio, the officer speaking, "Franklin, this is Jones. Yeah. He's running."

Barnes crouched and moved through the rain along the street toward the Fusion parked a block down. He got into the car, started the engine, and pulled up the street to the next turn. Headlights were coming down the street, both in front and behind. He hooked a left, drove a block, and pulled a quick right. He drove another block and pulled another left. He drove several more blocks and found himself at Eight Mile, where he turned right and drove slowly, blending into traffic.

He cruised for a few minutes, constantly checking the rearview mirror until he felt he was clear of tails. He kept up with the steadily thinning flow of cars until he found he was getting close to Whitehall Forest. The woods spread for miles to the north and east, stretching nearly to Lake Huron on the state's east side. At the spear-tipped bottom edge of the forest it crossed Eight Mile and died before reaching Seven Mile, heading south toward Detroit proper.

Barnes found his bearings easily, and soon he was at the entryway to the Flamingo Farms trailer park. He pulled down the two-track and located his old family trailer. It looked so small now. Impossible to believe all four of them had lived there. The trailer was just one of thirty or forty of the same style, all stacked together like matchsticks in a box. Somehow his childhood home looked wrong without Dad's Bondoed Camaro sitting out front. Mom and Dad had moved out some years back, found a similar trailer in a similar park in Florida, where they set up camp in the warm weather. What were they up to these days?

His phone rang.

UNKNOWN.

Barnes picked up the call and said, "I guess you're back to Shadow now."

"I'm sorry," Shadow said. "To not be Leo. Rather, *that* Leo."

"Who are you, then?"

"Are you still. Certain I'm not. In your head?"

"I don't know anymore," Barnes said. "I don't care."

"And what. About Ricky?"

"What about him?"

"Is that what. You thought. When you let. Him die? *I don't care?*"

A searing pain emerged at the base of Barnes's skull. It traced down through his neck and up over his head. "No. I didn't let him die."

"So you say. And so you would. Tell anyone. Who might listen. But down inside. Down where. The heart holds sway. Where the truth lives. You didn't care enough. To save him. You let him die."

Barnes cringed and bent forward, let his head fall to the steering wheel. "You don't know me. You don't know how I—"

"Six quarters. In that purse. Six. One-player games."

"He was right behind me! He should have made it!"

"But he didn't."

"You can't know these things."

"That chain gave out. Detective. That weak link. Was you."

"You rode my memory."

"I am your. Memory. Living and. Breathing. I will haunt you. As Ricky haunts you. All your days."

"That might not be so long."

"The riddle, please."

"Flaherty's going to die," Barnes said. He checked the time: 10:27 p.m. "In an hour and a half you're going to kill him."

"The riddle," Shadow said.

"Why?"

There was a pause on the line, and then, "It's no fun. Unless you try. To stop me."

"Fuck you," Barnes said. "You've had your fun."

"You can. Still save him."

Barnes gritted his teeth. "Will I get to kill you?"

"That depends."

"On what?"

"On whether. Or not. You believe. I'm a voice. In your head."

"Life presence," Barnes said.

Shadow chuckled. "Okay. Life presence."

"What about the girl?"

"You're still stuck. On her?"

"You know I am."

"The riddle."

"My age minus one," Barnes said. "Midnight's younger cousin."

"What's your age?" Shadow said.

"It doesn't matter," Barnes said. "It's Ricky's riddle. He made it up when he was ten, so the answer is nine. Another *I* on the decoder ring."

"WILL-I?"

"And if midnight is twelve, its younger cousin could be any number lower, but I'd guess eleven, making WILLIK."

"Does that. Mean anything. To you?"

"No."

"Are there. Any other clues?"

"I don't think so," Barnes said.

"What about. The watch?"

"What watch?"

"You said. There was a watch. In the envelope."

Barnes reached into his jacket pocket to find Ricky's old army watch. The battery was still plenty dead, but the face showed the time in twenty-four-hour format. It displayed noon with a value of "12" in the position where "6" would normally be, and midnight a value of "24" at the top. Barnes said, "Midnight's younger cousin is twenty-three."

"WILLIW?" Shadow said.

"That second *I* can't be right," Barnes said. "*My* age. She kept saying that." He grabbed the green note and read it, the circle around *my*.

"Who is *she*?"

"Candy Harper," Barnes said. "I thought Ricky was stressing that it was his age. But it wasn't his age, it was Candy's."

"How old. Was she?"

"At that time she was sixteen." Barnes turned the decoder ring on his finger to 16. *P.* "My age minus one." He turned the decoder ring back one slot to 15. *O.* "Willow."

The phone went dead.

28

Barnes returned to the dead end in the woods west of Featherton Road. The car's headlights exposed the white birch trees, pines, and windswept undergrowth. He cut the engine and sat for a moment in the car, taking in the silence. Sometimes, when he and Ricky entered the woods after having been away for a while, Ricky would stop him with an outstretched arm and say, "Wait." The two boys would stand still, Ricky with his eyes closed, taking in the scents of cedar, river, and soil, the sounds of rustling leaves and the calls of birds. After a few deep breaths Ricky would release Barnes's arm and say, "Okay, let's go."

Barnes got out of the car. No flashlight this time. He'd have to make his way through the trees in darkness. He waited for his eyes to adapt and then took it slowly, finding familiar markings on his way to the riverbank. Once there, he moved forward carefully and silently, ducking branches and climbing over fallen trees until he came to the familiar clearing.

The rain had stopped. The graffitied boxcar sat at the edge of the open space, the hard lines of its silhouette intersected by the shadowy shapes of trees, rocks, and bushes. The thought of the thing alone out here, night after night, touched a nerve.

He turned away from the boxcar and continued along the riverbank toward the willow. Soon he was there. The tree was still on the wrong side of the water, still tilting, still dying. He stepped into the water and barged across to the other side. Once again he located the two roots between which Ricky had buried the time capsule, a hole there now where Barnes had dug it out.

He looked around for a clue but found nothing of interest. He sat down with his back against the willow's trunk and cleared his mind of the case, the machine, the voices. The wind picked up, blowing cold against his water-soaked legs. He thought of Ricky here with Freddie Cohen, the two of them burying the time capsule. Hopeful young boys. Innocent, even as carnal needs spoke from within, directing thoughts and actions in misunderstood ways, mimicking what was learned from parents, what was seen on TV.

"I never meant to hurt him." Freddie Cohen's voice, still that of a twelve-year-old boy.

"I know."

"I love him."

"We all did."

"Where am I? Is this Heaven?"

Barnes laughed out loud. *"Afraid not."*

"I don't understand."

"Shhh."

Barnes tilted his head back and looked into the canopy. For a second he saw Leo up there, hiding. The false Leo.

William Franklin is telling you lies.

"Why?" Barnes said.

"The Madrox Project." The familiar voice.

The wind picked up again. It pushed the willow's canopy around, the weeping limbs like so much hair, splitting and colliding, exposing the dark sky and stars above. Barnes recalled Freddie stepping under the canopy to watch Ricky scale the willow until he was lost from sight.

He stood and faced the trunk, rubbed an open palm against the bark.

"Be careful." Freddie Cohen's voice.

Barnes began to climb. The tilt allowed him to easily find the first major branch and pull himself up. He moved from branch to branch into the depths of the canopy, feeling a surge of youth as he ascended. His muscles and bones recalled the movements. Their own memories. Memories from a time when a boy would climb a tree just because he could. But no, that was the adult-filtered version, wasn't it? A boy climbed a tree not because he could, but to conquer the damn thing, to attain new heights, to get to the top and look out at the world from a higher perspective. As a boy, Barnes had often wondered, whenever he put his foot down in a forest, had another foot ever been in that exact spot? Some Native American from years ago? Some kid just a couple of grades higher? It was impossible to know, but he liked the idea of his foot coming down in a place no foot had ever before stepped.

And what if no one but Ricky had ever reached the top of this willow? What if Barnes got to the final branch and occupied a space on this planet only he and his brother had ever occupied?

Barnes reached the last climbable limb. The trunk was thin here, and the branches were pliable but strong enough to keep him in place. From his vantage point he could see across great strips of Whitehall Forest, all dark now, the tumble and rumble of differently shaped trees swaying in the breeze like the chop of a black ocean.

But there, not too far away, back down the path he traveled to get to this spot, emerged a point of light. Headlights in the darkness. The light barely reached above the tree line, emerging like yellow fog. He watched the light for a moment, watched it play in the tops of the forest, and then, as fast as it appeared, it was gone.

"I'm here," Barnes said, tilting his head back and speaking into the night sky. "Ricky. I'm here." He found the Big Dipper and then rotated his head and arched his back to find the Little Dipper. He grabbed the trunk to stop himself from toppling backward. His hands clutched the bark as his fingertips found a knothole. The hole was small, just wide enough to allow his hand inside. He reached down into the hole and felt around. Debris at the base. He dug at it with his fingers until he found something that felt man-made.

Barnes pulled out the item, a lightweight ball of duct tape roughly the shape of a small puck. Barnes began carefully peeling back the tape, brittle from years of weathering. The first few strips ripped apart as he removed them, but once he got closer to the center the tape was less weathered, stronger. He got a good peel going and managed a long strip, reducing the puck as the tape uncoiled.

Black lettering appeared on the white inside of the tape. Magic Marker. Barnes peeled until the lettering stopped and then read what was written.

COME GET SOME, HURRICANE.

Barnes continued unraveling the tape to reveal two George Washington quarters buried at the center of the ball.

A two-player game.

Mano a mano.

Dynamite Ricky versus Hurricane John.

He looked back up toward the sky. "You're dead meat, Dynamite." He pocketed the quarters and began climbing down. He reached the bottom, crossed the river, and traveled the riverbank back toward his car.

He arrived at the clearing. Something was different now. A scent in the air like spray paint. He scanned the clearing to find that the boxcar was no longer a silhouette. The door was open a crack, and a yellow hue of light spilled out from within.

MADROX was spray-painted in huge letters on the boxcar's outer wall.

Barnes moved slowly across the clearing, giving the boxcar a wide berth. He returned to the spot beneath the pines from where he'd approached the car years before, when he'd apprehended Calavera and taken three bullets in the process. His scars burned at the memory. He touched the raised flesh above his heart as he moved closer, felt its heat like fire, felt the ache in his knee and his shoulder. He stepped toward the door, breathing heavily, hands shaking. His eyes were undistracted by movements in the trees, leaves turning in the wind. The cedar scent was suddenly stronger than the paint. The crickets stopped chirping. He gripped the boxcar handle and was set to pull it open when he heard a voice from inside.

"We can't keep going like this."

Jessica.

"We're living with a stranger," she said. "It's not just weird, it's dangerous. He has no loyalty to us, and why should he? He doesn't even know who we are."

"We offered to pull you," a voice replied. Franklin's voice. "You wanted to stick it out. We can pull you now, if you want. There's a safe house in—"

"Jesus Christ," Jessica said. "You're kidding, right?"

"If we felt you were in danger," Dr. Hill said, "we wouldn't have given you the choice. Remember who he is right now."

There was a pause. Then Jessica said, "I know. I'm sorry. I mean, to say he's dangerous with you sitting here, it's just . . ."

"Don't worry about it."

Barnes pulled the door open.

29

Barnes stepped into the boxcar to find Franklin, Dr. Hill, Jessica, and Richie sitting in folding chairs formed into a half circle. There was an empty chair in the middle, facing them.

"Hey, buddy," Franklin said. He gestured toward the empty chair. "Have a seat."

Barnes shook his head no.

"Suit yourself," Franklin said. "How are you feeling?"

"What is this?" Barnes said.

"You might call it an intervention," Dr. Hill said.

Barnes looked at Richie. The boy's feet were dangling from the chair above the wooden slats of the boxcar. He swung them back and forth in a chopping motion but stopped when Barnes's eyes came to rest on him. The brave kid held Barnes's gaze for a moment but then looked down. His long hair fell from his shoulders and dangled.

"You dragged my son into this?" Barnes said to Dr. Hill.

"The method is to—"

"I don't care about your fucking method," Barnes said. He reached halfway toward the gun in his armpit but stopped when Jessica gasped and Richie screamed. Barnes stared at his family, crying, Jessica's face contorted in confusion and pain.

"We had to minimize the other life presences in your mind," Dr. Hill said. "In order to do that, I've—we've—had to force you to question your ability to conceive reality."

Barnes turned to Franklin. "What's he talking about?"

"The Madrox Project," Franklin said.

"Bullshit."

"What do. You think. Now?" Dr. Hill said. He waggled a cell phone.

"I think you're a maggot," Barnes said. His hands began to shake. His core grew cold. "You knew all those riddles. You led me on this chase. For what? For these?" He held up the two quarters he'd acquired from the tree knot. "I guess Freddie Cohen's letter was fake, too, huh?" He looked at Franklin. "Huh?"

"No," Franklin said. "The letter was real. Ricky's time capsule was real."

"But you knew about it," Barnes said. "You knew what was in there and where it would lead me?"

Franklin nodded.

"We used it to help you," Dr. Hill said.

Barnes drew his weapon. He pointed it at Dr. Hill. "Shut the fuck up!"

Richie cried out. "No!"

"It's okay, son," Barnes said. He kept his gun aimed at Dr. Hill and offered Richie his half of their monkey bite handshake.

Richie didn't respond.

"Hey, bud," Barnes said, stepping closer. "Come on. It's me."

"No, it's not," Richie said.

Barnes squinted as pain shot from one temple to the other behind his eyes. His bones became cold steel, his guts constricted with stabbing pains like shards of ice, his muscles twitched with spasms. When he regained focus, he found Richie had been replaced by a young girl with long red hair. Her face was full of freckles.

"Richie?" Barnes said.

"My name's not Richie," the girl said. "It's Amanda."

Another bolt of pain behind Barnes's eyes. He grimaced and clutched his forehead, dropped to his knees.

"We had to get you back on the machine," Dr. Hill said. "We had to give power back to the other life presences in your mind. Give them the strength to minimize your piece of the pie."

The pain in Barnes's head grew worse. He trembled all over. He fought it back and focused on Dr. Hill, the gun still aimed. "Fuck you."

"I'm not your enemy," Dr. Hill said.

"We're here to help," Franklin said.

"Is that right, *partner*?" Barnes said, transferring his aim to Franklin's chest. "Here to help me what?"

"Let go," Jessica said.

Barnes turned to her.

"We're here to help you let go."

Barnes examined her dear face. So beautiful, and once so bright. Always full of pain these days, always dim. Her smile was a stranger, her laughter only an echo. He recalled the day he took her in for fingerprinting. The way she smiled at him in the rain. The way she ran across the police station parking lot, stopped at the door, and looked back at him. Back then he had thought, *Ricky would love her.*

Another shot of pain through his head. His body quaking madly, he dropped to all fours. When he opened his eyes and looked up, Jessica wasn't there. She'd been replaced by a woman he didn't know. A woman with red hair and freckles, just like . . . Jesus, just like her daughter. They were both weeping now, holding each other.

Barnes turned back to Franklin and Dr. Hill. "Who are they?"

"We had to give power to the others inside your mind," Dr. Hill said. "I had to make way for—"

"Who are they?" Barnes screamed.

Franklin gestured toward the woman and the girl. "Meet Joanna and Amanda Flaherty."

Barnes turned back to the two huddled together. Joanna, the mother, glared at him from the corner of her eye while comforting her child.

"You've been seeing things as you want to see them," Dr. Hill said. "Not as they really are."

Barnes felt weak. He dropped his gun and came up to his knees. He placed his hand on the scar above his heart. No tickle, no sting. No scar. His knee and shoulder no longer burned, no longer ached.

"Hey, partner," Franklin said.

Barnes refused to face him. He kept his eyes on Jessica. No, not Jessica. Joanna. Joanna Flaherty.

"John," Franklin said.

Barnes turned to him. He knelt before his old friend with his hands at his sides, clutching Ricky's quarters, unable to stand. He picked up the gun again, laid it against his thigh.

"Adrian spent a lot of time as you on the machine," Franklin said. "He had your Calavera memory cut into a binge. He thought it was making him a better detective. No one was aware of how much he used. We thought he was tapping into victims' memories, trying to solve cases."

"But it was me."

Franklin nodded. "After some time it occurred to him that you were gaining control. He was losing time, having blackouts. He wanted it to stop, but he was too late. He knew you might seize full control someday, so he let me know."

"'Barnes will know how to find me,'" Barnes said.

"Right."

"So what, then? I've been solving this Eddie Able case as Flaherty?"

Franklin and Dr. Hill exchanged a glance.

"What?" Barnes said.

"Flaherty was solving the case," Franklin said. "The break came when we got Freddie Cohen's letter, addressed to you. Flaherty rode the memory and pieced it together with what we had from the crack house on Caulfield Avenue. That Eddie Able in his memory had just killed Georgie and Alice of Sparky Time Amusements. The timelines matched up."

"The 911 call," Barnes said.

Franklin nodded. "It gave us a new angle on the cold case. We went back to the crime scene evidence and started to track down Leo."

"You said Flaherty created a cover-up. The Madrox Project."

Franklin shook his head.

"What?"

"The project was our creation," Dr. Hill said. "This whole thing." He gestured around the boxcar, at Franklin, at himself. "A way to knock you out of Flaherty for good. We've been working on Flaherty for months, hoping we could keep you from taking full control."

"But you caught on," Franklin said. "You invented a cover-up, redacted names from case files, and sent yourself on a personal snipe hunt."

"Why would I do that?"

"An unsolvable case," Franklin said. "Flaherty would defer to you. You'd be in control at all times."

"So we had to set you up," Dr. Hill said. "Give you a false Leo to arrest and solve the case. Give you less reason to stick around."

Another bolt of pain through Barnes's head. He ignored it. "Why didn't you give *me* the letter?"

Franklin smiled sadly. "You weren't around."

"Where was I?" Barnes said. "Jesus Christ, Billy, where am I?"

Again, Franklin and Hill exchanged a glance.

"I'm here," Barnes said. "Billy. Look at me. I'm here."

Dr. Hill nodded to Franklin.

Franklin turned to Barnes and said, "You never walked out of this forest, John."

Barnes blinked. He clutched Ricky's quarters in a sweaty palm. He felt like he was being zapped with electricity.

"That confrontation with Calavera?" Franklin said. "You didn't make it, partner. I'm sorry."

"But those memories," Barnes said, his eyes searching Franklin's face. "Me and Jessica at our new house. Painting the walls, takeout Chinese food . . . Jesus, the pregnancy test for Richie, the hospital."

"Flaherty's memories," Dr. Hill said. "You took them as your own and constructed a new reality around them."

Barnes's mind traveled back through the scenes he thought were his. He found details he'd never questioned before. Rainbow ponies on a boy's shoes? Richie's confused reaction to the Eddie Able birthday gift . . .

"Why have you done this?"

"We needed to reduce your slice of the pie," Dr. Hill said. "It was the only way for Adrian to regain control. The Madrox Project was designed to break your hold on sanity, thereby breaking your hold on Flaherty. We need you to release him." He nodded at Flaherty's wife and daughter. "*They* need you to release him."

Barnes felt Flaherty emerge from within, felt his hold over Flaherty's mind slipping.

"You've been convincing yourself," Dr. Hill said, "of a reality you needed to be true."

"That story you told," Barnes said. "Leo's mother. The maid. The man with ALS?"

"What about it?" Dr. Hill said.

"Was it real?"

Dr. Hill shook his head. "Just something an addict once told me. A dream he had."

"His eyes," Barnes said. "They pleaded so."

Dr. Hill nodded.

Forgive me. Barnes.

You're forgiven. The familiar voice. Flaherty's voice.

I knew your voice sounded familiar. Barnes.

"Me, too." Flaherty.

"What do I do?" Barnes said to Dr. Hill.

"You have to let go."

Barnes turned to Joanna and Amanda. "I'm sorry."

Joanna closed her eyes and dropped her head.

Barnes looked at Franklin, saw the big man's eyes going red, tears forming and welling.

"We did good things," Barnes said. "Didn't we, partner?"

"We did," Franklin said. His voice was choked.

"Jessica?" Barnes said to Dr. Hill. "How is she? Is she okay?"

Dr. Hill nodded.

"Is she happy?"

"She's happy."

"I get to be with Ricky now," Barnes said, turning back to Franklin.

"That's right," Franklin said.

"You still got that eulogy?" Barnes said.

Franklin smiled. "Dumbass went and got himself killed."

"Amen," Barnes said.

And then he let go.

His body suddenly felt light, like a gust of wind had picked him off his feet. He felt calm and warm. He unclenched his fists. His gun slid off his thigh and clattered against the floor. Ricky's quarters fell to the boxcar planks and rolled. One bounced off Franklin's shoe and dropped flat. Heads. The other rolled in a circle until it collided with its brother and fell next to it. Tails.

30

Adrian Flaherty watched the two quarters roll along the boxcar floor. Once they stopped moving he looked up. Before him sat Lieutenant Detective Franklin and a man he vaguely knew. A doctor? He looked to his left to see Joanna and Amanda there, clutching each other with tears on their cheeks.

"Jo?" Flaherty said. "What's happening?"

"Daddy!" Amanda said. She hopped from her chair and hugged her dad.

Joanna stood. She approached her husband slowly, eyes searching his face. She knelt down next to him.

"What is it, honey?" Flaherty said.

Joanna reached out and placed a hand on his cheek. She leaned in and kissed his lips. Her touch was light and soft, tentative as a bird. She smiled. "It's you."

"Leo's machine," Dr. Hill said, using his cane to help him stand. "Where is it?"

Flaherty looked up at the doctor. He blinked and shook his head when he realized he recognized the man, after all. Not a doctor, but Detective John Barnes.

"You're supposed to be dead," Flaherty said.

"We needed that version of Barnes," Franklin said, "the one inside you, to believe he was dead, else he'd never let go."

"The machine?" Barnes repeated. "Where is it?"

"In the toolbox," Flaherty said. "Back of my truck." He threw Barnes his keys.

Barnes hobbled toward the boxcar door, leaning on his cane with each step.

"You'll get him home?" Franklin said to Joanna Flaherty.

She nodded.

"He's still confused," Franklin said. "Keep him calm, let him rest."

"I will."

Franklin and Barnes left the boxcar.

31

Barnes shoved one of Flaherty's keys into the toolbox in the bed of the booted truck in Roosevelt's parking lot. The top popped open. He threw back the lid to find a machine among the boxes of nails along with a tow bar and drill. His elbow pits went cold, his scalp tingled. He pulled the machine out of the toolbox and set it in the truck bed. He rubbed his hands through his hair.

"Sure you can do this?" Franklin said.

"I have to," Barnes said. He looked at his partner. "Don't I?"

"We can find someone else," Franklin said. "I'm sure Gabriel Messina has a lineup of Sect members who'd love to hook in and help Little Cher. Maybe even Messina would do it himself."

"No," Barnes said. "She may not have that kind of time."

Franklin didn't disagree. He picked up the machine and walked toward the front door to Roosevelt's. "Come on."

"Right behind you," Barnes said.

Franklin went into the bar.

Barnes hopped up and sat on the tailgate, cringing at the pain in his shoulder. Six years had passed since his showdown with Calavera. The wounds had healed into ugly scars, the shattered bones replaced with titanium implants. The doctors said the pain would eventually fade, but Barnes knew better. The voices in his head might be quiet now, but the death of a dozen or more life presences leaves traces.

Death doesn't heal.

He pulled out his phone and typed a text to Jessica.

I have to go back under. Cherry Daniels.

Three little dots appeared below his message, indicating she was replying. Barnes looked up as he waited. In the distance were the projects on Keisel Street. Machine City. A pumping heart of decrepit buildings pulling in innocent people, pushing out insanity. A living example of why the machine had been outlawed. A census taker walking those halls would find himself on a nightmare trip. Everyone was a movie icon, a high-profile athlete, a reality-TV star. Men were women, women were men. Adults were children and vice versa. Come back through a half hour later and they'd all be someone else.

His cell buzzed with Jessica's reply.

Save her.

Barnes put away his phone and started toward the bar. The place was desolate, having closed its doors to the public a half hour before. Generally it turned into an after-hours cop hangout until dawn, but Franklin had asked that they clear the venue out. On the way over he'd called in a favor on their old tech, Warden, asking him to come help administer the machine. Warden had moved on to a clerical position at a city building once the machine was made illegal, making it years since Barnes had seen him.

Franklin came out before Barnes arrived at the door. He said, "We got a problem."

"What's up?"

"No serum."

"You're kidding."

"Nope."

Barnes turned around to think. He leaned on his cane and gripped the bridge of his nose. "There's that memory shop over on Fenkell. They gotta have serum."

"Gonna be closed at this hour."

"Does it matter?"

"Go," Franklin said. "I'll wait here for Warden."

Barnes drove to Three Aces on Fenkell, situated across from his child-hood haunt, Mancino's Diner. The scent of bacon wafted across the street as he tore into the memory shop parking lot.

Most of the time there'd be protesters out front, Melodians and Brittanians, but all was quiet since the shop was closed. For propriety's sake, Barnes checked the front door. Locked. He peeked inside through the plate glass. Memory shops were generally set up like tattoo parlors—the walls covered in art, a few comfortable chairs with machine kits at the side, drinks and snacks for sale. This one was no different. He'd marginally hoped to spot some kind of contact information so he could get ahold of the owner. No soap. He could call dispatch and run a check to find the proprietor's name, but arousing that kind of suspicion would force Captain Darrow to bring down the hammer. The precinct policy was no machine usage, ever.

This trip would have to be a backdoor operation.

Barnes went around back with a mind to shoot through the lock, get in, snatch some serum, and get out, but it appeared he was the runner-up on that thought process. The back door of Three Aces had been pried open. The jamb was bent and mangled, the door still open a quarter of the way.

Barnes drew his weapon and approached slowly. He pushed the door open with his elbow, gun aimed inside the store's back room. The lights were off. He focused his eyes for movement but found only black shapes, boxes, and shelves.

He called out, "Police!"

"Oh, shit," a whispering voice said.

"Dude," another voice said, "we gotta run."

"Don't run," Barnes said. "Just chill out. I'm turning on the lights."

"Fuck that!"

"No," Barnes said. "*Not* fuck that. Relax. You have a chance to do something good here tonight, understand? You have a chance to save Little Cher. Stay put and shut up."

No answer.

Barnes reached over and flicked on the lights.

Two protesters stood before him. One was a Melodian, the other a Brittanian. The Melodian held a crowbar in one hand, the Brittanian, an ax. About their feet were the scattered remains of three or four machines chopped and beaten to death. Artificial hearts were cracked on the floor surrounded by pools of serum, like white blood. Most of the bottles of serum on the shelves behind them were punctured and drained, but a few remained intact.

"Look," Barnes said, gesturing with his head toward the remaining bottles, "I just need some of that serum right there. That's it."

The Brittanian plucked a bottle off the shelf. He raised his ax blade. "This?"

"Yes," Barnes said, realizing the two could take out the remaining bottles of serum with one combined swoop. "Don't get smart. Throw it over and I'll walk away, say I saw nothing."

"No," the Melodian said. "You'll use it on a machine."

"To save Little Cher," Barnes said.

"Who cares about Little Cher?" the Melodian said. "She's dead by now. We're trying to stop scum like you from riding the machine."

"Scum like me?" Barnes said, moving his aim to the Melodian. His shoulder ached from keeping the gun steady. His knee burned. "That's cute coming from a guy sporting a reverse Mohawk, hanging out with another guy dressed as a teenage girl."

"At least we're honest about who we are."

Barnes checked the guy's left hand, saw a wedding ring. "You got a wife and kids? Where are they right now? What are they gonna do while you're sitting in a jail cell for the shit you pulled here tonight? Vandalism. Destruction of property. Sure you're being honest with yourself?"

The Melodian sneered. "Don't talk about my family."

Barnes turned his aim toward the Brittanian. "And what about you, pigtails? Is that rouge on your cheek? Eyeliner? What's your name?"

"Fuck you," the Melodian said, answering for the other. "That's his name."

Barnes kept his eyes on the Brittanian. The man glanced at his partner and then back at Barnes. He said, "My name's Randy."

"Randy, I'm giving you an opportunity to avoid jail time and save a little girl's life. Just give me that bottle."

"Don't give it to him, Rand."

"Randy," Barnes said, "look at my head. Look at my hair. Do you see shaved temples? No. Because I'm not a munky, okay? Look at my badge." Randy looked down at the badge hanging chest-high from a dog-tag chain around Barnes's neck. "I'm a cop, and I'm trying to do the right thing here. Think I want to go back on that machine? Think I—"

"Wait," Randy said. "You're John Barnes, aren't you?"

Barnes nodded.

"You caught Calavera?"

Barnes switched his handgun to his right hand, used his left to pull back his shirt and reveal the scar above his heart. "You're goddamn right I did."

Randy tossed him the bottle.

Barnes pushed through the doors into Roosevelt's.

"Hey, Barnes," Warden said, offering his hand to shake. A few years older now, Warden's features had softened. His eyes were less intense, less jaded. His hair was cropped short, and his skin was glossy pale. Broken capillaries could be discerned around his nose. An addict for sure. Maybe a munky?

Barnes shook Warden's hand, handed him the serum.

They'd already set up the machine on the cushions of a long booth. Warden brought over the serum bottle and attached it. The fluid gurgled as it emptied from the bottle into the innards of the machine, filling the artificial heart.

"Do I want to know how?" Franklin said, indicating the bottle.

"No."

The serum was attached, the needle and tubes were ready to go, and the suction cups were clean and glistening. The table was cleared for Barnes to lie down.

"Take a look," Franklin said. He pointed at the machine's small screen. "There's only one local file that has never been transferred."

Barnes examined the list on the screen. A file named Bliss displayed a zero in the Transfers field, while the other files numbered in the hundreds. In the Plays field, however, the number on the Bliss file was more than a thousand.

"You ready?" Franklin said.

Barnes looked at his partner, who was now holding a set of battery-operated clippers. Barnes chuffed and shook his head. "Flaherty thought he quit the force, right?"

"Technically, that was you," Franklin said. "Near as the tech boys can figure it, you took over completely while Flaherty was working on his kid's jungle gym. You mentally blackjacked him and decided you were a construction worker."

"Why would I do that?"

"Do what, blackjack Flaherty?"

"Quit."

Franklin held his partner's eyes for a moment and then said, "Because this shit is goddamn hard."

Barnes looked off. "I talked with him, man. I got the feeling he knew some things he couldn't possibly know. I mean . . . *I* couldn't possibly know."

"Like what?"

"How could I, or that version of me, be aware of anything that happened to me after Calavera? Richie, Jessica, it was like he knew them."

"You said it yourself," Franklin said. "The new personality doesn't understand that the host body's memories aren't his own. Think about it. You and Flaherty are about the same age, been married about the same amount of time. Hell, your kids even go to the same school. It'd be simple to confuse his own memories with the kind of life that version of you wanted."

"It's the life I hoped for when I thought I was dying."

"Exactly. And then, presto-change-o, you're walking around in a body living precisely the life you dreamed. It wasn't confusing. It made perfect sense to him. To *you*."

"But he saw me with Jessica," Barnes said. "How could he not recognize . . . I mean . . . how could *I* not recognize me?"

"He saw what he needed to see," Franklin said, turning up his palms.

Barnes took a moment, and then he said, "If we can't save this girl, I'll have killed her. I took Flaherty off track when he was about to nail this bastard."

"No," Franklin said. "A different version of you did that."

"But it was still me."

Franklin gestured at the machine. "Can we focus, please?"

Barnes rubbed his hands through his hair. "All right, let's go." He peeled off his jacket.

Franklin flipped on the clippers and got to work. In a matter of minutes Barnes was once again bald. He rolled up his right sleeve, lay back on the table, and closed his eyes.

"Want this?" Warden said.

Barnes felt something small and light on his chest. He opened his eyes. A dowel-rod bit. He placed it into his mouth and crunched down on the wood. He breathed evenly as Warden attached the suction cups and brought the needle toward his arm. His hands were shaky.

"Should I sing?" Warden said.

Barnes shook his head, eyes on the needle.

"Here we go," Warden said. His shaky hand went calm as the needle approached Barnes's skin. A prick of the skin and the needle found the vein. The cold serum traveled up Barnes's arm and through his body.

Warden turned the dial.

32

The scents of rope and wood and paint. Stage lights in the rafters. The man sat backstage on an overturned milk crate, elbows on his knees. From his vantage point Barnes could see some of the kids in the audience with their happy catatonic stares as a life-size Eddie Able gesticulated before them. A wave of nostalgia washed over Barnes as he recalled *The Eddie Able Show* and its characters, its sets. He and Ricky with their butts on the edges of cheap furniture, action figures and Hot Wheels cars around their feet, dropped at the precise moment the show began to air.

The man was filled with happiness. A sense of completion and acceptance. He reminisced that he'd found a home in the studio, a place to belong. The producers liked him. They said he was good with his hands and that he understood what kids wanted. They'd even listened when he spoke up during the preproduction meeting.

"What's Eddie's sign-off?" the show director had said.

"Let's just keep it simple," the actor in the Eddie Able outfit replied. They'd just run through a final dress rehearsal and he'd taken off the fiberglass head, was holding it under his arm like an astronaut with his helmet. He was handsome and tall, and he had great teeth. The actor turned on his high-pitched Eddie voice and added, "So long, kids. See you next time. Don't grow up too fast, okay?"

"We tape in a half hour," the director had said. "If that's the best we've got, we need to roll with it, but . . . damn, I wish we had something more memorable. Anyone?"

The cast exchanged looks and shrugged shoulders.

The man raised his hand.

The director looked at him. "Leo, what have you got?"

Barnes felt an uprising of Leo's fear, felt his sphincter loosen. "I just think . . . ," Leo said, looking around fearfully. "I just think. That no kid. Really wants. To get old."

"Okay," the director said, "and?"

Leo looked at the man who would play Eddie Able. He was perfect. Leo wanted him to say great things, wanted him to be extraordinary. Leo opened his mouth to speak, but his jaw just quivered.

"Come on, buddy," the actor said, "spit it out."

"Leo," the director said, "if you've got something, let us know. Otherwise, we—"

"Wouldn't it. Be *bliss*," Leo said to the actor. "If you never. Got old. Like me?"

The actor turned to the director.

The director smiled. "I kind of like that." He patted the actor on the shoulder. "Try it out."

The actor slid on Eddie's fiberglass head and backed away from the assembled crew. "So long, kids," he said, waving to an imaginary audience. "See you next time." He waggled a finger in admonishment. "Don't grow up too fast, and hey, come to think of it . . ." He tapped his lips, tilted his head, and said, "Wouldn't it be *bliss* if you never got old, like me?"

Leo's heart had hopped with each syllable of the actor's phrasing, each utterance. It was as though the sun had risen in his chest.

The cast exchanged smiles and nods.

They loved it.

They loved *him*.

Darkness and silence.

"End of transmission."

The Vitruvian Man test pattern.

Please Stand By.

33

"Mort Jenkins," Barnes said. He was sitting on the edge of the booth table at Roosevelt's, holding his bit in one hand, rubbing his head with the other. His teeth ached. His mind was filled with fog. Warden removed the suction cups from his temples.

"WXON news anchor, right?" Warden said.

Barnes nodded. "He'll know our guy."

"How?" Franklin said.

"*The Eddie Able Show,*" Barnes said. "Jenkins was the man in the suit."

"We already covered that," Franklin said. "The crew, the cast, everyone."

"This guy, Leo," Barnes said, "he was there. We don't need everyone. Just Jenkins. He'll remember."

Franklin got out his phone and turned away. He began walking toward the bar's front doors. "Dispatch, this is Detective Franklin, badge 4-7-8-2. I need a residential address for Mort Jenkins."

Warden removed the needle from Barnes's arm, replaced it with a cotton ball. "Hold that in place."

Across the room, Franklin spoke into his phone, "Yes, the news anchor!"

"You haven't lost your touch," Barnes said, offering a conciliatory smirk.

"Like riding a bike," Warden said, alcohol on his breath. He stripped a Band-Aid and placed it over the cotton ball on Barnes's arm.

Barnes hopped off the table and grabbed his jacket. He winced in pain as he slid a sleeve over his surgically repaired shoulder.

"Those old wounds still bother you?" Warden said.

"Sometimes," Barnes said. He curled his arm up, closed his fist, opened it again, wriggled his fingers. From within his mind came a new whisper.

"*Where am I?*" Leo.

"*Shhh.*"

"How's the new gig?" Barnes said to Warden as he picked up his cane.

"Great," Warden said. He scratched at his elbow pit.

Barnes watched the move curiously, then looked up at Warden's face. He couldn't help but steal a glance at the man's closely cropped temples.

"Don't judge me," Warden said. "You have no right."

Barnes reached into his jacket pocket and produced a business card, handed it to Warden.

Warden took the card and read it. "You're a sponsor now?"

"My name is John," Barnes said, acting as though he were speaking in front of a group, "and I've been off the machine for"—he looked back at the machine on the chair cushion—"what, sixty seconds?"

Warden chuckled. He looked at the card again and then slipped it into his pocket.

Barnes placed a hand on Warden's shoulder. "Whenever you're ready."

"We got Jenkins," Franklin said, standing just inside the bar door. "Let's go."

◆　◆　◆

Mort Jenkins looked rough without his television makeup, never mind that it was 4:00 a.m. and the cops had dragged him out of bed. He stood in the doorway of his Birmingham estate wearing a black silk robe. "What was that name again?"

"Leo Vance," Franklin said. "He worked with you on *The Eddie Able Show*. We've had his name for a while, plus an old address, but we haven't been able to locate him."

Jenkins shook his head. "No one named Leo worked on the show. I'd remember."

"Is he. Talking about me?" Leo.

"Shhh."

"Your first show," Barnes said. "At pretaping, he was there. He suggested Eddie's final line."

Jenkins blinked. He looked up and over. "Wait. Oh yeah. He had a lisp or something?"

"I don't. Have a lisp!" Leo, using Barnes's mouth.

Mort Jenkins looked strangely at Barnes. "What?"

"Ignore that," Franklin said.

Jenkins held Barnes in a perplexed gaze.

Franklin snapped his fingers before the news anchor's face. "You remember him or what?"

Jenkins turned his eyes to Franklin. "Yeah, I remember now. He was a stagehand, I think. Only lasted one day with the crew. I guess I forgot."

"What happened to him?" Franklin said.

"He gave us that awful sign-off line. There was such an uproar from the parents in the audience that we had to refund some tickets. The next morning someone went to find this Leo—it was Joe Smitty went to find him, I think—and let him know he was fired, but the guy never showed up for his second day."

"After. What happened. How could I?" Leo.

"Shhh."

"He never even picked up his paycheck," Jenkins said.

"Wait, what?" Franklin said.

"I'm sure it wasn't worth much, but I remember Smitty saying he never even came back to pick up his paycheck."

"The show was produced by WXON, right?" Barnes said.

Jenkins sighed. "Let me get my coat."

34

"Hey there, Arnie," Mort Jenkins said. He waved to a small security camera mounted above the back door to WXON studios in Southfield. A blinking red light could be seen just below the camera's lens.

A voice came over the speaker. "What's up, Mort? It's nearly five a.m."

"My friends would like a tour," Jenkins said, rolling his eyes as he gestured to Franklin and Barnes. They showed their badges to the camera.

A buzzer sounded.

The news anchor pushed the door open, and they stepped into the studio to find themselves backstage. Huge mounted cameras sat dormant and dark among the white screens, prompters, and taped X marks on the floor.

They moved past the news desk, which seemed tiny compared to how it looked on TV. Arnie was waiting for them at the door to the control room. He was a solidly built man with the initial makings of love handles. Likely a former cop as well as a gym rat. He adjusted his gun belt. "What's up, Mort?"

"These guys would like to take a look at some old employee records. Can we get access to the room?"

Arnie made a pained face. "Hate to ask, but can I see those badges again?"

Franklin put his badge so close to Arnie's nose he had to back up to read it. He smiled and gripped a key ring attached to his belt by a retractable chain. "Follow me."

They left the studio and walked down a hall to a door marked RECORDS. Arnie opened the door, flicked on a light, and motioned for them to enter. "It's chronological by year, and then alphabetical by employee name. Who are you looking to find?"

Mort opened his mouth to reply, but Franklin cut him off. "Thank you, Arnie. We'll take it from here."

Arnie stepped out of the room and closed the door.

"I thought you already had an old address on him?" Jenkins said.

"Just what we dug up on a machine registration form," Franklin said. "Led us to a landfill in Northville. This guy's been a ghost for thirty years."

"He was weird," Jenkins said. "I remember that now. Good with his hands and gadgets and things, but . . . I don't know, just the kind of guy that gave you the creeps, you know?"

"How'd he get the job?" Barnes said.

Franklin knelt down to examine the label on a file box.

"I guess he was pretty good with kids," Jenkins said, "and handy as shit, come to think of it. He rigged up the Eddie head with a device that would say Eddie's catchphrases for me. I just had to press a little joy buzzer inside my glove and a speaker in the head would sound off. It was crucial. Being inside that head was suffocating, and it was nice to be able to interact without always having to use that stupid high-pitched voice."

Franklin pulled out a box. "Here we go." He took it over to a table and flipped off the top. He began riffling through the manila folders until he found *V*. He pulled out the folder and opened it, laid it flat on the table, slid aside pay records and check stubs for a variety of employees whose last names began with *V* until he came to Leonardo Vance. The check was still there, uncashed. The address was 1857 Heidelberg, Detroit, MI.

Franklin raised an eyebrow.

"What?" Mort Jenkins said.

"The Heidelberg Project?" Barnes said.

"Is that the block where all the houses are pieces of art?" Jenkins asked.

Franklin closed the folder and stuffed it back into the box. "Yep."

"This guy lives there?"

"One way to find out."

35

The dawn brought more rain. The night sky gradually shifted from black to a drab gray as the sun ascended from behind cloud cover. The nearby homes and buildings were painted like things out of a children's book—polka-dot patterns, colorful squares, numbers and letters in a jumble. A distant house was covered in stuffed animals and action figures stapled to the siding, one of which was an Eddie Able fireman edition. A chain-link fence was draped in discarded shoes. Sidewalks were painted with giant faces and paw prints.

Franklin pulled the sedan over to a curb on Heidelberg Street.

"What's the point of all this?" Barnes said.

"Make people think," Franklin said. "Get a reaction."

"It's beautiful." Leo.

"Shhh."

"Which one is it?" Franklin said.

Barnes pointed to a tiny house on the corner, one block off what was considered the Heidelberg Project. The yard was overrun with six-foot-high weeds. The roof was in dire need of re-shingling. The siding was a simple brown, much of it eaten through by termites. Cracked windows were duct-taped in lightning patterns.

A man in a trench coat emerged from the front door of the house. He popped open an umbrella and walked down the porch steps, started down the sidewalk in the direction away from the sedan's position.

The detectives got out of the car.

Barnes followed behind Franklin through the rain, a little slower than his partner due to his limp. His knee and shoulder ached.

"Sir," Franklin called out.

The man stopped and turned back. His face was in shadow due to the umbrella. Barnes switched his cane to his left hand. With his right he reached into his jacket and produced his Glock, held it close to his thigh as they approached.

Franklin stopped twenty feet short of the man's position. He pointed at the house from which the stranger had emerged. "You live here?"

The man nodded.

"Can I have your name?" Franklin said.

"Jim," the man said. "Jim Dobbins."

Franklin showed the man his badge. "Can you come back here, please?"

"What's this about?" the man said.

"Just come back."

"I'm going to be late for work," the man said, gesturing with his head in the direction he was going.

"Get back here," Franklin said, employing his booming voice. "Now."

Barnes caught up to Franklin as the man came back. He stood a few feet away from the detectives under his umbrella, looked at the gun in Barnes's hand.

"You own this house?" Franklin said.

"No," the man said. "I rent."

"From who?"

"I don't know," the man said.

"You don't know your landlord's name?"

"Look," the man said, "I've got a record, okay? I got popped for DWI while I was on probation for assault. Been out a month and I found a job sweeping up at Saint Bradford." He thumbed over his shoulder, again indicating the direction he was going. "This guy tells me he'll let me rent, no paperwork, no questions asked. I jumped at it."

"Let's see some ID," Franklin said.

The man got out his wallet and began fishing for his card.

"This landlord," Barnes said. "What's he look like?"

"Older guy, I guess," Jim Dobbins said, handing a state ID card to Franklin. "Fifties, maybe?"

"The name Leo doesn't ring a bell?"

Dobbins shook his head.

"Vance?"

"No."

"How'd you meet him?" Franklin said.

"Man, this is gonna cost me my job," Dobbins said. "I can't be late."

"Answer our questions and you can go. How'd you meet him?"

"All right, you know that project on the southwest side?"

"Machine City?" Barnes said.

"Yeah," Dobbins said. "I guess that's what they call it. Anyway, they got some kind of abandoned arcade room in the basement of one of the buildings. I stayed there a few days after I did my stint. Ran into him while I was there."

"What do you mean you stayed there?" Barnes said.

"I needed a place to crash," Dobbins said. He indicated the rain. "To stay out of this shit. Back door was unlocked. I snuck in there after the courtyard quieted down for the night. Met him once I was inside. Scared the hell out of me to find him down there."

"Are you saying this guy lives in that basement?" Franklin said.

"I think he's the maintenance man," Dobbins said.

"Which building?" Barnes said.

"A, I think."

"How do you pay him rent?" Franklin said.

"Bitcoin," Dobbins said. "I buy it and send it to his account. Gotta use a computer at the church, but they're cool with it."

Franklin handed Dobbins back his ID. He side-nodded toward the house. "He's not in there right now?"

"What do you want him for?" Dobbins said.

"Answer the question."

"No, he's not in there," Dobbins said. "What do you want him for?"

Franklin looked at Barnes.

"Little Cher," Barnes said.

Jim Dobbins closed his eyes, his lips curled in anger. He opened his eyes again. "The man I assaulted?" he said. "Stepdad to my little girl. One day she tells me he touched her, and I . . ." He looked off and clenched a fist, raked his upper teeth against his lower lip.

"We get the point," Barnes said.

"Go to Machine City," Dobbins said. "He'll be there."

36

"Leon Vince," the dispatcher said. "Name's been on their employee records for ten years. Maintenance man."

"*Vince?*" Franklin said.

"Could be a typo," the dispatcher said.

"Son of a bitch," Franklin said.

Barnes clicked off the radio. Franklin pulled through the Machine City parking lot, bounced over a curb, and sped through the concrete courtyard, scattering the people there. The dealers ran the fastest.

"Nothing like making an entrance," Barnes said.

Franklin veered toward building A and drove all the way to the far end of the concrete, stopping before the tires hit the grass. "You take the back door. I'll take the front."

"Wait for backup?" Barnes said.

Franklin shook his head. "If she's in there, we need to move."

They got out. Franklin hustled through the downpour back up the parking lot toward the building's front doors. Barnes left his cane in the car and limped toward the back.

The door was unlocked, just as Jim Dobbins had said. Barnes pushed it open and crossed the threshold into a small hallway with a door on one side. His bald head dripped. He pushed the door open slowly, gagging at the scent. A bathroom. He aimed his weapon at the single stall. A quick search revealed nothing but a toilet buzzing with bluebottle flies.

He moved deeper into the building.

The basement's main floor carried the scents of sawdust and grease. Pipes hung overhead, flanked by shelves stacked with drills and saws, hammers, boxes of nails and screws, cut plywood and particle board. Overhead fluorescent lights dangled from chains, their bulbs knocked out and shattered on the floor.

Hell of a maintenance man.

Barnes moved forward slowly, moving flashlight and weapon first around shelving units, nitrogen canisters, and a table saw.

He held his breath when a flashlight beam appeared at the far end of the room. Barnes watched for a moment, and then whistled "shave-and-a-haircut."

The returning whistle was not the natural "two-bits" but a repeat of "shave-and-a-haircut," indicating it was Franklin. The big man emerged from behind a stack of boxes and signaled silently to Barnes, indicating a door that read EMPLOYEES ONLY along the eastern wall.

The detectives moved across the room toward the door. Along the way Barnes felt a tug at his feet. A trip wire. "Shit."

"Guess he knows we're here," Franklin whispered.

"Then fuck it," Barnes said. He charged toward the door as fast as his bum leg would let him. He kicked it open and stepped to the side, expecting a blast from a shotgun or some other such thing. Instead, a peek revealed a set of stairs leading into darkness.

"I got you covered," Franklin said, aiming his gun down the steps.

Barnes descended to find a dead-bolted door at the base of the staircase. "Police!" he called. "Open up!"

No answer.

Barnes tried the door handle, found it unlocked. He turned it and pushed the door open. A dark room. He aimed his beam. The light revealed swirling dust over the black backs of arcade cabinets. He moved inside the door and aimed the light to reveal that the cabinets had been seemingly arranged into a maze, covering what appeared to be the entire length of a second basement lower than the first. The space was possibly the remnant of a previous structure knocked down when the projects went up.

"You all right?" Franklin said.

"Yeah," Barnes said. "Come on down."

Franklin started down the steps, but the basement door slammed closed behind Barnes. The dead bolt snicked into locked position. Barnes heard the muffled thumps of Franklin's feet as he ran down the steps.

"Locked," Franklin said. His voice was nearly muted by the reinforced door. "I'm gonna shoot it."

"Don't!" Barnes said. He illuminated the dead bolt from his side, saw that it was a bulletproof model, saw the wiring connected to the lock and the closing arm at the top. A live trap. Anyone coming in wasn't meant to come out. "Call for backup."

"Gotta go back upstairs to get a signal," Franklin said. "Stay put."

A sound from behind drew Barnes's attention. Breathing? No. The hum of electric machinery. He turned away from the basement door and started through the twisting maze of dormant arcade and pinball games. His flashlight illuminated *Donkey Kong* and *Galaga*, their colorful panels hovering over the iron sights of his handgun. He stepped slowly, checking for trip wires along the way. *Ms. Pac-Man, Street Fighter.* The maze twisted left. *Arkanoid, Rampage.* And then back right again. *BurgerTime* and *Mania Challenge.* He came to an open spot on the north side of the room.

His light exposed the far wall, which was stacked with cardboard boxes and piles of fiberglass Eddie Able heads in various states of decay. Monster masks. Some were full of rat holes, others were turned upside down. Mesh eyes were torn out, noses knocked in, ears missing. One mask had an old brown stain about the width of a gloved finger trailing from below its nose down over its lips and chin.

Cherry Daniels lay on a padded table in front of the boxes and Eddie heads, hooked into a machine. Her hands and feet were bound.

275

Her tiny body arched with the electric flow. She had a leather bit in her mouth, stretching her lips to cracking beneath fluttering eyelids. The suction cups were attached to her temples, a needle in her arm.

A voice came over a speaker system. "I'm Eddie, and I'm able!"

"Come on out, Leo," Barnes said, stepping closer to Cherry, sweeping his weapon across the boxes and discarded fiberglass heads, pressure on the trigger. His heart pounded hard enough to shake his arms.

"Being friends is twice as nice," the recorded voice responded, coming from what sounded like multiple speakers.

Barnes approached the machine near Cherry. The stacks of Eddie heads watched him from the shadows.

"You're looking. For me." Leo.

Barnes reached the machine and turned the dial from "Transmit" to "Idle." A moment passed, and then the little girl came blinking out of her coma. When she saw Barnes standing over her, Cherry screamed through her bit.

Barnes put a finger to his mouth. "Shhh."

The girl continued screaming.

Barnes showed her his badge. "It's okay," he said. "I'm here to help."

It was the last thing he said before every video game and pinball machine turned on. The room burst into a disorienting cacophony of colorful lights and sounds. Barnes stumbled backward, found his balance, and spun a full circle, his finger ready to squeeze. The sounds of the games ignited the voices in his head—a dozen people screaming, yelping, hooting. The lights were like a laser show, shooting bursts at his eyes, causing him to blink and shake his head.

There must be a fuse box.

Gotta find it. Cut the electric.

The girl on the table howled.

Barnes kept turning, aiming, blinking. Ghost visions of each Eddie Able head emerging to reveal a body below, standing, coming toward him.

"Untie me," Cherry cried, almost unintelligibly through her bit. "Please!"

"Calm down," Barnes screamed, his eyes still on the Eddie heads, trying to pick out movement, trying to spot the fuse box. His lungs expanded, collapsed shakily.

"Please," Cherry said.

Barnes dropped his flashlight on the table and pulled out her bit. "Where is he?"

"I don't know."

"I'm going to cut you loose."

"Hurry."

One-handed, still covering the Eddie heads, the games flashing and catcalling, Barnes produced his jackknife, flicked open the blade, and cut through the plastic ties on her wrists and ankles. She sat up and ripped the suction cups from her shaved temples, yanked the needle from her arm. Blood and serum splattered the table and the floor.

Barnes handed her a handkerchief. "Wrap it around."

"Don't take. Her away." Leo.

"Fuck you."

Cherry Daniels tied off the handkerchief using her teeth. She slid off the padded table to her feet. She clung to Barnes's waist, her face buried in his hip.

"Why do. You hate me?" Leo.

"You kill innocent children."

"I have never. Killed any. Children."

The childlike voice on the speaker was louder than the pinball and arcade machines, louder than the voices in Barnes's head. It said, "Wouldn't it be *bliss* if you never got old, like me?"

"How old are you?" Barnes.

"Twenty." Leo.

"Stay behind me," Barnes said to Cherry Daniels. He corralled her behind him as he backed through the room toward the entrance to the video game and pinball maze, gun aimed and sweeping.

"You'll be a killer someday." Barnes.

"No. I have never. Hurt anyone." Leo.

"You will."

"Anyone. But mother."

"I can help you. I can stop you."

"How?"

"Tell me where you would hide."

Barnes kept backing up with Cherry, moving her along. The Leo in his head remained silent among the whispers and shouts of the other voices. Again, Barnes thought, *"Tell me where you would hide."*

"I wouldn't."

The lights of the games and pinballs went out. All sound stopped. The girl screamed. Barnes cursed. His flashlight was on the padded table, several feet away. The beam was focused on a few of the Eddie Able heads against the wall.

Out of the shadows came a *cli-cli-clicking* sound. A safe dial turning. Barnes aimed his weapon in the direction of the sound. He continued to back up with Cherry behind him. They flattened against a row of arcade cabinets.

The squeal of a hinge.

"To your right," Barnes whispered to Cherry. They slid along the cabinets until they found the opening that led back through the maze toward the stairs.

A cardboard box fell and banged against the padded table. It knocked the flashlight to the floor. The light rolled and came to a stop, the beam left aiming at a life-size Eddie Able standing in the center of the room, pointing a handgun at Barnes.

"Run!" Barnes said. He pushed Cherry back and leaped to the side. Gun blasts strobed the room. Leo shooting.

Barnes rolled along the floor.

Sparks burst and glass shattered from where Leo's bullets ripped through the arcade cabinets.

Barnes rolled to a stop. Ears ringing.

Aim where you last saw him.

Shoot.

Barnes's weapon bucked in his hands.

The flash of light revealed that Leo was moving, the fiberglass head facing Barnes as the body was caught turning, retreating. Barnes moved his aim and fired again. Another miss. Leo was revealed in the strobe of light, diving behind the mass of boxes and Eddie heads.

Barnes scuttled quickly across the floor and scooped up his flashlight. He rolled and took cover behind the padded table, covering the flashlight's beam with his hand while turning away to keep it from Leo's sight.

Leo fired three times, opening holes in the poured concrete wall where Barnes and the flashlight had just been.

Barnes's ears rang in the silence. No way to know if Leo was moving again.

Create a distraction.

Barnes dropped low, reached up, and placed the flashlight on the padded table, the beam aimed at the pile of Eddie heads. He pulled his hand away quickly, expecting shots.

Leo didn't take the bait.

Barnes chanced a look. The flashlight revealed the rows of heads, any one of which could be occupied. He sought movement as he scanned the eyeholes, searching for a glint in the darkness.

Only dead black eyes stared back.

But one head was different, wasn't it? The one with the bloody finger mark beneath its nose and over its lips. The one that scared Freddie Cohen in Whitehall Forest while Ricky lay knocked out in the leaves.

Leo may have watched Ricky that day from across the river, may have seen him there, helpless. It would have been so easy to take him.

He *had* taken him, though, in a way. Leo's presence in those woods, at that moment in time, caused Freddie Cohen to drop that coin purse. The goddamn coin purse that stopped Johnny and Ricky from spending the afternoon building a ladder to their tree fort. Instead they took the purse and ran, first to home, then to Calvary Junction.

Instead Ricky died.

Barnes took aim at the Eddie head. He leveled his sights on that old brown blood over the fiberglass lips and squeezed the trigger.

The head rocked back from the blast but didn't fall. A hole appeared just below the nose. Burnt cordite in the air.

Suddenly the head rose up from the pile of others like a ghost. The body beneath stood to full height and staggered out and away from its hiding spot. It dropped its weapon and put up two hands to what remained of its real face beneath. Blood fell in gouts over the man's chest, down across his belly and waist. He stepped out of the light from the flashlight beam and merged into the shadows.

Barnes heard a whump over the ringing in his ears. Leo hitting the floor?

A hollow thunk followed, then a sound like a bowling ball. The Eddie head rolling away?

Barnes came up to his knees, gun aimed at the dark spot where he'd heard Leo go down. His chest heaved. Adrenaline pulsed. The ringing abated. Scuffling sounds. Writhing sounds. In the corner? He aimed there. Heard ragged breathing. He closed his mouth and breathed through his nose to hear better.

A wet, whistling sound.

Words.

"Eht . . . hu- ur- ur . . . sss . . ."

"It hurts." Leo.

"Shhh."

280

Barnes found Cherry Daniels curled in a corner near the basement door, shivering. The contrast between the girl cowering before him and the confident contestant on *Starmonizers* almost unnerved him. He helped her to her feet and lifted her into his arms while the uniforms used a battering ram to knock down the door. He carried her up the steps and out of the basement beneath building A into an ambulance. She refused to release him as he set her down on the gurney.

"It's okay," he whispered into her ear.

For a while she kept him in a vise grip, trembling madly, but eventually she loosened and allowed her weight onto the bed. She held Barnes's gaze but flicked her eyes to his bald temples and the circular suction cup marks.

"You're safe now," Barnes said.

The girl blinked and shook her head. She tried to sit up on the gurney, but Barnes held her down.

"Mother, stop!" the girl said. "You're. Hurting me."

Barnes continued to hold her down. Two paramedics joined him as the girl kicked and flailed at them, snapped her teeth at them. "You. Can't take her. She's mine!"

Barnes put his body weight on the girl's chest while the paramedics strapped her legs down. She went into a full body seizure, which lasted for half a minute, and then she went still.

More paramedics entered the ambulance.

Barnes started toward the back door to give them room to work.

"You were there," the girl whispered.

Barnes stopped. He came back to her. "What's that?"

"In his memories," Cherry said, calm now. "At the arcade. You and another boy." She closed her eyes, fought back a shiver, and seemed to hold on to herself. "He watched you from behind the counter. You were always playing that wrestling game."

"At Vacationland?"

Cherry nodded.

A memory bloomed in Barnes's mind. He and Ricky exchanging dollars for quarters with the man who never spoke. Ricky had nicknamed him Boo Radley, while others called him Stinkpot due to his constant smell.

"He gave me his memories," Cherry said. "'Cause he wanted me to know he was once good."

"He was a bad man," Barnes said.

"He was broken," Cherry said. "That other boy at the arcade. He was your brother?"

Barnes nodded.

"He was nice to Leo. The other kids were unkind."

"Ricky was a good kid."

Cherry gripped Barnes's hand. "So were you."

37

Jessica was sitting cross-legged on the couch reading a book when Barnes came through the front door. He noted that the book was upside down. She hopped up and met him on the foyer tiles before he could kick off his shoes. She hugged him tightly. "Oh, thank God."

Barnes returned her hug, held her for a moment, and pulled back. Their foreheads came together, their eyes closed.

"Is she safe?" Jessica said.

Barnes nodded. "She'll be fine."

Tension fled Jessica's body. She opened her eyes and looked into his, rubbed her hands over his bald head. "Are you okay?"

"No." Leo.

"Shhh."

"Yes. Where's Richie?"

"Down for a nap."

Barnes finished kicking off his shoes and took Jessica's hand. Together they walked down the hall to Richie's bedroom. The door was open a crack. Barnes pushed it open another couple of inches to reveal his sleeping son's face in a shaft of soft light. He put his arm around Jessica's shoulders, pulled her close. Together they watched their boy for a moment, just as they did their first night home from the hospital. They'd giggled about how cliché they were, standing over their newborn like a couple of mushy dopes, people from a commercial. Jessica had quit teaching to stay home with the baby and taken to motherhood unexpectedly well. Having spent her youth on the run from substandard parenting, Barnes half expected her to withdraw from the responsibility, but her own experiences seemed to make her that much more dedicated to making sure Richie was well taught, well groomed, well loved.

For John it hadn't been so easy. It felt like betrayal as Richie grew into the spitting image of Ricky, displaying at a young age the same head-butt-the-world attitude of Barnes's kid brother. He felt like he was in some sci-fi story where a couple replaces their dead child with an android in the boy's image, all to some horrible end.

But the feeling of betrayal was erased when Richie, only three years old at the time, asked, "Dad, do you love me?"

"Of course I do, kid."

"Why?"

"Because you're my son."

As the words left his mouth, it struck Barnes how true they were. This was his son. Not his kid brother, not some dream of what might have been, not some apparition, but a human being. A life. A boy who needed his father.

"I stopped by the apartment," Barnes whispered. He gestured with his head toward the kitchen as he pulled the bedroom door quietly closed. They went back down the hall and sat across from each other at the kitchen table. He reached into his pocket and pulled out a wad of facial tissue. He situated the tissue in the center of the table and peeled it open like a gift. Inside was a half-carat round diamond. He smirked to recall Flaherty coming at him in the parking lot of that shuttered Kmart. "Almost got my ass kicked for it."

Jessica smiled. She picked up the diamond and examined it. "I can't believe they didn't just sell it."

"Some people know a cubic zirconium when they see one."

Jessica rolled her eyes. She compared the diamond to the empty prongs on her engagement ring just the other side of her wedding band. She would reset it herself, Barnes knew. She'd picked up a set of handyman skills in the years since walking away from teaching. She'd even been hired a few times to fix porches, repair roofs, and wire a surround-sound system for one of the neighbors. He could already see her setting the ring between the clamps of the vise on the workbench in the basement, one eye shut and biting the tip of her tongue as she examined the issue up close. "Where did they say it was again?"

"In a crack between the boards on the back deck," Barnes said.

She snickered and shook her head. "How many people would have just taken it?"

"Not everyone is a thief," Barnes said.

She smiled sadly. "I guess we see too much of the bad around here, eh?"

Barnes looked off. "Maybe."

"Tell me," Jessica said.

He held her gaze. "I shot him."

Jessica looked down.

"He's dead."

She set the diamond in the wadded tissue and took his hand.

"He never had a chance, you know?" Barnes said. "His father was a john he never knew, his mother was a hooker keeping up appearances as a maid. She couldn't have cared less for him, was cruel. Smart kid, though. At eighteen he took out a life insurance policy on her. Paid off big when her body was found in a dumpster outside the Corktown casino."

"He killed her?" Jessica said.

"Yes."

"Probably," Barnes said. "We're still working it out, digging through his stuff. She dumped him when he was sixteen. I guess he lived on the streets and then spent some time in juvie, which is where he met up with Tyrell Diggs. Got himself a job with *The Eddie Able Show*, but it didn't pan out. Things went south from there. He'd already bought one house with his mother's payoff, the one on Heidelberg. He gave Diggs the money to buy another in his own name."

"The crack house on Caulfield," Jessica said.

Barnes nodded. "He slowed down after the bodies were discovered there. Must have been low on funds. Must have been scared. My guess is he worked odd jobs for a while, enough to pay the taxes and utilities on his houses, until he found maintenance work at Machine City and set up his funhouse in the abandoned basement. Kept a low profile, though I'm sure we'll be able to pin some missing persons on him going back twenty or thirty years. Anyway, by selling memories on the Sickle Web, suddenly he could make serious money again, get himself a car, get his operation back. All thanks to the machine."

"*The machine?*"

"*Shhh.*"

"He's with you now," Jessica said. "Isn't he?"

Barnes nodded.

She squeezed his hand. "We'll be okay?"

"I don't know."

Jessica waited.

"When I first got that letter from Freddie Cohen's estate, I was afraid to go back on the machine, remember?"

Jessica nodded.

"We used the letter to help Flaherty, but I recommended it because I had to find out what Freddie wanted me to know."

"And did you?"

"From what I gathered from Flaherty, Freddie wanted me to know he was sorry for hurting Ricky. Something he couldn't say while he was still alive."

"Some things are too hard to admit," Jessica said.

"But that's just it," Barnes said. "I needed Flaherty to ride that memory because I still can't admit that Ricky's death wasn't my fault. I had to know if there was some loophole that would set me free." He took a rattling breath, regarded his wife. "But I'll never be free, will I? I'll always be chasing Ricky's riddle."

There was a knock at the front door.

Barnes checked the time. It was nearly noon, though it felt like next Tuesday. He pushed out his chair, went to the door, and opened it.

Adrian Flaherty stood on the porch.

His skin was pale, and he had bags under his bloodshot eyes. Barnes looked past him to see Joanna in the driver's seat of the car parked at the curb, Amanda in the back.

"You all right?" Barnes said.

Flaherty nodded. He held out a fist, something clenched in it.

Barnes opened his palm.

Flaherty dropped Ricky's watch and decoder ring into Barnes's hand. "They were really his, weren't they?"

Barnes nodded.

"What do I do now?" Flaherty said.

Barnes produced one of his Machine Anonymous business cards and handed it over. "I know I already gave you one, but . . . well, you were me at the time."

Flaherty took it and read it.

Barnes rubbed a hand over his bald head. "Maybe we can start over together."

Flaherty looked up. "No offense, but I think I'll pick a different sponsor."

ACKNOWLEDGMENTS

I'd like to start by thanking my old yellow Labrador, Moose. He's no longer with us, but for more than thirteen years he was my loyal companion and good friend. He was there when I started putting the proverbial pen to paper, always by my side, and always a willing chum for whatever antics I got into. When he was—ahem, when we were—young we used to wrestle and play like brothers. When he got old we would sit together and conspire. He carried me through lean years, taught me a thing or two about patience, and showed me what unconditional love looks like. I wouldn't be where I am without him.

Of course, I'd like to thank my wife Nichole and my girls. There are hundreds of reasons why, but it comes down to the simple things. A smile. A hug. A home full of music and laughter.

I'd like to thank Jessica Tribble for always giving it to me straight. You were right about those chapters.

I'd like to thank Sarah Shaw, Ashley Vanicek, and my editors at Thomas & Mercer.

I'd like to thank the reviewers on Amazon and Goodreads who said nice things about *Punishment*, and even those who slammed it. Sorry, but I love you, too. I guess I'm supposed to say that writing my second book was super hard compared to the first, but I don't feel that way. Writing novels is super hard in the same way raising kids or trying to be a good person is super hard. It's just satisfying when you're doing it right. Every moment of every day is a struggle as well as a new adventure, a reason to cry, a kick, a laugh. The highs are only as high as the lows are low. They require each other. That said, in regards to level of difficulty, I don't really know first book from second book, only that I love to tell stories.

ABOUT THE AUTHOR

Scott J. Holliday was born and raised in Detroit. In addition to a lifelong love of books and reading, he has pursued a range of curiosities and interests, including glassblowing, boxing, and much more. He is the author of *Punishment*, the first book in his series featuring Detective John Barnes; *Stonefly*; and *Normal*, which earned him recognition in INKUBATE.com's Literary Blockbuster Challenge. He loves to cook and create stories for his wife and two daughters. Visit him at www.scottjholliday.com.